OUT OF THE
Shadows

Also by *Tiffany Snow*

OUT OF THE
Shadows

A TANGLED IVY NOVEL

TIFFANY
SNOW

Montlake
Romance

Published by Montlake Romance, Seattle

www.apub.com

Amazon, the Amazon logo, and Montlake Romance are trademarks of Amazon.com, Inc., or its affiliates.

ISBN-13: 9781503949522
ISBN-10: 1503949524

Cover design by Eileen Carey

Printed in the United States of America

To Emily—and women like her—who make their voices heard and take back their lives.

Your courage and strength are an inspiration.

PROLOGUE

Devon drove through the night as though the devil himself was at his heels. A part of his mind couldn't stop replaying the images he'd seen in Beau's apartment. Ivy, fighting for her life against Clive, then again against the FBI agent and his men. It had taken every ounce of training and self-discipline he had not to storm the hallway and kill those who'd taken her from him.

From him.

He didn't know when he'd begun to think of her as his, but it didn't change the fact that Ivy belonged to him now. Perhaps it had been the moment he'd first walked into that bank and seen her, so beautiful and lovely, she'd taken his breath away. And she'd been completely unimpressed by him. Even now, as deadly serious as things were, a smile tugged at his lips as he remembered the barely concealed disdain she'd treated him with, as though he was as far beneath her notice as a mere peasant to a princess.

Or maybe it hadn't been love at first sight, but had been the night she'd lain in his arms and told him of the horrors she'd endured as a child. Her voice matter-of-fact as though recounting a laundry list. Completely unaware of her own strength, delicate in form and appearance, but underlain with a refined steel, she was a package of resilient femininity whose inner beauty and light hadn't been dimmed by the tragedies of her life.

Becoming something more than what you thought you could be, that was something Devon could relate to. Adversity tended to bring out the reality of what someone was made of, either turning them bitter and angry at the vagaries of fate, or taking whatever was good within and refining it, turning it into a more pure distillation of their being.

Ivy was the latter, and he liked to think he was, too. He'd also like to think he'd been good for her, helping her to see herself as he did. But at the moment, he was more concerned about her physical well-being than her emotional and psychological one.

It was a twist of fate that Ivy should be the one the old man had chosen to vaccinate against the virus his father had created, so many years ago. Devon winced when he thought of what could have become of her had he not been the one to realize what had been done. But the vaccine that had saved her life now made her invaluable to too many deadly players.

The streets were empty of traffic at this hour as the wheels ate up the miles from the city center to the suburb where Devon knew Vega would be temporarily housed. It always amazed Devon, the places where the Shadow kept offices around the world to be used strategically on a moment's notice. St. Louis was ideally located, situated nearly dead center in the US.

Vega already knew of Ivy's immunity and had ties to the Americans that could work in Devon's favor to locate Ivy. Given her prevailing interest in the Shadow's control over the virus, Vega should be as willing to regain custody of Ivy as Devon was.

And Clive. Devon couldn't forget Clive. A shudder went through him. He'd been careless. He hadn't made certain Clive was dead that night in Kansas, and Ivy could have died because of it.

Instead, he'd taken her. But where? To Vega? And why hadn't he been the one to bring her back?

All these questions and more were swirling through Devon's mind as he pulled into the vacant lot of the small, three-story office building. The ground was wet from rain, and his shoes slapped against the pavement as he went inside.

The empty hallways were well lit but sterile, as Devon entered the lift. Holding the button for the ground floor, he waited. The light blinked twice, then a small panel slid open. Pressing his hand to the screen it revealed, Devon waited for the scanner to finish. A voice then came from the speaker inside the lift.

"Agent identification complete. Welcome. Please proceed."

The screen disappeared and the doors closed.

The car descended two levels before coming to a stop. When the doors opened, Devon was quick to exit, his steps sure as he walked to a door at the far end of the hallway. He rapped twice, then let himself in.

The office was a far cry from the linoleum floor and fluorescent lights of the exterior. Devon's shoes sank into plush carpet as he entered the office, closing the door behind him. It was a large room, big enough to hold a couch and two chairs, plus an expansive maple desk. Windows lined one wall, though underground, their glass displaying an image of a bright morning in the city of London, beamed across the ocean so the woman who sat behind the desk would feel at home no matter her location.

If someone saw her on the street, they'd never guess who she was or of what she was capable. Of average height, she was an attractive woman, but not striking. Exceedingly well preserved, there was faded beauty in her features, from her carefully coiffed hair that never was allowed to touch her shoulders, to the expensive tailored suit in a warm ivory. Pearls she rarely went without gleamed at her throat. Always in sensible, low-heeled shoes, Vega was the high school English teacher that no one ever talked back to because, frankly, they were too afraid of her.

Though Devon had never fallen into that group of people who feared her. Vega had taken him in when he'd been stripped of everyone he loved in a brutal IRA bombing, leaving him an orphan. They'd had a stronger, closer relationship than any of her other recruits into the Shadow. She'd given him a purpose and identity, and never let him go about feeling sorry for himself.

"Sometimes life doesn't turn out how you expect, Devon," he recalled her saying to him. *"You have to take the hand that's been dealt to you and make of it what you can. No one can do it for you. It's your decision to make. It's your life, but I can help you live it."*

Devon had taken the advice to heart. He'd dedicated himself to the Shadow—to Vega—completely. Had trained and done his job better than any other agent, without ever once questioning Vega's orders. He'd trusted her implicitly, with his life, for as long as he could remember.

"Devon," Vega said, glancing up from a file she was perusing. "It's rather late for a visit. To what do I owe the honor?"

Devon took a seat in one of the two leather chairs opposite the desk, unfastening the single button on his suit as he sat down.

"We're in a spot of bother with the Americans," he said. "They took something of mine."

"Oh?" A pair of reading glasses was perched on the end of Vega's slim nose and she removed them, sitting back in her chair to view Devon. "And what is that, pray tell?"

"More of a who, actually," he said, careful to keep all emotion from his voice. It wouldn't do for Vega to know how panicked he was at the thought of Ivy being beyond his reach. "Ivy. The FBI has become aware of how . . . special . . . she is and in their usual clumsy way have blundered into kidnapping her under the guise of national security."

Vega regarded him silently, waiting, he assumed, for an explanation as to why she should care about this development.

"I want her back," he said.

"Our relationship with the Americans is tenuous at best," she said.

"I'm aware of that."

"And why would you want me to jeopardize it for this one woman? Who isn't British, I might add, but an American herself?"

Devon chose his words with care. "It's my fault she's in the position she is," he said. "I feel responsible to free her, set things right. Her involvement wasn't of her choosing."

"I'm not sure I would agree with you," Vega said dryly. "I doubted your judgment when you took her to Amsterdam and I'm doubting it now."

"Then perhaps you'd concede that it is in our interest to have her under our control rather than allowing her to remain with the FBI."

"My scientists were able to get a blood sample from her and are studying it as we speak. I'm not certain she'd be of any more use to us whether the FBI has her or not. Or whether she's necessary period, dead or alive, for that matter."

Devon realized that what he'd suspected had been correct after all, and his heart gave a lurch. Clive had taken Ivy to Vega as his own bargaining chip. "Clive been around lately?"

Vega didn't blink at the abrupt change in topic. "He was, but left some hours ago. I sent him to Geneva on a mission."

Devon nodded. "And what mission is that?"

"Not yours, in case you're wondering," she replied dryly, closing the file that had been lying open on her desk. "In fact, I don't believe you're required stateside any longer."

Devon's sixth sense was kicking into high gear, not only at the casual and flippant way Vega had dismissed Ivy, but also at how she wanted him out of the US. And Clive was in Geneva? Ridiculous. The man had been in no condition to be given a mission.

"So you expect me to leave Ivy? You know I'm ready to exit this business. I was hoping to do so . . . perhaps with her." Devon had once told Vega he was fond of Ivy and was ready for a change. At the time, she'd taken the news with little comment.

Vega sighed. "Yes, that's what you said. Are you really fancying that you're in love again? With this girl, no less? I'd expect it of someone who was your equal, but she most certainly is not." Her disdain could not have been more clear.

Devon frowned, studying the woman who'd taken him from nothing and given him a profession, a meaning for living, and made him an extremely wealthy man in the process. Her cynicism took him slightly aback.

"You disapprove?" he asked.

Vega shrugged. "What you choose to do in your personal time is your business, as is who you do it with. But you're an extremely valuable agent. I have put considerable effort, not to mention expense, into your training. I am not overly enthusiastic at the prospect of your retirement."

"Enough to tell the Americans about Ivy?"

There was a pause as Vega regarded him. "Are you accusing me, Clay?" she asked, her voice deceptively calm.

"I find the timing of Ivy's disappearance terribly . . . convenient for you," he replied.

"I think you forget your place," Vega snapped. "I'd tread carefully, if I were you."

"Or else what?" Devon replied. "You'll fire me? I've already quit."

"Quitting isn't an option. This job isn't like you're working in a shop." Vega's voice had turned steely. "You don't *get* to quit."

A hard knot formed in the center of his gut, but Devon's face remained blank. "So when I signed up, it was for life," he said.

"Exactly."

"I considered retirement when I married Kira. You didn't have a problem then," he said.

"Oh, didn't I?" Vega sat back, resting her elbows on the arms of her chair. "Another foolish relationship. I must say, too many of my agents seem prone to flights of romantic fantasy. Surprising, considering you kill people for a living."

The memory of finding Kira's broken and bloody body flooded Devon. He had left her alone and unprotected and could never forgive himself for that. Heartbreak, despair, and crippling regret echoed through him as he thought about her sightless eyes, which had seemed to accuse him of failing her. The dawning of a terrible thought nibbled at his mind as he looked at Vega.

"Kira," he began, but his voice broke and he had to stop to clear his throat. "Kira's murder. No one knew where I'd hidden her. No one . . . except you."

Vega's gaze was unflinching.

"Tell me," he said, horror giving way to rage. "Tell me you didn't betray me. That you didn't send them there to torture and kill her while I was away doing the mission *you* had sent me on."

"Your allegiance is to *me*," Vega said, her voice cold and hard. "And cannot be questioned. I've done what was necessary to ensure the Shadow's continued existence . . . and yours."

"You comforted me, told me it was too dangerous for me to be with anyone. That Kira was dead because of me," Devon accused, not wanting to believe the truth, though it was spelled out there for him. He'd been so happy with Kira, unable to believe he'd found someone who cared for him as much as he had cared for her. Although he'd been nervous about telling Vega of his decision to marry, wondering how it would affect his job with the Shadow, it hadn't once occurred to him that she'd be anything but pleased.

Devon stared at her. "How? How could you do that to me?"

The question, the pain in the words, caused the first break in Vega's composure. Her demeanor cracked.

"It was in your best interest," she said, her hands fluttering slightly, as though she were flustered. A condition Devon had never before seen afflict her. "You were going to throw away everything for an ephemeral emotion that had temporarily made you lose your senses. Kira's death was necessary, though regrettable."

"Regrettable?" Devon's fury made his hands clench into fists, his voice rising. "They raped and tortured her! She died in agony, and you call it *regrettable*?" The knot in his stomach turned to lead, threatening to overcome him with the pain of the past.

"I trusted you." His voice was a rasp of sound, full of rage and despair.

"That's your problem, Clay—you trust. Trust no one. That was the first lesson I taught you. You would have done well to heed it. I'd hoped Kira would be a permanent lesson, but it appears even a man as clever as you needs to be told twice."

Needs to be told twice. The words reverberated inside his head, turning around and over as he replayed events from a different perspective now.

"How long have you known about Ivy?" he asked, already thinking he knew the answer.

"Long enough to know I needed someone close enough to watch you."

"It's the agent, isn't it?" Devon said. "The FBI agent. It was never a coincidence that he took such an interest in Ivy."

Vega's lips curved in a thin smile. "See what I mean? Clever. Of course, not as much as me. The agent's presence was . . . fortuitous."

"So did he come willingly into the fold, or did he have to be persuaded?"

"The Shadow has sleeper agents that are activated when required," she said. "An American FBI agent is a particularly valuable asset to have."

"Was Anna's death also regrettable? Don't tell me you also didn't conveniently allow her location to slip to Heinrich."

"Clive made the same mistake you did," Vega retorted. "And I've had to spend entirely too much time running about cleaning up the ties you and he made to civilians."

"And where is Clive now?"

"Clive was used as a lesson to your precious Ivy," Vega sneered, gripping the arms of her chair and leaning forward. "I'm fonder of you and had hoped to spare you the pain of another death. I persuaded Ivy that it would be better for your continued good health if she ended things between you. Clive helped me . . . illustrate the point."

Clive was dead. And it was only by the whim of the sociopath sitting across from him that Ivy wasn't dead, too.

The tension in the room was palpable as Devon and Vega stared at each other. After a moment, she relaxed her posture and settled back again.

"Are we going to have a problem?" she asked, the deadly calm of her voice sent a chill through him. "I let Ivy live, but that can change. It's up to you."

"You're threatening me," Devon said.

"I'm *reminding* you," she countered. "Of your duty, and your purpose, which is not to marry the girl and ride off happily into the sunset. Those dreams are fairy tales meant for children."

Devon stood, refastening the button of his jacket. "I'm getting Ivy back. Once that's done, I'll end my association with her. But I will not let you determine that her fate now be in the hands of those who'd use her as a science experiment."

Half of that was a lie. He would not be dictated to by the woman who'd murdered someone so dear to him. It was only through the self-control honed by years of biding his time that he was able to hide the rage burning through his veins. He wanted nothing more than to reach across the table and strangle with his own hands the woman who'd betrayed him. But he was well aware of the danger lurking behind these walls. Someone was always watching. He'd be dead before his fingers even touched her skin.

Vega nodded slowly. "I'll allow it. Providing you follow through with your intention to rededicate yourself to the job. To me."

Devon's smile was cold. "Always. For Queen and country."

"Me, the Shadow, then Queen and country," Vega corrected.

Their gazes locked and Devon gave a slow nod. He felt her eyes on his back as he exited the room.

Returning to the lift, he pushed the button and glanced to his right as the doors slid open.

Two men were heading Devon's way. They were the same men who'd taken Ivy back to her apartment.

Devon smiled affably, holding the lift until the men had joined him inside. "Long night?" he asked casually.

One of them gave a short nod and tight smile, quickly averting his eyes.

Devon waited, every sense on alert. Casually, he unbuttoned his jacket, glancing at the small camera mounted in the corner, its eye silently watching.

His fingers fairly itched to make the first move, but he didn't want to if he could help it. If Vega doubted his loyalty, now would be the perfect time to eliminate him. She wouldn't have done it herself while he was in her office—no, she never got her hands dirty. She'd have these men kill him. He couldn't let that happen. If he was dead, Ivy would be at the mercy of Vega's double agent and whatever government or pseudo-government agency had taken her.

The doors slid open and the men parted to allow Devon to exit.

"Good evening," Devon said, taking the step that would pass him between them. The hair on the back of his neck stood on end and his skin tingled at having to put his back to them.

He took a breath . . . held it . . . but they made no move to interfere. Another second and he was clear of the lift. The doors closed behind him.

Devon felt exposed in the bright light of the hallway. Anyone could take a shot at him and he wouldn't even see them until his body hit the floor. He kept his steps sure and even as he walked toward the exit that seemed a mile away.

Nothing happened. Nothing prevented him from walking out those doors and getting into his car. Vega must have figured he'd been properly chastised and threatened. No doubt she also didn't want to lose two highly trained agents in as many days. Letting her think he'd been cowed hadn't come naturally, not when he'd wanted to rip her apart with his bare hands. But reacting emotionally would help no one, least of all Ivy. So he'd played the game and pretended.

However, the problem with having a tiger on a leash was . . . it was still a tiger.

CHAPTER ONE

I used my fingernail to scratch another line into the wall alongside the other two. I had no watch, no windows, and no clock. All I had to mark the passing of time were the meals pushed through the slot in my door. Three regular meals served like clockwork. Breakfast. Lunch. Dinner. Nine meals since I'd been taken. Three days.

The door to my cell opened and I sat up on the sparse twin bed. I knew what was coming. Two people entered, their gender indeterminate due to their yellow hazmat suits. They never spoke to me as they wheeled in the cart with the needles and tubes. With ruthless efficiency, they strapped me down on the bed and took their blood samples.

I'd tried fighting them the first time. That had been a mistake. They'd dosed me with something that had knocked me out for hours. The lethargic feeling had taken a while to wear off so I hadn't fought the next time they'd come, never wanting to be so powerless again.

Then I'd tried talking to them.

"Who are you?" I'd asked. "Why are you doing this? When am I going to be let go? Where's Agent Lane?"

Lane. Special Agent Scott Lane of the Federal Bureau of Investigation. Erstwhile supposed friend, then the man who'd betrayed and imprisoned me. He'd not shown his face since the night he'd helped them haul me away. He'd said it was "for my own good."

For my own good, my ass.

The two people took my blood and my vitals, then departed, all without speaking to each other or to me. It was scary how accustomed I was to being a human pincushion. Actually, it was more than scary. It was terrifying. But if I thought too long and too hard about it, I ended up in a panic. That kind of fear was paralyzing.

What *was* I going to do? That was the more pertinent problem. Staying here for the indefinite future was out of the question. The space was like an anesthetized hospital room, though even more sparse. Bathroom, bed, and chair. Generic clothes that were clean. No television. No phone. A small stack of books, notebook paper, and some pens and pencils were all they'd given me to while away the time. I was about to go stir-crazy.

To top it off, I was worried about Devon.

He'd been so angry the last time I'd seen him. Storming from my apartment in the mistaken belief that I didn't want to be with him. Mistaken because I'd had no choice but to lie to him since Vega had made it clear she would kill him before she'd let him escape her clutches.

I missed him. I missed him so much there was an ever-present ache in my chest. Every time the door opened I couldn't help hoping, no matter how farfetched, that he'd enter my cell and rescue me from the hell I was living.

Tears stung my eyes but I blinked them back. They would not see me cry. And I had no doubt I was being monitored. A small camera in the corner of the ceiling kept an unblinking eye on me.

What if it went on like this for longer? What if days turned into weeks and weeks into months? What would my friends and family think? I'd just disappeared. Would they think I was dead? Would anyone look for me?

Would Devon ever return and see that I'd gone missing?

He'd know something wasn't right. He'd know what to do. I couldn't help hoping, even if logically I knew that hope was futile.

The door opened again. Usually they wouldn't come for more blood until morning. A man entered, and to my surprise, he wasn't wearing a hazmat suit. Instead, he was dressed in khaki pants, a dress shirt, and white lab coat. He left the door open behind him.

"Good evening, Ivy," he said, pulling a chair next to my bed. "I am Dr. Nayar."

"Hi," I said, and I wasn't real friendly about it. I pulled my knees to my chest and wrapped my arms around my legs.

"How are you feeling?"

I stared at him as though he'd lost his mind. "Trapped," I said. "How do you think I feel?"

"That's understandable," he said sympathetically. "And I apologize that we have to do this for now—"

"I'm a US citizen," I interrupted. "You can't just keep me here like this, with no cause. It's a violation of my civil rights."

"Unfortunately, the danger you pose supersedes your rights at the moment," he said.

"What kind of danger?" I shot back.

"The virus you carry, of course."

"I'm not carrying a virus," I said. "I have the vaccine."

"A vaccine unknown to anyone and never before tested," he countered. "Considering what we know of the virus, unleashing you on an unwitting populace hardly seems wise."

"So where's your suit then?" I asked. "Everyone else has come in here with those hazmat suits. But not you."

"They've been displaying an overabundance of caution," he explained politely. "But I wanted to talk to you and thought the suit wouldn't be conducive to that."

"You want to get to know the lab rat?" If I'd hoped to break his calm with the jibe, I failed. The man seemed unflappable.

"You're not a lab rat, Ivy," he said. "You're doing an incredible service to your fellow man. Perhaps you've seen firsthand what that virus can do to someone, perhaps you haven't."

I remembered Anna and how she'd looked, blood pouring from her nose, lips, and eyes. It had been horrible, and I couldn't imagine how painful her death must have been.

"But trust me when I say that it's an awful way to die," he continued. "The virus itself can only survive in the open air for a very short time, but long enough to infect. In the wrong hands, this could decimate entire populations."

"Is it always fatal?" I asked.

He shrugged. "It's impossible to tell. I'd hope there was some allowance for survivability, but there's no way of knowing."

"I still fail to see why you need me to stay here," I said. "I've been around people for months, interacting with the public, and no one has taken ill because of me."

"Not yet, no."

"So you're just going to keep me here? Indefinitely?"

"Why don't you tell me more about the night you were vaccinated," he said. "You went to the home of Mr. Galler, correct?"

I gave a heavy sigh, but saw no reason not to answer him. "It was a quick pinprick. That was all. I felt sick a couple of hours later but was fine by the next day."

The doctor wrote this down as though I'd spouted prophecy.

"You can re-create it, right?" I asked. "The vaccine? That's why I'm here. So you can re-create it."

The doctor smiled. "Of course." He slipped his pen into his pocket, but it fell from his fingers to the floor. When he bent to retrieve it, I took my chance.

One of the books they'd left for me to read was a hardback, a real heavy tome. Snatching it up with both hands, I swung with all my strength. It smacked the doctor on the side of his head as he straightened.

He toppled out of the chair onto the floor and didn't move.

I knew I had mere moments before whoever was watching came for me. I snatched his ID card, which looked like it doubled as a key card, then rummaged frantically through his pockets, finding and grabbing a set of keys. Then I was out the door and running like hell down the hall.

An alarm sounded, loud and grating. As I neared a door next to a window in the hall, I heard footsteps behind me. Turning, I saw two men in hot pursuit. Though they had guns at their hips, they didn't pull them. I'd been right in assuming they wouldn't want to kill me.

I swiped the key card in front of the reader at the door, looking through the glass to see a man and woman staring at me. The woman's mouth was open in shock, while the man was on a phone, talking frantically.

The door buzzed and I shoved through just as the woman stepped out of the doorway.

"You can't—" she began.

I hit her. My fist sank hard into her gut and she doubled over. I clasped my hands and brought my elbows together, than rammed them down into the back of her neck as hard as I could.

She collapsed to the floor and I didn't waste time seeing if she'd get up. I felt a flicker of regret for hurting her, but I was fighting for my life and my freedom. Nothing else mattered.

I burst into the room just as the man was backing up. He was still on the phone. I grabbed the base and yanked. The cords ripped out.

"Stop!" he yelled, making a grab at me, but I swung the phone with both hands and smashed him in the face. Blood spurted from his nose as he reeled back. I swung again and this time he went down on all fours.

I glanced to my right, searching, and spotted the control switch for the door. I slammed my hand down on the lock button just as the men pursuing me appeared outside the window. I watched, heart in my throat, as they swiped their key cards. The door buzzed, but did not open.

Grabbing a piece of broken plastic from the now-ruined phone, I turned the sharp broken edge down and raised my arm, wrist up. In a quick swipe, I cut a four-inch gash halfway down my forearm. It wasn't terribly deep, but neither was it a paper cut. Blood began flowing freely.

Reaching down, I got a big chunk of the guy's hair and yanked his head up so he'd look at me. His eyes were glassy, but he was still conscious.

"You know what's inside me," I said.

He nodded, his vision clearing. Blood was smeared across his face and dripped from his nose. I held up my arm so he could see.

"You do what I say, or I'm going to make certain you get contaminated. Got it?" Not that I thought I was contagious. I just wanted him to buy it.

Understanding dawned, then panic. He nodded frantically.

"Give me your keys and your key card."

He fumbled in his pockets and I glanced through the window. The two guys were working at the lock. One of them was watching me, and he didn't look nice.

"Hurry up," I urged the guy, who finally handed everything over.

"Back on the floor." He complied and I hurried out of the room and began running down the hall.

A door with an actual lock that had no keycard swipe blocked my path. I tried key after key on the ring he'd just given me. There was a buzzing noise. The men had gotten through that door and were closing in fast. I scrambled through the keys, willing one of them to work. Two more didn't, then one finally turned. Rushing through the door, I slammed it shut, then shoved the key in the other side of the lock and broke off the end. Praying that would slow them down, I turned and ran, my bare feet slapping against the linoleum floor.

There was an elevator ahead. Relieved, I ran toward it, hoping it would lead me to freedom. When I was ten feet away, the doors slid open, and a man stepped out. I skidded to a halt so fast that I slipped and fell on my butt. I stared up, horrified.

It was Beau.

Beau had no business being here. Beau was a salesman and my nosey neighbor. If he was here, that meant only one thing: he'd been lying to me all this time and was working for the very people imprisoning me.

All this went through my head in an instant. I scrambled back, still on the floor, aghast at coming so far only to be thwarted this close to freedom by someone I'd thought a friend.

He spotted me on the floor and ran toward me, weapon in hand.

"Ivy! Holy shit. I didn't expect this." He reached for me.

"You're a liar," I said, slapping his hand away and scrambling to my feet.

He grabbed my arm as I tried to back up.

"Yeah, I'm a liar. I'm also here to bust you out. You coming or not?"

I looked behind me. The men were working on the door, alarm

still blaring. I had no choice. I let him pull me into the elevator just as a crash sounded down the hall. They'd gotten the door open.

Panic spurred me to punch the button to shut the elevator doors and Beau hit the button for level one.

"Take this," he said, handing me a gun from the small of his back. "But don't shoot anyone."

"You're giving me a gun and don't want me to use it?"

"Right."

The doors opened before I could question him further. Beau peeked carefully out of the elevator, weapon at the ready, but no one appeared. My heart was in my throat as I followed close behind him. The metal of the gun was warm in my grip. Blood flowed down my arm to coat my hand.

It was dark outside. A car skidded to a halt outside the door at the same time as someone yelled.

Beau spun around, firing as he yanked me behind him. Beau fired twice more, backing me up until I hit the door. "Into the car!" he yelled at me.

I rushed to the waiting sedan and yanked open the rear door. I threw myself inside and Beau followed. The driver stepped on the gas and the door banged shut behind us. Tires squealed as we tore away from the building.

My eyes shut in relief. I was breathing hard, blood thundering in my ears. What had started as an impulsive, desperate gamble to escape had actually succeeded.

Beau was reaching for my hand and taking the gun from me. He had to pry my fingers off before I realized what he was doing and let go. A gun meant safety, a way to defend myself, and I didn't want to give it up.

"Where's the blood coming from?" he asked, looking at my arm. "Did you get hit?"

I shook my head. "No. It's just a cut." I glanced up front. "Who's driving?"

"You can call me Ty," the man said. "I'm in the same business as Beau."

I turned to Beau. "And what business is that exactly? You're supposed to be a salesman."

"Actually, I'm CIA," he said.

I stared at him. "CIA," I repeated in disbelief. "You. *You're* a CIA agent."

A hurt look crossed Beau's face. "I'm a little offended," he said. "It's not *that* unbelievable."

"Yeah it is," Ty interjected.

"Shut up," Beau said without heat, then turned back to me. "Yeah. I've been keeping an eye on you for Devon."

Devon.

My heart skipped a beat at hearing his name.

"You've seen Devon?" I asked.

"Who do you think helped arrange this little rescue?" he replied.

Hope leapt inside me. Devon hadn't forgotten about me, in spite of the horrible things I'd said to him.

"Where is he?" I asked, hoping he hadn't left the country.

"We're meeting up with him," he replied.

"Why didn't he come?" Why hadn't he been the one to rescue me instead of Beau?

"I've got a get-out-of-jail-free card," Beau said. "The FBI and CIA may not be buddies, but if things had gone badly, they couldn't have kept me. Devon doesn't have that kind of out, plus, he needs to keep his head down and profile low right now."

"Why?"

"I'll let him tell you that," Beau said, looking out the window. We pulled into the parking lot of a strip motel. Ty parked in front of one of the rooms on the end just as the door flew open. It was Devon, standing there watching us.

My hand was on the door handle, but I hesitated, unsure of the reception I'd get. Telling myself it didn't matter—at least I was free—I pushed the door open and got out.

Devon's gaze landed on me with an intensity I could feel. I took a tentative step toward him, then he was striding toward me and I was running to him.

He caught me in his arms, lifting me off the ground and holding me so tightly it was hard to breathe. Not that I cared.

"Thank God," he murmured in my ear, and the relief in his voice brought tears to my eyes.

"I don't know if I should cry or vomit." Beau's dry comment got a laugh out of Ty.

"Sod off," Devon said, easing his hold until my feet touched the ground.

"Let's get inside before a drive-by brings a swift end to this touching reunion," Beau said.

Taking my hand, Devon drew me inside the motel room, with Beau and Ty bringing up the rear.

"You were quicker than I thought," Devon said to Beau.

"Well, she'd done most of the work for us," Beau replied with a nod to me. "She was practically on her way out when we got there."

"Really," Devon said, looking at me. A glimmer of a smile played about his lips.

I shrugged. "Desperate times call for desperate measures."

He caught sight of my bloody arm and frowned. "You're hurt."

"Just a scratch. They were afraid of me, that they'd catch it or something."

Devon disappeared into the bathroom as Beau and Ty sat in two plastic-cushioned chairs. He returned with a wet washcloth and reached for my arm.

"No, don't," I said. "I'll do it. I don't want you to get infected."

"Nonsense," he said, taking my hand and sitting on the edge of the bed. "If your bodily fluids were going to infect me, they would have done so before now." He tugged me down next to him.

"Totally TMI, buddy," Beau piped up.

I rolled my eyes, smiling as I let Devon clean up the blood. I drank him in. He wore jeans and a cotton shirt, the color a deep navy that made his blue eyes even more startling in color.

"So what now?" Beau asked. "They're going to be looking for her, and it'll only take a few hours before the surveillance tape shows who I am."

"It's late," Devon said, glancing at the clock. "Let's get some rest and discuss the way forward in the morning."

Beau and Ty got to their feet. "Yeah, that's probably best. You two have a lot to discuss anyway. Catch you in the a.m." They exited the room with little fanfare, the door closing quietly behind them.

Neither Devon nor I watched them leave, both of us still staring at each other. I was relieved that Beau and Ty had left, and apparently Devon felt the same because he pulled me into his arms again, one hand cupping the back of my neck as he kissed me.

I felt that kiss down to my toes. Lacking all pretense of seduction, it was relief and thankfulness and love poured from him to me.

He pulled me sideways onto his lap, his hands cradling my face as he kissed me. I buried my hands in his hair, pressing as close to him as I could. When we finally came up for air, I didn't move from his lap. He cradled my head in the crook of his neck and held me.

"I was so scared," I confessed. "I was afraid they'd keep me there forever."

"I wasn't about to let that happen," he said, kissing the top of my head. "Didn't you think I'd come for you? Have you so little faith in me?"

"After the things I said, I didn't think I'd ever see you again." Brutal honesty. I didn't want any more lies between us.

"Ah yes, the resounding kiss-off you gave me. I should have seen through your little ploy quicker than I did."

I rested my head against him again, the scene in my apartment replaying inside my head, as well as everything that had led up to it. "Vega killed Clive," I said. "Right in front of me. She said she'd kill you, too, if I didn't make you leave."

Devon sighed. "I know. And I was a bloody idiot not to realize what you were doing and take you with me right there and then. It would have spared you the past few days."

"How did you know I was gone?" I asked. "I thought you left."

"I was with Beau," he said. "We couldn't stop them, not without killing them, and it's taken this long for him to work his contacts to find out where you were. I've been going out of my mind with worry."

Shrugging, I said, "They didn't hurt me. Just took blood and kept me prisoner. I haven't even seen Scott since he brought those men into my apartment."

"The next time I see him, he's dead." That sent a chill through me. I didn't doubt Devon meant every word.

It was later than I thought, nearly midnight, and I realized my inner clock had been off by about six hours. But that also explained why Beau and Ty had come when they did, when the shift at the facility would be lowest, rather than during daylight hours.

"I don't know what's going to happen to me," I said. "It's not like I can undo what Galler did, and now everyone knows. No matter what I do, they're going to find me eventually and put me back inside that place, or another one just like it." I felt as though my life, as I'd known it, was over. Any chance I'd had for happiness was gone. My life was no longer my own to control.

"Shh, don't say that," he said. "I won't let them."

"They'll kill you if you try and stop them. And even if we do get away from them, Vega won't let us be together. We're living on borrowed time."

Devon pulled back to look at me. "Aren't you the fatalist," he teased. "We'll find a way out of this. I love you, and I'm not letting you go. We'll be together. No matter what."

It sounded too good to be true, but I wanted to believe him. I decided that no matter what happened, we had right now. I kissed him, the feel of his lips against mine grounding me in a way that was comforting. We were together, and despite everything, Devon loved me and wanted to fight for us. I couldn't ask for more.

Tugging at his shirt, I pulled it up over his head and tossed it aside. His skin was warm and smooth under my hands. I ran my palms over his shoulders and down his arms, admiring the hard expanse of muscle that curved and contracted as he moved.

"You've been through a lot," he murmured against my lips. "You sure you wouldn't rather take a nap?"

"Why waste time sleeping?" I asked. "Besides, I trust you. You won't hurt me." And I didn't just mean physically. Devon understood me, the Ivy I'd hidden away all these years who'd pretended everything was okay. He'd found her—found me—and made me face and conquer all that had kept me prisoner inside.

"Never," he breathed.

He undressed me carefully, kissing every inch of skin he revealed. His lips gently traced the cut on my arm, as though he could heal the wound himself. Skin glided along skin, our bodies touching, and it was more than arousal, more than desire. It was coming home.

"I thought I'd never see you again," I whispered as his mouth brushed a kiss along my jaw. My hair was spread on the pillow as he settled above me.

"I was a bloody fool to let you go," he murmured. "I won't make the same mistake twice."

Making love had been a phrase I'd always shied away from, the words feeling melodramatic and overwrought to describe the physical act of sex. But I'd been wrong. I'd just never felt this way, never had a man who felt the same in return, and that transformed everything into more than the physical. Devon gazed into my eyes, pressed light kisses to my cheeks, and murmured words of love in my ear as he moved inside me. I held him close, glad beyond words that I'd stuck with him even when it looked like our relationship would never amount to anything.

He wrung two orgasms from me before allowing himself to come, his body shuddering against mine. Our bodies were slick with sweat, his chest heaving as our lips clung together.

Spent, I lay cradled in his arms. He played with my hair and I listened to the sound of his heart beating.

"I don't want tomorrow to come," I said, my voice quiet in the dim motel room. "I wish we could stay like this and pretend nothing else existed." A ridiculous, childish hope.

"It'll be all right," Devon said.

"You don't know that." I turned, resting my chin on my arm as I lay on his chest and looked up at him. "Can we just run away? Far away, somewhere they'll never find us."

"We have the means, yes, but I don't want to be constantly looking over our shoulders, waiting for the day they track us down, because they certainly will. That's no way to live."

He was right and I knew it, but I was still disappointed. I noticed he'd placed his gun under the pillow and his right hand lay tucked beneath his head. Devon keeping a weapon within easy reach even as we slept only reinforced the danger we were in.

A deep sense of foreboding hung over me, and I couldn't help being afraid that one or both of us wouldn't make it out of this alive.

CHAPTER
TWO

Morning came too quickly, and when I woke up, Devon had already gone and come back, bringing me clothes and a cup of coffee.

Beau and Ty showed up soon after I'd showered and dressed, also sipping from paper cups of steaming black coffee.

"So Beau said he'd been keeping an eye on me for you," I said to Devon. At the time, the interest Beau had taken in my life had seemed so strange. He'd given new meaning to *nosy neighbor*. I'd thought him eccentric—friendly but odd. Now it turned out he'd been spying for Devon.

"I didn't like leaving you alone," Devon said. "Beau lived right across the hall from me, so he kept tabs on you, yes." He didn't sound apologetic.

"So even after you said we were through and left me the apartment . . ."

"Yes," he said, his palm brushing my cheek. "Even when I didn't think I'd be back, I couldn't help wanting to know how you were, what you were doing."

I pulled back. "How nice for you," I said stiffly. "Whereas I was left to wonder each day if you were still alive or not."

"Awkward," Ty mumbled under his breath. I shot him a look and he shut up.

"We can argue about it later," Devon said. "For now, we need to plan." He turned to Beau. "What did you find out?"

"Well, you were right. Vega's ticked off some people in pretty high places. They think she's become too powerful and want her taken out. Unfortunately, she's got too many balls in vises."

"What does that mean?" I asked.

"She's got too much dirt on too many people," Devon said. "She's spent the past forty years collecting every secret and skeleton in the closet of every politician in Britain. No one dares oppose her."

"Which is why the CIA is willing to help," Beau said. "Off the record, of course. I let The Powers That Be know that you've gone rogue and are looking to terminate your association with the Shadow and Vega. They like the idea of the British owing us one, so they'll help you and turn a blind eye, even keep the FBI off your backs for a while."

"To take Vega out, I need to get back to London," Devon said. "There's no way that's going to happen on a commercial flight."

"Agreed. But if you drive down to Key West, we can put you on a boat to Gitmo in Cuba. From there, we can fly you into London under the radar and outside of prying eyes, both theirs and ours."

"Drive to Key West. How long will that take?"

"From here? About twenty-four, twenty-five hours," Ty answered.

"We can put Ivy in a safe house—" Beau began.

"No," Devon interrupted, his voice hard. "Absolutely not. She'll come with me."

Beau looked surprised. "But it'll be dangerous—"

"So will leaving her behind. I trust you, but no one else. Leaving her behind is out of the question."

I was thrilled at this, my heart having sank when Beau talked about a safe house. I didn't want to let Devon out of my sight, even for a moment. And it appeared he felt the same way.

"Okay then," Beau said. "I'll give you the name of the contact in Key West."

"Wait," I interrupted. "What about my job? My friends and family? Won't they have the cops out searching for me by now?" I couldn't imagine how worried Grams had to be after not hearing from me for the past few weeks. Or Logan.

"The FBI took care of that," Beau replied dryly. "You decided to quit your job and go on sabbatical with the Peace Corps in Venezuela."

My eyes widened. "Are you kidding me? No one who knows me would buy that." Did they even have air conditioning in Venezuela?

"They're less concerned about people buying it than just having a plausible reason for your disappearance," Ty clarified. "Sketchy cell service in South America. And the Peace Corps isn't known for providing its workers with five-star hotel accommodations, so it's not like you can call home frequently. All in all, not a bad cover story."

I shook my head, knowing that there was no way Logan would believe such a story. He had to know it had something to do with Devon, which would be just as bad, because he wouldn't think to raise any alarm about my disappearance.

Beau and Ty got to their feet. "Good luck, my man," Beau said to Devon. He turned to me. "Take this," he said, handing me the gun he'd given me the day before. "You may need it."

"Thank you," I said, impulsively giving him a hug. "Thanks for coming to get me."

"No problem," he said with a grin. "You were the one going all Sarah Connor. Way to be badass."

He fist-bumped me, which I half missed because no one I knew did that. I laughed, pleased at the compliment anyway.

Ty gave me a finger wave, then they were out the door and heading to their car.

"We should go, too," Devon said.

A few minutes later, we were driving out of the lot, heading in the opposite direction of Beau and Ty.

"Where'd you get the car?" I asked. We were in the latest model of a high-end black SUV.

"I thought we could use something less obvious than what I'd prefer to drive," he said. "It's not awful."

I gave a little laugh. No, I certainly wouldn't call a car that cost almost a hundred grand "awful."

"So you know the way to Key West?" I asked.

"It's south, a little east," he replied, glancing at me.

"That's kinda vague," I said, eyeing the navigational system in the car. "Why don't I just punch in the address and let it map it for us?" God forbid a man would need directions, even Devon, apparently.

"If it'll make you feel better," he said with a shrug. "But I don't need it."

I hid a smile, working the menu until the computerized female voice came on over the speakers.

"When possible, make a U-turn," she said politely.

I snorted a laugh, turning it into a cough when Devon shot me a look. But he did as the computer told him, spinning the car around to head in the opposite direction.

We drove for a while in silence. There was a lot to discuss, but I wanted to enjoy just being with Devon. His hand reached for mine, loosely slotting our fingers together, and it made me smile.

A while later, we drove through a small town and stopped for gas. A restaurant across the street was open and my stomach growled.

"Can we get something to eat?" I asked when Devon got back in. I pointed to the restaurant.

He grimaced slightly. "We're likely to get hepatitis, but all right. There aren't a lot of choices, it would seem."

"You're such a snob," I teased. "You're not going to get hepatitis."

"You can hardly know that," he said, maneuvering the car across the street and into a vacant parking spot. "And if I do, you'll be saddled with caring for your ailing boyfriend."

Boyfriend. What an odd term to apply to Devon. He felt like so much *more* than that, especially after all we'd been through.

The place smelled like coffee and bacon, and I took an appreciative sniff as a waitress led us to a booth by the windows. I slid into the vinyl seat as Devon sat opposite me.

"Coffee, please," I said, taking a menu from her.

"Hot tea," Devon ordered.

Everything looked good—I was starving—and when the waitress came back, I ordered a ham and Swiss omelet with hash browns and a side of biscuits and gravy.

Devon raised an eyebrow as he listened to me, then ordered poached eggs with bacon and rye toast.

"What exactly is biscuits and gravy?" he asked once she'd gone.

"It's nirvana," I answered with a grin. "My Grams used to make me homemade biscuits and sausage gravy all the time." At the memory, my smile faded.

"What's wrong?" Devon asked.

I shrugged. "I just miss them, that's all. They practically raised me, but I don't see them much anymore since I moved." With all that had happened, I craved the normalcy of home and my grandparents.

"And you never told them about Jace," he said.

I shook my head. "Why would I? It would just hurt them and bring back the past for me. That part of my life is done."

"And what do you see for the next part of your life?" He took a sip of his tea.

"Is this a trick question?"

His lips tipped up in a half smile. "No. But it occurs to me that you've never mentioned career aspirations."

"I don't really have any," I confessed. "I was just glad to get out of my hometown and be somewhere else. I've always been good with numbers so the job at the bank seemed like a good entry-level position." While other teens had been discussing colleges and career plans, I'd just wanted to leave. It hadn't mattered what my major was, only that it had taken me away.

"Did you go to university?"

"Yes. The University of Kansas. I studied business." Not terribly exciting, but my grades had been decent. "Why are you asking?"

The waitress brought our food then, so he didn't answer until she'd left. I dug into the biscuits and gravy first, which were almost as good as my Gram's.

"After this is over, we should have a plan," he said, shaking salt and pepper onto his eggs.

I didn't answer for a moment as I chewed. "You really think we're going to come out of this okay and go live life like normal people?"

Devon glanced up from his eggs. "Of course. Don't you?"

I was careful with my words. "I hope so," I said. "But the odds aren't in our favor."

He looked at me, his expression grim. "Then why are you here?" he asked.

I stared at him in confusion. "Excuse me?"

"If you think you're going to die, then why stay?"

It took a moment, but then I understood. He took my lack of faith in our chances of survival as a lack of faith in *him*.

"I'm here because I love you," I said. "And if anyone can keep me safe and get us out of this mess, it's you. But Devon, Vega has people everywhere, and now the FBI is looking for me. It seems . . . hopeless."

He leaned across the table and took my hand in a firm grip. "You can't lose hope," he said. "Don't lose sight of what you want, and don't be afraid."

I looked in his eyes, his expression gravely serious, and gave a slow nod.

"Okay," I said. "I won't."

He studied me a moment more, as though ascertaining the validity of my words, before sitting back again and taking another bite of his breakfast.

Maybe we could maneuver our way out of this for a happily ever after.

"Try this," I said, holding out my biscuit-and-gravy-laden fork to him.

He looked dubious, but leaned forward and ate the bite, chewing slowly.

"Well?"

The look on his face said it all and I couldn't stop a laugh. "You don't appreciate fine cuisine," I teased.

"Neither of those words apply to that dog's dinner," he retorted.

I shook my head and went back to my breakfast, then caught him looking at something over my shoulder, his attention fixed.

"What is it?" I asked, turning to see what had him so mesmerized.

There were only a handful of customers, and I didn't see anything out of the ordinary. I glanced in the corner to where a television was hung, then promptly dropped my fork.

My face was on the screen, along with a caption: "Wanted by the FBI." The TV wasn't loud but I could hear, ". . . escaped late last night from an FBI detention facility and is considered armed and extremely dangerous. The public is cautioned not to approach her if spotted, but to call 911 or the FBI tips hotline at once."

The picture of me they used was one that had been taken for my ID badge at work. I was smiling, my hair very long and blonde. And it felt as though I was looking at a stranger.

I'd changed so much since the day I'd met Devon. For the better, I thought.

"Turn around," Devon muttered. "Don't draw attention to the television."

I did as he said, staring at the food on my plate that had suddenly lost its appeal.

"No one paid any attention to that, I think," Devon said. "But let's get out of here, just the same." He tossed some money onto the table. Scooting out of the booth, he took my hand and pulled me after him. Our exit from the diner was ruthlessly unhurried, when all I wanted to do was run. But we caught no one's attention, as was the intent.

Once we were back in the car, I let out a sigh of relief. Devon started the engine before pulling out of the lot.

"Now what?" I asked. "If they plaster that everywhere, there's no way we'll make it all the way to Key West."

"We need to change your appearance," Devon said. "People notice you already, so you stick in their minds. You're quite right. Someone will figure it out."

My looks. Most women would be glad to have them, but they'd caused me nothing but trouble. Being pretty—a curse that should have been a blessing. I'd been born with pure-white blonde hair that now hung to the middle of my back, and golden bedroom eyes. I was tall and model-thin, which I *had* always appreciated because it was really the best figure for wearing the designer clothes I coveted.

Devon spotted a drugstore a couple of blocks down. "Get in the backseat and lie down," he said.

I did as he instructed, climbing over the seat rather than stepping outside. We were only about fifty miles from where I'd been held, and it wasn't outside the realm of possibility that they'd spread the search this far.

"I'll be right back," Devon said.

I anxiously waited for him, the car gradually warming as the sun shone into the front windshield. Yet I still jumped, startled, when he opened the driver's side door. He handed me a bag.

"Hold this," he said.

I peered into the plastic bag as Devon pulled out of the lot. "Hair color for men?" I asked, holding up the box.

"Too obvious if I bought hair color for women," he replied.

There were also a pair of glasses, a comb, a deck of cards, and scissors. I could see where this was going and I tried not to be upset. But I liked my hair. The thought of dyeing and cutting it made me want to cry. Which was ridiculous, even I could see that. Hair grew back. If I were dead, it wouldn't really matter much what color or length my hair was, now would it?

"The shop assistant said there was a town with a hotel about ten miles down the road," he said. "We'll stop there."

I didn't say anything as Devon drove, and neither did he. No doubt both of us were too preoccupied wondering what we'd do if stopped by a roadblock. But nothing and no one blocked our path on the two-lane blacktop, and we only passed the occasional car. Soon, Devon was ushering me into probably the worst motel room I'd ever been in.

"Not exactly the Ritz," he said ruefully. "My apologies."

"It's fine," I said, eyeing the stained carpet. It really didn't matter where we were, so long as I was with Devon. Though not being incarcerated was a definite bonus.

He locked the door behind us and drew the drapes closed while I sat gingerly on the bed.

"This place took cash and I used a fake name," Devon said, digging through the plastic bag. "But I still want to be on the road again soon."

I eyed the box of hair dye as he ripped it open.

"So . . . you like brunettes? I hope?" I asked, trying to keep my voice light.

Devon glanced at me. "I like alive," he said flatly.

Point taken.

"Let's do this," he said.

I nodded and stripped off my shirt, wearing only my bra. No sense getting dye on my clothes. Going into the bathroom, I wet my hair, taking one last look at it.

By the time I returned, Devon had pulled out a wobbly chair from the corner and sat it in the middle of the floor. He'd laid a towel on the floor behind the chair and motioned for me to sit.

I took a deep breath as I sat down. "You have to have a license to be a beautician, you know," I joked, trying not to think about what was going to happen.

"I'll add it to my list of transgressions."

A smile tugged at my lips.

"How short?" he asked, and I appreciated him asking.

"Um, I guess we'd better go above the shoulders," I said. No way was I going to try something super short and spiky. It took a real hairdresser to know how to cut it like that and I didn't trust Devon. At least, not with my hair.

I winced at the tug on my hair and the snipping sounds, but Devon was quick and a few minutes later, the heavy weight of my hair was considerably lighter. My neck felt weirdly exposed.

"Is it even?" I asked.

"Mostly," he said.

I turned to look at him, but he just winked. "Kidding. Sorry."

Glancing down, I saw my hair on the towel and couldn't repress a sigh.

"It'll grow back, darling," Devon said. His fingers brushed under my chin, lifting my gaze to his.

"I know. I'm being stupid," I said. "Time for the dye, I guess."

That was harder. And messy. But a couple of hours later, I'd rinsed it out, blown it dry, and stared in the mirror, trying to get used to the "midnight black" Devon had chosen. The color made my eyes stand out and my fair skin was like porcelain ivory.

"What do you think?" I asked Devon, who'd come up behind me.

"I think it's incredibly difficult to make you look anything short of stunning."

It was the perfect thing to say to make me feel better.

Devon brandished a pair of glasses. "Put these on."

The lenses were just glass, not corrective, and the frames were dark. I made a face at myself.

"Not bad," Devon said. "You look quite different. It should help."

"Do you think they're searching for me everywhere in the States? Or just around here?"

"Not only are they searching for you everywhere, they're enlisting the public to help," he said. "I must confess, I didn't think they'd go that far."

"Can't the CIA make them stop?" I asked.

"The agencies don't always share information and sometimes don't even have the same agenda," he said. "The CIA's goal is to help disarm Vega. The FBI doesn't care about that. They just want you. I'm sure Beau will do what he can, but in the end, the search will go further up the line than he'll be able to influence.

"We'll wait until dark, then hit the road again," he continued.

"Okay." Key West seemed a long ways away.

Devon left the bathroom while I studied my reflection. I heard the sound of cards being shuffled. Coming out, I saw he'd taken up a spot on the bed and was busy mixing the deck of cards he'd bought.

"A way to pass the time?" I guessed, perching opposite him and crossing my legs underneath me.

"I'd rather have sex, but didn't think that was a viable option for the entirety of the trip," he said dryly.

"Well, you're not exactly twenty-five anymore," I teased him.

"Twenty-five-year-olds know nothing about sex," he replied.

"So how old are you anyway?" I asked as he dealt the cards.

"How old do you think I am?"

I studied him, considering. Men only looked better as they aged, and Devon was no exception. The softness of youth had been replaced by a lean strength of character in the line of his jaw and the set of his eyes.

"I'm going to guess . . . thirty-five?"

His lips twitched. "Close enough."

"So you *are* robbing the cradle," I said, picking up my cards.

"I don't hear you complaining."

"Certainly not." I layered on a so-so copy of his British accent, prompting a full smile from him. "So what are we playing?"

"Texas Holdem," he said. "Do you know how to play?"

"I know the basics of poker," I said. "Like Five Card Draw. But not Texas Holdem."

"Then I'll teach you."

We whiled away an hour or two playing various poker games, with Devon teasing me about my poorly done poker face. Finally, after trying to bluff my way through a bad hand, I tossed my cards aside and climbed onto his lap.

"You're terrible at bluffing," he said, his soft smile indulgent.

"Maybe I'm fantastic at bluffing, and you're just really good at reading me," I countered.

"Possibly."

I rested my head on his shoulder, my good mood fading as I looked out the window.

"You're worrying again," he said, his palm gently rubbing my back.

"And you're not?"

"One problem at a time, one day at a time, one hour at a time. That's how you deal with it. Look too far ahead and the obstacles can feel insurmountable. It's like climbing a mountain. Take it one step at a time."

"And what about after?" I asked. "If we do make it out of this, what then? Where will we live? How will we live? What will we do?"

Devon rested against the headboard and stretched out his legs, pulling me into a more comfortable position on top of him.

"You tell me," he said. "I've been everywhere. If you had to pick, where would you want to live?"

It was one of those questions people play for games, but this was for real.

"I've never thought about it," I said. "I wanted to get away from home, but I don't want to go so far away I can't see my grandparents very often."

"Please don't ask me to live in Kansas."

His dry comment made me laugh. No, I couldn't imagine a man like Devon living in Kansas.

"I won't," I said.

"Do you like the snow or the sun? Mountains or the ocean? Trees or plains?"

"Yes."

He chuckled deep in his chest. "Not at all difficult to please, then," he said.

My eyes were drifting shut, the exhaustion and stress catching up to me, and I mumbled a reply. The sound of his heartbeat underneath my ear was comforting to me, as was the steady rise and fall of his chest as he breathed. His hand was still lightly rubbing my back, and before I knew it, I'd drifted off.

It was dark by the time we left and I was starving, but even the hunger pangs in my stomach paled in comparison to my nerves.

Devon and I found a Salvation Army store in the small town, and we stopped to replenish our wardrobes. Though he'd had clothes with him, he'd ditched them in a dumpster because custom-tailored suits may have helped blend in with the crowd inside a city, but driving through Middle America, they'd stand out.

"You actually expect me to wear that?" Devon asked, raising an eyebrow at the plaid shirt I held up for him.

"It's your size," I said, "and it's not bad. American Eagle brand, not bad at all."

"It's *checked*."

"We call it *plaid* here and I adore plaid."

"Bollocks."

I snickered, shoving the hanger at him anyway. "Stop whining," I teased. "They say plaid is the new black. Now be good, or I'll buy you plaid in *flannel*."

"God help me," he muttered, trailing along as I moved from rack to rack. By the time I was done, we had several days' worth of clothes in generic denim, cotton, and yes, plaid. I found some used tennis shoes for myself that fit well, and, for Devon, a pair of work boots that he didn't complain overly much about.

"Expensive shoes stand out," I said, "especially on a man."

"Yes, that's why I buy them," he groused as he discarded his Ferragamos.

I had the suspicion that Devon knew all this as well as I did, and was only giving me a hard time to make me laugh and take my mind off things. And it worked, mostly. But there was still no denying the fact that the only reason we were buying the clothes was because I was being hunted by the FBI.

"Go out to the car and wait while I buy these," he said, handing me the key. "There are only a few security cameras here, but the best ones—the ones with the clearest video—will be at the register, and I don't want your face to be recorded."

"Okay," I agreed, my nerves coming back with a vengeance.

I looked at the ground as I headed for the SUV, not meeting anyone's eyes as I passed. A man was behind me, maybe twenty yards, also walking through the parking lot. I couldn't see what he looked like without being obvious, but I was acutely aware of him. The temptation was strong to walk faster, but that would make me stand out. Besides, there were other cars in the lot. Maybe it was just coincidence that he happened to be going to his car the same time I was going to mine.

Yeah, because that's just how my luck had gone lately.

It occurred to me that leading him right to my vehicle wasn't the best plan. All he'd have to do was overpower me—not difficult—throw me inside, and take the car.

I walked past the black SUV, which was parked in the farther reaches of the lot, and headed for another car. The man followed, only now he was gaining on me.

So much for coincidence.

I broke into a run, hoping I could outdistance him. What I didn't have in strength, I could make up for in speed. My legs were long and ate up the pavement. Unfortunately, his did, too.

Doubling back, I dodged amongst the parked cars. I ducked behind a big pickup, crouching down as I scurried between vehicles, using them to conceal my location. Finding a shadowed spot next to a minivan, I stopped, getting as low to the ground as possible and yet still ready to run. I couldn't see my pursuer any longer, but in the sudden quiet, I could hear him.

His feet crunched slightly on the asphalt as he searched for me. His steps were slow and deliberate, as though it were only a matter of time before he found his prey. And it was true. I couldn't outrun him and I had no weapon. Even if Devon came out of the store in time, I was too far away for him to help me.

The footsteps were close, right on the other side of the vehicle where I was hiding. I held my breath and didn't so much as twitch. If he'd just move on to the next car, I'd make another break for it and head back toward the store and Devon.

Hands came down on my shoulders and I bit back a scream, whirling with a fist cocked. Whoever he was, I wasn't going down without a fight. But I froze.

"Devon?"

"What are you doing?" he asked. "Why are you hiding?"

I glanced around frantically, looking for the man, but he was gone. "There was someone following me," I explained. "He chased me and I ran between the cars to hide."

Devon's eyes narrowed as he scanned the lot, but the only people around were heading into the building, too far away to be the man who'd chased me.

"Let's go."

I obeyed Devon's curt command, allowing him to hustle me into the SUV. But even as we sped out of the lot, my hands were still clammy with sweat as I stared out the back window, searching for the man. He couldn't have just disappeared. But it seemed he'd done exactly that.

CHAPTER THREE

The incident outside the Salvation Army store had really thrown me. I couldn't understand why the man hadn't attacked or where he'd gone. Maybe he'd seen Devon and decided against it? Maybe it'd had nothing to do with the FBI search and he had just been a random predator targeting a woman walking alone?

As if my luck would be that good.

"You don't think I'm making it up, do you?" I asked.

Devon glanced over to me, his brow drawn in a frown. "Why would I think that?"

"Because you didn't see him," I said. "Maybe you think I'm being paranoid or imagining things."

"By now, I think you're fully capable of knowing when you're being pursued," he said. "I can only assume he saw me and decided to wait for a more opportune time."

My blood chilled. "Do you think he's following us?"

Devon shrugged. "I don't know. We'll have to deal with that as it happens. I don't see anyone, but with satellites and drone technology, anything is possible."

Satellites and drones. I hadn't even thought about that. But all those things were at the government's disposal, so wouldn't they use them?

"We're still alive and not in custody," Devon said, reaching across the seat to take my hand and give it a reassuring squeeze. "There's a reason for that."

I nodded, trying to feel comforted by his words, but it was hard.

It was evening when Devon pulled off the highway into a truck stop for gas, which appeared to be the only business for miles around. Over a dozen semis were parked in the lot and more were edging the off- and on-ramps to the highway.

Devon navigated to the fuel pumps. Cars were on the opposite side from the semis with a large building housing a convenience store, fast-food restaurant, candy store . . . and a place selling western-style boots.

Hmm. I didn't have any of those.

"I can see it on your face," Devon said in a resigned sort of way. He was leaning in the open driver's side door, waiting for the tank to fill.

I pretended innocence. "What do you mean?"

"You want to go in the boots store."

"Pffft," I waved him off. "Don't be silly. What would I do with cowboy boots?"

"You know, most women would go for the sweets," he said.

"I like candy."

His lips curved in a half smile. "Go on. You've got ten minutes, and no, I'm not buying whatever you fall in love with."

I grinned and popped out of the car, feeling almost like my old self.

"Ten minutes!" he called after me.

I could do a lot of damage in ten minutes.

The bell over the door tinkled merrily as I walked in, and my nostrils were filled with the warm scent of leather that permeated the shop.

"Wow," I breathed, taking it in. There were rows and rows of boots lining the walls, along with a small section in the back of leather belts, and a case displaying buckles of every size and shape imaginable.

I drifted toward the rows, taking it all in. It was like a nirvana for cowboy-boot lovers. One red pair in particular caught my eye and I couldn't resist touching them, my fingers sliding over the detailed drawings of flowers and vines etched into the leather. I may not own any cowboy boots, but I could appreciate good quality and craftsmanship in any kind of footwear.

"I bet I have those in your size."

Glancing behind me, I saw a wizened old man had approached, a smile buried under his gray beard and moustache. Eyebrows that could use a trim flanked eyes that assessed me as only a seasoned salesman could.

"Oh no," I protested rather weakly. "I'm just looking." My eyes were drawn back to the boots like magnets and I was still touching them.

"Might as well try them on," he said. "You're an eight?"

Wow. He was good. I nodded. "Yes."

"I'll be right back." He disappeared into the back at a faster clip than I would have thought him capable. I considered that I should probably leave, but it would be rude to just walk out on him, right? Plus, I hadn't used up my full ten minutes yet. And I was cheerful, a condition that had become all too rare lately. I was loath to give up the feeling so readily.

"Here you go," he said, returning with three boxes. He set them down on the floor next to a bench. "I brought those plus a couple of other pairs I thought you might like."

Oh, this was bad. Really, really bad, I thought as I sank onto the bench and started pulling off my tennis shoes. Yet I reached for the boot he handed me and slid it on. It fit perfectly, as did its mate. I tucked my skinny jeans inside and smoothed the denim.

"Take a look at those, now," he said proudly, gesturing to a full mirror attached to the wall. "They sure do look good on you, don't they."

Yes, yes, they certainly did.

"Try these," he suggested, holding out another pair. They were a deeper red, and black, with more elaborate etchings. I snatched them up like an addict being offered a hit.

"They feel better than the others," I said, parading in front of the mirror. Okay, I was totally rocking these boots.

"I have a buckle that would go perfectly," he said, getting up from the stool he sat on. His knees creaked when he moved, but that didn't slow him down as he went for the glass case in the back.

I saw Devon in the mirror as he walked up behind me.

"I think the *plaid* has gone to your head," he said dryly.

I grinned. "Haven't you ever wanted to do it with a cowgirl?" I teased.

"Somehow I believe real cowgirls rarely wear red boots."

Pointing at him in the mirror, I said, "You're so wrong. I bet they do wear red boots."

"And how much are these shining specimens of American culture?" he asked.

Good question. I dug around in the box for the price tag, swallowing hard when I found it, then I quickly pulled off the boots.

"So I guess you're ready to go?" I asked, being super careful as I put the boots away. They must have been inlaid with gold under that leather to justify the price.

"Whenever you are."

"Did you decide on the boots?" the salesman asked. "This buckle would look mighty fine with 'em."

I smiled. "Thanks, but I think I'm going to pass."

"Are you sure? We're having a sale. Buy a pair of boots and the second pair is twenty percent off."

I hesitated, looking longingly at the boots, then Devon gave me a shove out the door.

"I'm going, I'm going," I muttered. "Just looking at them, that's all."

"Of course you were," he said.

We headed into the convenience store part of the building and I used the bathroom, then grabbed a soda and a bag of potato chips while I waited for Devon. Tinny country music played over the speakers and bright fluorescent lighting lit the aisles.

Wandering around the place, I saw they had all kinds of kitschy souvenirs and knickknacks, though why someone would want to buy a two-foot-tall metal chicken made out of recycled Coke cans was beyond me. I paused by the dream catchers, done in every color of the rainbow. Now those I could've used a few months ago.

Three truckers were milling about the coffee machines, chatting. Wearing worn denim, baseball hats, and various stages of facial hair, it wasn't hard to peg their occupation. I couldn't help half tuning in to their conversation as they sipped from their steaming Styrofoam cups.

". . . bear in the bushes up the road a ways," one of them said.

I paused in my browsing, the term catching my attention.

"Shit. All the way out here?" another asked.

The first man nodded. "Yeah. Word is smokeys are as thick as bugs on a bumper. Gotta be in Louisville by mornin' and I can't waste time with a brake check."

The door to the convenience store opened and a cop stepped inside.

I sucked in a sharp breath, freezing in place.

What if he recognized me? There was nowhere to go. I couldn't even leave the store because I'd have to pass him to do it. I was trapped.

"Easy there, missy," one of the truckers said to me in an undertone.

"Look somewhere else. You're about to give yourself away, staring at him like a deer in headlights."

My startled gaze met his. He gave a little nod and nudged me toward the candy rack. I took the hint, dropping down to hunch by the candy and pretending to give much consideration to Kit Kat versus Snickers.

The men casually stood close, their legs obscuring my view of the rest of the aisle.

"Evenin', officer," one of them said. I heard the officer mumble something in reply. A few seconds later, the truckers moved back.

"He's gone," the same guy said.

I got to my feet, my knees a little too shaky for my liking. "Thank you," I said.

"There's a lot of smokeys out there looking for somebody," he said. "I reckon that might be you?"

It was rather obvious by my reaction so I didn't bother lying and just nodded. "But I didn't do anything," I said. "I swear. I'm not dangerous."

One of the men snickered. "You got that right," he said, his voice gruff. "You look about as dangerous as my Aunt Mae."

The others seemed to agree, with rounds of "Yep" and "No shit."

"You headed down 65?" he asked. I nodded. "You traveling alone?"

"No. I'm with a . . . friend," I replied, not really wanting to call Devon my "boyfriend."

"Where you headed?"

I thought about not answering, but decided they might be able to help. After all, they already had. "Florida."

"You got a CB?" he asked. I shook my head. "Get one. It's a good way to keep up with what's ahead of you. My handle is Slackjaw. This here's Meatloaf." He jerked his head to the first guy. "And Kentucky George." The last of the trio. "You can keep in touch with us. We're all headed down south."

Given the names, I assumed those were all CB handles. "Okay," I said. "Thanks. I appreciate it."

"Got a handle?"

"Um, no . . ."

"Make one up and we'll keep in touch," he said.

I was immediately at a loss. A handle was like a nickname, right? I'd never had a nickname in my life.

"Uh, I-I don't know—" I stammered.

"Outlaw Annie," Meatloaf interrupted.

Everyone turned to look at him.

"What?" he asked. "She needs a handle."

Slackjaw shrugged. "Outlaw Annie good with you?"

I nodded. "Yeah, sure." Who didn't love Annie Oakley? I'd grown up out west, I knew who she was. She'd been a badass. "Thanks, guys."

"You be careful now," Slackjaw cautioned.

I met Devon at the counter and set my things on it for the cashier to ring up. I told him about the cop and what the truckers had said about police being all around. His expression turned grim.

"Add a state map to that, please," he said to the cashier, who obliged.

Once we were back in the SUV, we spread the map open on the dash.

"Best to turn off our navigation system," he said. "Big Brother and all."

I hadn't thought of that and now I realized why he'd bought the map. I felt better being able to see where we were going, which was a heck of a lot easier with a paper map. And knowing the government couldn't track me was also a huge plus.

"Did they say how far away they were?"

I shook my head. "No. Just 'a bear in the bushes.'"

"Slang for a police car hiding," he said.

"We need to buy a CB," I said. "That way we can hear about stuff like this."

Devon glanced at me. "Exactly what I was thinking," he said, a twinkle in his eye. "Perhaps I should be alarmed at how your mind is starting to work like mine."

I didn't tell him that Slackjaw had been the one to suggest it to me. "Great minds think alike," I said with a shrug.

We Googled the nearest Wal-Mart, which had us double back about five miles, but they had CBs so it was worth the trip. Turning it on, I put the channel on nineteen.

We drove in silence for a while as I listened to the chatter on the CB. I noticed lots of semitrucks around. Traffic on the highway picked up as the evening wore on and more truckers were awake to avoid the daytime drivers.

It was about an hour after we'd left the convenience store when something on the CB caught my attention.

"Breaker one-nine, this here's Slackjaw. You got a copy on me, Kentucky George?"

His accent was the same thick Southern I remembered from the convenience store. The CB speaker crackled again.

"Ten-four, Slackjaw. Kentucky George here, c'mon."

"There's a checkpoint Charlie up 65 a ways. They're stopping everybody. A manhunt goin' on."

"Copy that, Slackjaw. How bad is the brake check?"

"'Bout a mile now. Outlaw Annie, if you copy, you in particular might wanna get off the boulevard."

Devon and I glanced at each other. "That's me," I explained. "They gave me a handle, said I was Outlaw Annie."

"I thought it was your idea to get a CB?" he asked.

Damn. So much for my mad spycraft skills. "Okay, so maybe they suggested it, but I agreed."

A smile flitted across his face. "A checkpoint and manhunt," Devon said. "That's not good."

"And if he's calling me out by name, then they must be show-ing my picture around." I had to thank my luck that we ran into the truckers.

"And they recognized you."

"So much for the disguise." I sighed. Cut and dye for nothing, it appeared, if even random truckers could spot me.

"Outlaw Annie, you copy the checkpoint Charlie?"

Picking up the CB, I pressed and held the button. "Annie, here. I copy your checkpoint, Slackjaw. Thanks for the heads-up." I released the button, then remembered how you were supposed to do these things and quickly pressed it again. "Over." I glanced at Devon. "That's how you do it, right?"

He was hiding a smile and gave me a mockingly serious nod. "Absolutely. You sounded exactly like a truck driver."

I gave him a narrow-eyed look, which he ignored while navi-gating us a lane over in between traffic that had slowed to a crawl. An exit was up ahead and he aimed for it. It was only as we were sliding out of traffic that we saw the flashing lights at the top that indicated more cops waiting for those doing exactly as we were try-ing to do—get around the checkpoint.

Devon jerked the wheel and maneuvered back into the lane, bypassing the exit.

"Better to stick with the motorway," he explained before I could ask. "They'll be under more pressure to move quickly there, what with traffic tied up like this."

I was nervous as we crept along, wondering what was going to happen. What if they recognized me? Would they arrest me on the spot? I assumed they would. What would happen to Devon?

"Annie, this is Slackjaw. You off the boulevard?"

I pressed the button and spoke. "Negative. Bears all around." I hoped that meant what I thought it did.

"Copy that. Meatloaf and Kentucky George, you copy?"

The CB crackled. "That's a big ten-four, Slackjaw. Mealoaf here. Any ideas for rescuing Annie?"

"There's a bull hauler in front of me. I reckon we can convoy us a spot of trouble, come back."

"Roger, Meatloaf. I'm comin' up on your donkey now in the granny lane. Kentucky's got eyes on the gumball machines. Annie is in front of me. Annie, I hope you got your ears on."

I couldn't decipher most of that except the last part, and I thumbed the button.

"Annie's here," I said. Now I noticed the semitrucks surrounding our SUV. I figured Meatloaf was in front of us while Slackjaw and Kentucky were behind.

"Keep up, Annie. We're about to put the hammer down. You copy?"

"Ten-four." I was getting good at this, though I still didn't know what was going on. "What are they doing?" I asked Devon.

"I believe they're going to run the checkpoint," he said, "with us in between them."

I stared at him, open-mouthed. "But . . . why would they do that?"

"They're American truck drivers," he said dryly. "You probably have better insight into their behavior than I do, my dear. I'm guessing their love for the law is less than their desire to assist a damsel in distress."

I couldn't fathom it, so I decided to just be grateful for their intervention as the truck in front of us sped up. The headlights from the one behind us were blinding as they blazed through the rear window, right on our tail. Devon sped up and I could see the checkpoint up ahead.

My palms were sweaty as I clamped my hands on my seat, my nails digging into the leather. I didn't speak, not wanting to interrupt Devon's concentration as he stayed right on the bumper of the truck in front of us, accelerating.

The police saw the trucks coming—they were kind of hard to miss—and started scrambling to get out of the way. Beyond the checkpoint, the highway was clear.

People were yelling and drivers of the cars we passed watched in open-mouthed wonder at the caravan of three semitrucks and an SUV barreling past them. The trucks blew their horns and I couldn't help covering my eyes as we crashed through behind Meatloaf. There was the screech of metal against metal and the sound of tires squealing. I held my breath, waiting for the crash. But nothing hit us, and a moment later, I chanced a look.

"They're barricading the road behind us," Devon said. The SUV was still going top speed and accelerating.

I twisted in my seat to look behind us. All three truckers had stopped, parking their rigs across the road to prevent any quick chase from the police. They had indeed covered for us.

"Peach, are you through?" I heard over the CB. I quickly thumbed the button.

"Ten-four. Thank you all for doing that." I had no idea how much trouble they'd be in, but I hoped it wouldn't be more than a slap on the wrist.

"You take care now. Watch for bears. They're thick as bugs on a bumper, searching for this woman named Ivy."

I swallowed hard. "Copy that, Slackjaw." I let the button up with a sigh of relief.

Devon drove fast, and took the next exit, handing me the folded-up map.

"Going off the motorway will cost us time, but will be worth it to avoid the police," he said. "Look and see the secondary route I've marked. See if it looks right to you."

I was no stranger to two-lane country roads, the winding curves and trees flashing by reminding me of where I'd grown up. Beyond the trees loomed impenetrable darkness that only thickened as the hours passed. It made my imagination work overtime, probably from watching too many episodes of the *X-Files* growing up. If I wandered past the initial barrier into the inky blackness, would I find evidence of the unexplained? Aliens and mothmen and Bigfoot?

Doubtful. More likely mosquitoes, snakes, and feral possums.

"What are you thinking that's making you smile like that?" Devon asked.

I glanced over at him, realizing I was indeed grinning a little at my fanciful imaginary forest expedition.

"Just thinking about what's out there," I said with a shrug, nodding my head toward the trees. "When I was little, I was always fascinated by the idea of monsters. Mythical creatures out there, evading detection and leaving only clues as to their existence. They could hide forever, it seemed."

"Monsters are real," he said grimly, "and they do hide amongst us. Disguised as normal people you love and trust."

The darkness in his voice had me studying his profile. "You're talking about Vega, aren't you," I said. He didn't answer, but he didn't have to. "You told me once before that she's the one who helped you when your parents were killed." This time I waited, hoping he'd open up to me. It took several long moments, but eventually my patience paid off.

"The murder of my parents had a profound effect on me," he said. "I retreated into myself, turning into a sullen, angry, silent boy. A couple of years passed and I started getting into fights, trying to find an outlet for the anger, I think. I . . . beat one child so badly, he ended up in the hospital. He was all right, but I was to be removed from the orphanage and placed in a YOI, young offenders institute, which is much like your juvenile detention centers.

"That's when Vega appeared," he continued. "I was fifteen and friendless. Smart, but unmotivated. If I'd been removed to the YOI, I am quite sure I'd have run away and become a full-blown criminal on the streets of London. She placed me in another location that I later was to learn belonged to the Shadow. I lived there, was trained there, for the next four years."

I did the math. "You were nineteen. So . . . then what did you do?"

"I killed someone."

He said it matter-of-factly, but I could detect a hint of something else. Regret, maybe? Disillusion?

"They'd trained me to be a ruthless killer, but also had taught me spycraft, and above all, unwavering and unquestioning loyalty to the Shadow. For the first few years, I did a lot of recce. After that first kill, it was easier, but assassinations didn't come until later. I left a bloody trail in my wake and became Vega's top operator."

I wasn't sure how to respond. *Congratulations* wasn't really what he was going for, I thought. His hand lay on the console between us, so I folded my palm over his. I stayed quiet, letting him say things I knew almost for certain he'd never told another living soul.

"I did my job faithfully for six years. Excellently. Then I met Kira. It didn't occur to me that I wouldn't be able to be with her. We were in love." There was no mistaking the bitterness in his voice. "I was a fool."

Devon's grip tightened on my hand.

"Vega told me . . . she was the one who'd had Kira murdered."

I stared at him, both shocked and unsurprised at Vega's actions. I remembered the easy, almost casual way in which she'd had Clive killed. How she'd spoken of giving Heinrich the whereabouts of Clive's wife, Anna, which had led to her infection and tortuous death.

I wished Devon wasn't driving so I could put my arms around him, but I settled for squeezing his hand instead.

"I'm so sorry," I murmured.

"I trusted her, obeyed her, gave my life over to her, for *years,*" he said. "And she betrayed me. What she did . . . what she *allowed* them to do to Kira . . . " He looked at me and I sucked in a breath at the rage and pain in his eyes and on his face. "She's the monster, Ivy. And we're going to take everything from her."

The conviction in his words sent a chill through me. I understood Devon's wanting vengeance, but I didn't want him to die because of it.

It was after midnight when we pulled into a motel in the middle of nowhere that looked like a reject from *Psycho*. Devon turned off the engine, but I made no move to get out.

"What's the matter?" he asked.

It would have sounded ridiculous for me to be all, *I'm skeered*, like a kid who'd watched too many horror movies . . . but apparently I'd watched too many horror movies.

"Maybe there's like a Holiday Inn or something a bit further," I suggested. "I could drive, if you're tired."

"Holiday Inns have records and computers and cameras," he said. "This place does not."

"I also doubt they have running water," I muttered as he got out.

"Wait here," he said before closing his door and walking into the dingy office to rent a room.

"No problem," I said under my breath, eyeing the flickering neon sign proclaiming "Vacancy," except the *N* and *C* were both out, so it looked like "Vacay."

"Far from it," I said to myself, remembering the wonderful hotel in Maui at which Devon and I had stayed. Although I had champagne taste on a beer budget (as my Grams was so often telling me), I didn't think I was being all snotty about *this* place. Anyone in their right mind could see it was a total dump.

"Should've bought Lysol at Walmart." Oh well. I'd have to pick some up the next time we passed the ubiquitous shopping center.

Devon returned a few minutes later, bearing a key. He drove us toward the end of the strip of rooms, stopping in front of number thirteen. I glanced at him.

"Thirteen? Really?"

"Surely you're not superstitious," he said, his lips twitching at the corners.

"Why tempt the universe?" I countered. "We're already on its bad side."

Leaning over, he pressed his lips to mine in a quick, hard kiss. His hand cupped my cheek as he gazed into my eyes. "I promise, I'll protect you from the universe," he softly murmured.

My heart promptly melted.

I followed him inside as he carried the duffel bag containing our clothes. The room was clean, but old. The linens thin and worn, the carpet stained in spots with God only knew what. I perched gingerly on the edge of the bed.

Though I hadn't done the driving today, I was exhausted. I swiped a hand tiredly over my eyes.

"Are you all right?" Devon asked, his brow creased with concern.

I smiled. "I'm fine. Just need to get some sleep, I think."

He seemed to accept that, turning away and bolting the door, then wedging a chair under the knob. I watched as he checked the windows, too.

"Do you think anyone is following us?" I asked, the man from the parking lot coming to mind.

"I think it pays to be cautious."

Abruptly I wondered what would happen if we did make it out of this. Devon had lived a life I couldn't begin to imagine. Would he find the day-to-day normalcy of no longer being a spy boring? And what would he do if he decided he'd made a mistake and couldn't live just a normal existence?

I thought about this as I brushed my teeth and got ready for bed. I stripped off my jeans, then inspected the sheets and bedcovers before climbing into them. Devon was checking his weapon and didn't take anything off before settling down next to me.

"Aren't you going to take off your shoes?" I asked, bewildered. But he shook his head.

"If I need to move quickly, I don't want to take the time to put them on. Better to be prepared."

Well, that sounded alarming.

"Should I put my shoes on, too?" I asked.

"No, darling." He drew me into his arms and pressed a kiss to my forehead. "You sleep and don't worry."

His arms were strong, the muscles hard, and it made me feel safe. His weapon was underneath his pillow and his right hand lay within easy reach of it. I relaxed, my body molding itself to his, and closed my eyes.

I woke with a jerk, gasping as Devon bounded out of bed. In seconds he was at the door, and before I could utter a word or ask a question, he was outside.

Confused and trying to clear the cobwebs of sleep from my brain, it took me a moment to get to my feet and follow him. That's when I saw the headlights outside, burning bright enough to blind me.

Devon was going somewhere without me?

But no, he was there, and the car . . . someone was stealing it.

Gunshots made me jump, my heart climbing into my throat. I couldn't see, couldn't tell what was going on, but then the car was tearing out of the lot, gravel spewing from behind its wheels, and Devon was firing more shots. I heard glass breaking, but then the car was gone, the taillights a dim red disappearing down the road.

I stood in the sudden silence, still trying to wrap my foggy brain around what had just happened. Someone had stolen our car and Devon . . .

I looked around, my eyes adjusting to the darkness, and saw him. He was standing about ten yards away, arms at his sides and hand still grasping his gun.

"Devon?" I asked, my voice cautious. "What . . .what's going on?"

He turned back to me. "Ivy," he said, "do get back inside. I don't think there are more of them, but you're an open target, standing there like that."

I hesitated for a second, then stepped back into the dark room. Hurrying to the bed, I pulled on my pants and was tying my shoelaces when he came back inside.

"So someone just stole our car?" I asked.

"It appears so." His voice was grim.

"That's so . . . random," I said. "I mean, we're in the middle of nowhere."

"Exactly."

I hesitated, trying to decipher what he was thinking. "What does that mean?"

"It means I don't think it was random."

Alarm shot through me. "You think they found us?" The thought of going back into that facility to be poked and prodded, separated forever from Devon, made me physically ill.

But Devon shook his head. "If it had been Vega or the FBI, they wouldn't have left us and taken the car. No, I think we're dealing with a different element here." He removed a box of bullets from the duffel and reloaded his gun. I was really glad he hadn't left the bag in the car.

"So what are we going to do?"

He rammed the full magazine home and I started at the sound.

"I'm going to get it back."

He headed out the door again and I jumped to my feet, following him. He turned around, but I spoke first.

"Don't even think that you're leaving me behind in this creepy motel by myself," I said. "No way."

My stubborn insistence softened the hard expression on his face. "I keep forgetting you're not one to sit idly by and wait for life to suit you," he said, taking my hand with his free one. "All right. You can come, but you must do as I say. Agreed?"

"Agreed." Unless he told me to leave him and save myself or something dumb like that, of course.

The office door was unlocked when Devon pushed it open, a rusted bell announcing our presence. No one was behind the counter and it was quiet, the only sound that of the buzzing fluorescent lights overhead.

Devon's steps were silent and he squeezed my hand and let go, a glance telling me he wanted me to stay put. I stopped, watching him lift his weapon, elbows bent, as he rounded the counter to a door just beyond.

Someone coughed and Devon paused, moving to the side of the door and waiting. Sure enough, a few seconds later, the door opened and a man stepped out.

I barely had time to notice his scraggly beard, stained T-shirt, and lip and nose piercings before Devon had him by the throat and shoved up against the wall. The muzzle of the gun was pressed against his temple and Devon was in his face.

"Where the fuck is my car?" he growled.

The guy looked terrified, but struggled not to show it. "I don't know what you're talking about, man," he said.

Devon pressed the muzzle harder into his head, until he flinched.

"I'll ask you one more time, then I'm going to shoot you." Devon's tone was cold, and sweat broke out on the man's brow. "Where is my car?"

"I don't know—"

The gunshot made me flinch, but Devon hadn't shot the guy.

Instead, the bullet was lodged into the wall behind his head. Blood dripped from his ear, and I realized the bullet had taken a chunk of flesh with it.

"Oh God! Oh God!" The guy was crying now, his hand covering his injury. "Please don't kill me! I know who took it! I'll tell you! Just don't kill me!"

"Then talk," Devon bit out.

"Th-they pay me a thousand bucks to tell them about any good cars. Then they come and steal them. I don't know what they do with them, I swear."

"Who are they?"

"I don't know their names," the guy said, his eyes swiveling to where Devon still held the gun close to his face. "They live about a mile from here, in the trailer park. They're a bunch of meth heads and dealers, brewing that shit up and selling it."

"A mile in which direction?"

"S-south," he stammered.

"Excellent."

Devon moved fast, the butt of the gun coming down hard on the guy's head. His eyes rolled up and he dropped to the floor like a rock.

"He's not dead, is he?" I asked, eyeing the body.

"No. Just out for a while. I don't want him to warn them."

"Warn them about what?"

Devon looked at me like I was an idiot. "That I'm coming."

"You can't go take on a bunch of drug dealers alone," I protested. "It's just a car. We-we can rent a new one."

"Where on earth do you think we'll be able to rent a new one out here?" he asked, raising an eyebrow.

Okay, well he had me there. Maybe we could sneak into the park, find the SUV, and steal it back. No muss, no fuss.

Yeah, right.

I sighed. "Okay. Let's go." I pointed at him. "And no, I'm not staying behind."

"I wasn't going to suggest you should," he said, sounding affronted.

I snorted. "Sure you weren't."

"All right. Perhaps I was thinking it would be safer—"

"We're in this together," I interrupted. "Where you go, I go. Whether it's dangerous or not. We're not separating." I knew what happened when you separated. I'd seen enough movies. It was always bad. Like getting up in the middle of the night to check out the strange noise downstairs in a horror movie. Always a bad decision. "Agreed?"

I waited, crossing my arms and staring at him until he finally caved. "Agreed."

Devon searched the clerk's pockets until he turned up a set of car keys, which went to a beat-up VW Bug we found behind the building. I slid into the passenger seat and gagged on the overwhelming odor of weed.

"Good lord," I said, rolling down the manual window. Hadn't seen one of those in a while. "Is getting high all he does?"

"What else is there to do around here?" Devon replied, starting the engine.

Okay, he may have had a point.

We drove south, following the same direction they'd taken the SUV, for about a mile. I scanned the darkness ahead, then pointed.

"There it is."

It was a dilapidated wooden sign proclaiming the entrance to "Hunter's Glen," and beyond it I could see the outline of trailers lined up in a row. At this hour, I'd expect them all to be dark, but lights glowed from so many windows, it was as though it were merely seven o'clock in the evening instead of only a few hours from the approaching dawn. Very weird.

Devon pulled off the road and killed the engine. He handed me the gun Beau had left, racking the slide for me.

"It's loaded with a round in the chamber," he said, "so be careful. Don't point it at anything you wouldn't want to shoot."

I nodded, my mouth suddenly dry. If Devon did actually need me to help him, I hoped I could.

"I want you to stay here," he said. I opened my mouth to protest, but he cut me off. "I'm going to do a recce, see what we're dealing with. Easier and quieter with just one person. Then I'll be back."

Okay, well, I couldn't really argue with that, so I just nodded, but I wasn't happy.

Devon switched off the overhead light so it wouldn't come on when he opened the door. When he got out, he didn't slam the door shut, but pushed it lightly until it latched.

The road was empty and silent, and I watched until he was swallowed by the darkness.

God, I hated the waiting.

My nerves were on edge and I started at every little noise. The smell inside of the car grew nauseating with each minute that passed, even with the windows down. Finally—afraid I was going to vomit from the sickly sweet odor—I couldn't take it anymore. I got out the same way Devon had, making sure to be as quiet as I could.

The weeds were thick on the side of the road and I tried to watch my footing carefully, not wanting to tumble down into the ditch. Walking a few yards down the road away from the car, I took a deep breath and cradled the weapon in my hands. Crouching down to better conceal myself, I waited.

The humidity was thick, and sweat trickled down my spine, tickling me. The cicadas were out in force, their sound filling the night air. Grass moved off to my right and I prayed it wasn't a snake. Though I'd grown up on a farm, I hated snakes.

Then the sound of a scream split the air, followed by a gunshot.

CHAPTER FOUR

The scream cut off as abruptly as it began, and then there was a flurry of activity.

I watched in horror, terrified that Devon had been spotted. Several men gathered in one area, talking animatedly. One of them pointed at a particular trailer and after a moment's discussion, that's where they went. I heard a screen door bang shut and more voices arguing.

I waited for Devon to appear, sweat trickling down my back and mosquitoes feasting off my exposed arms. Surely he'd have heard the commotion and would be hightailing it out of there. But minute after minute passed with no sign of Devon. Anxiety and fear clawed at my belly. What if they had caught him? Killed him? Was that what the gunshot had been?

Just when I thought I'd go insane, I saw him.

The screen door banged open again and two men dragged Devon outside, one under each of his arms. His head hung low toward his chest, and he was barely supporting his own weight.

Oh God . . .

They dragged him down the ramshackle stairs of the wooden deck and into the forest of trees behind the trailer lot. I thought frantically of what to do. Was he dead and were they taking him into the woods to bury him? Or was he alive and were they going to finish him off?

I couldn't let them kill him. I had a gun and the added advantage of them not knowing I was there.

There were too many of them for me to take on at once. This would require a bit more finesse than going in there, gun blazing.

I hurried back to the car, searching the rank interior until I found something I could use—a ratty scarf. Quickly jerking up the shirt I was wearing, I used the thin scarf to tie my weapon against my side, tightly knotting the fabric so it wouldn't slide. Then I grabbed a puffy vest emanating so much weed aroma, I could hardly stand it. I pulled it on and, as I'd hoped, it concealed the lump.

Panic made my hands shaky and it took longer to accomplish all this than I'd hoped. Taking a deep breath, I headed for the trailers.

The steps creaked underneath my feet as I climbed them, then I banged on the screen door. The front door was open, and I could hear a television playing loudly in another room.

At my knock, footsteps hurried toward me, bare feet slapping against the worn linoleum.

A woman came into view, a baby clad in only a sagging diaper on her hip. She wore a pair of stretched-out gray sweatpants and a T-shirt so worn the emblem on the front was nearly invisible. She looked me over in one quick pass, not opening the screen.

"Who're you?" she demanded. The baby was fussing and stuck a fist into her mouth. She looked maybe eight or nine months old.

"Um, I'm Mackenzie," I said. "Mac for short."

"Whaddya want?" Her accent was thick hillbilly, which is different from redneck. Most people think they're one and the same, but they're not. Regardless of her accent, her second question was no less rude than her first.

"My car broke down," I said, echoing a trace of her accent as I waved vaguely toward the road. "Was hoping I could use your phone."

"We don't have one," she said curtly. "Sorry. You can keep walking. I think there's a house up yonder. They's got a phone." She stepped back like she was going to shut the door.

"Wait." I held up a hand and she paused. "I'm real tired," I said, improvising on the spot. "Been driving all night. Do you think I can crash here for just a bit, then I'll walk up later on?"

Her gaze narrowed suspiciously and she studied me. I looked as innocent and tired as I knew how and finally, she gave a reluctant nod.

"Alrighty then," she said. "C'mon in. But this is only for a bit, ya understand? Ah got things ta do."

"Yeah, no problem at all. Thanks."

She pushed open the screen door and I grabbed it as she turned away. Before going inside, I glanced at the woods where the men had disappeared with Devon. They hadn't returned.

Inside, the television was blasting *Spongebob* and a little boy about four years old lay on the floor in front of it, asleep. The kitchen had piles of dirty dishes in the sink and a pot of something brewing on the stove.

I followed the woman and she led me to a blue sofa with sagging cushions. With her free hand, she grabbed a pile of unfolded clothes lying across the seats and shoved it to one end. A black dog of indeterminate breeding with a limp came up to me and nuzzled my hand as I stood there.

"Ya can rest here," she said, once she'd cleared a spot. "I'm Liza, if'n ya need anythin'."

"I'm sure I'll be fine." I patted the dog, who'd begun to whine softly as it looked at me. That's when I noticed the milky eyes and realized the dog had to be blind.

Liza paused, her face betraying surprise as she looked from the dog to me and back.

"What's wrong?" I asked.

"This here is old Maisie," she said. "She been around for almost twenty years. Blind as a bat, but she knows when folks is sick. Real sick." Liza's expression turned sympathetic as she looked at me. "I reckon you do need your rest if you'se sick. Take your time, honey. I'll be in the back trying to git this one ta sleep if ya need me."

I was at a loss as to what to say other than, "Thanks." I sat cautiously and watched as she headed down the narrow hallway to the back of the trailer. Maisie lay down at my feet, her unseeing eyes still fixed on me, a low whine coming intermittently from her throat. It was odd behavior from a dog, and likely some old wives' tale, but still unnerving.

The woman and her kids were sitting ducks for me to use as hostages, and for a split second, I thought about it. It wouldn't be hard to do. But then I thought of Devon, and knew he wouldn't want me to do that, no matter how much danger he was in.

The door flew open and in came the guys who'd taken Devon along with three more. They were talking.

" . . . in the shed for now, 'til we figger out what to do—"

"Who the fuck are you?"

One of them had spotted me and stopped short. The rest of them swung their gazes my way as one, their expressions ranging from curious to downright malevolent.

"I-I'm Mac," I stammered. "Liza let me in for a while. My car broke down up the road, but she didn't have a phone for me to use." My pulse was racing with fear and adrenaline, but hope flickered at what I'd overhead. Devon was in the shed.

Please still be alive, I thought.

One of them stepped forward, marking himself as the leader of the rather motley crew. They ranged in age from what I guessed to be around eighteen to mid-forties. The leader fell somewhere in the middle.

"You from around these parts?" he asked.

I shook my head. "I'm from Kansas. Just traveling through to visit family in Florida."

"Why ain't you on the highway?" He sounded suspicious and my nerves ratcheted higher.

"I'm not in any hurry." I shrugged. "It's family, ya know? Only so much time I can take listening to my ma tell me to get a job."

The leader got a crafty look in his eye. "Really? You lookin' for work?"

Not knowing where this was going, I went with it. "Yeah. You know of any?"

The guy glanced at his buddies as though communicating something, then looked back at me.

"I'm Jeb," he said, holding out his hand, which looked none too clean.

Eww.

I took it anyway, keeping the handshake as brief as possible and concealing my distaste.

"We're looking for someone to fill a position," he continued.

My eyes widened and my heart skipped a beat. God only knew exactly what *kind* of position they meant.

I cleared my throat. "Um, you mean like a job? Doin' what?"

"Deliveries," he said. "We do deliveries in places that aren't the best. Lots of cops around. They see one of us, they get suspicious. Profiling and shit. But they see you . . . a pretty little thing who looks like she couldn't hurt a fly . . . why they'd just be leavin' you alone, I reckon."

I pretended to think about it. "So . . . how much would I get paid?"

Jeb glanced at his buddies again. "Five hundred a delivery," he said.

I felt my jaw drop open and I shut it with a snap. "That's a lot of money," I said. "What exactly are ya'll delivering?"

"Nothin' you need to worry about," Jeb said.

Yeah, right.

"Just drive to where we tell you, wait for the truck to be unloaded, take the envelope they give you, and drive back," he said. "Think you can do that?" His tone had turned slightly belligerent and threatening.

"Um, it doesn't really sound like my thing," I said, getting to my feet. Now that they were all in here, I'd take a chance on getting Devon out of the shed.

"Have a seat . . . Mac," Jeb said, shoving me hard in the shoulder and pushing me back onto the couch. "We're not through with you yet."

I sat down hard, bracing my hands on the cushions, and didn't take my eyes off him. Adrenaline was hitting me, the rush of cold felt like I'd been dipped in ice water as I stared at the five men looming over me. I didn't want to think of just how badly this could go.

"We know you're with that man we caught sneaking around," Jeb said. "We have lookouts everywhere. You gotta, with what we do."

I decided it wasn't worth trying to play dumb. I didn't need time. I needed to know that Devon was okay. "What did you do to him?" I demanded.

Jeb's grin was malicious. "Don't worry about him. He'll survive. Probably. But if you don't do as I say, I can guarantee he won't."

The gun at my side felt as though it was burning a hole in my skin. My fingers nearly twitched to grab it and it took a supreme amount of self-control not to. I knew there was no way I could get to it before they realized what I was doing, but my panic wanted to overrule my brain.

"So what do you want me to do?" I asked, glad that my words were even, betraying none of the fear twisting in my gut.

"Come with me." Jeb jerked his head toward the door and I stood. The men parted a path for us, falling in behind me when I passed by. I could feel their eyes on my back and it made my skin crawl, every sense on alert for one of them to grab me.

Jeb took me behind the trailer, the path lit by the glow from the windows in the trailers flanking the path. A dog barked a few trailers down, which started another dog barking, then someone yelled at them. It was obvious no one was sleeping in this crazy place, even at this ungodly hour.

The breeze moved the trees, and the whisper of the leaves was eerie. I had no idea if Jeb was really taking me somewhere to deliver what I assumed were drugs, or if they were going to do something else to me. The drugs were obvious once we went deeper into the trailer park. The telltale odors of rotten eggs and ammonia that usually emanated from a meth lab permeated the air. If it hadn't been for some white-trash neighbors who'd spent every weekend from Friday night through Sunday cooking their favorite drug, I wouldn't have known what it was. But once I'd smelled it, it wasn't something I could ever forget.

To my relief, Jeb led me to two parked cars: an old Dodge van and the SUV they'd stolen from us. The paint job on the van was peeling and duct tape held on the driver's side mirror. He led me to the SUV.

"Flynn is going to ride along with you to show you where to go," he said.

One of the men stepped up to us. He had a shaved head and a tattoo around his neck, some kind of line art I couldn't see clearly. If I could've picked the least threatening of the bunch, Flynn would've been my last choice.

"I can see why the cops might red-flag you," I said dryly. The smirk on Flynn's face faded. I turned to look at Jeb. "I'm not doing anything until I see that my friend is all right."

"You're not in any position to be making demands," he said.

"I think I am," I said. "You need to make this delivery. And I'm guessing the people you're delivering it to won't take it well if you don't show up. The cops are watching for you so your operation is hanging by a thread. So I'd suggest you take me to see my friend." All of this was a shot in the dark. But they'd taken a chance, stealing our SUV, and I hoped I wasn't wrong.

I held my breath, waiting, trying to appear more confident than I felt.

"We could just kill you," Jeb said with a shrug, "and dump you in the woods. Critters around here will have your bones picked clean by tomorrow night."

"Go ahead," I said, looking him square in the eye. I took a step closer and lowered my voice. "Because if you've killed my friend, drug dealers are going to be the last thing you need to worry about."

And I meant every word. If Devon was dead—if this piece of shit had killed him—then he might as well kill me now because I wouldn't rest until only one of us was left standing.

Jeb must have read the look in my eyes because he studied me for a moment. At last, he gave a curt nod.

"Fine. This way."

I struggled to keep the relief from my face as he led me into the woods. Only Flynn and one other man followed us, the other two remaining behind.

We stopped in front of a metal shed with a guy standing guard by the door. Jeb nodded to him and he stepped aside, looking at me curiously. Jeb unlocked the padlock on the door. After what felt like forever, it finally swung open.

It was dark inside and Jeb reached in, flicking a switch on the wall. When I saw what it illuminated, I gasped, then ran inside.

"Oh my God, Devon," I murmured, dropping to my knees where he lay on the packed dirt floor.

He was unconscious, and I was glad of it. They'd removed his shirt and a bandage was wrapped around his chest. Dried blood flaked the pristine white, and I could see brown streaks against his skin. Scratches crossed his arms, from some sort of animal.

"What happened to him?" I asked.

"Bobcat," Jeb replied. "There's some that like to hang around these woods. The middle of the night, that's when they go huntin'. Your man got off a shot but the critter was busy sinking his teeth into him when we found 'em."

I peeked underneath the bandage, careful to not disturb the wound. A gray, mushy substance was smeared on his skin and gave off a powerful odor.

"What's this?" I asked, indicating the stuff.

"Medicine," Jeb replied. "Our kind, which is the best kind. Keeps out the infection."

Good lord. Had they done a chant over him, too, and put in some eye of newt? "Did it knock him out, too?" I asked.

"No. Morphine we give 'im did that."

Hmm. "So you . . . helped him?" I asked. He nodded. "Then why are you keeping him locked up in this dirty place?"

Jeb looked me in the eye. "We aren't about to let a gift horse get away," he said evenly. "We could use you, and looks like we won't have any trouble keeping you in line since we got him, too."

Nothing like laying your cards on the table, I supposed.

"Now you've seen him. Let's go," he urged. Flynn pulled me to my feet. I jerked out of his grip.

"Don't touch me," I snarled. Flynn's eyes narrowed dangerously and he stepped closer, looming over me.

"Leave her be," Jeb snapped.

Flynn froze, our gazes locked in a staring contest, then he backed down.

"Let's get this over with," he growled, stalking by Jeb and out of the shed.

I cast one last glance over my shoulder at Devon, then followed Flynn.

I didn't know how long Devon would be out, but if they'd given him morphine, then chances were it'd be several hours.

It was up to me to get us out of this mess.

Jeb led me back to the SUV and handed me the keys while Flynn got in the passenger seat. He was toting a huge handgun and another was strapped to his thigh. He saw me looking.

"You ain't in Kansas anymore," he said.

Tell me about it.

"Keep an eye out," Jeb warned Flynn, who nodded.

I started the engine and Flynn directed me out of the trailer park. He didn't talk much, just told me when and where to turn. Eventually, I was on a backcountry road, the tires throwing up gravel in the SUV's wake.

"Where are we going?" I asked. I'd been keeping track of the route as best I could, but was afraid I'd still get turned around in the dark.

"Just drive."

My hands were tight on the steering wheel, but I kept my silence. To my surprise, though we were far out in the country, we were suddenly in a small town, seemingly sprung up out of nowhere.

"Take a left at the light," Flynn said.

Not hard directions to follow since there was exactly one stoplight in the town, dangling lethargically over an empty four-way stop.

I took a left, noticing right away a dark police car parked on the side of the street ahead of us. Flynn must have, too, because he stiffened.

"Drive normal," he said.

I shot him an irritated look. "No kidding."

"Pull in to that bar at the end of the block."

I did as he said, noticing several other cars and trucks in the lot. Nice, new cars, too, not the older kind usually found in a rural southern town.

After I'd parked, Flynn said, "Let's go."

I followed him up the steps of a short deck and into the building. The sign on the outside proclaimed the bar to be open until three in the morning, which seemed like overkill for a town this size. But once my eyes adjusted to the darkness, I realized I might have been wrong because there were at least a dozen customers.

Flynn paused, scanning the faces that turned our way, then directed me to a booth in the corner. Two men sat in the booth and a chill went up my spine. While Flynn and Jeb were all *Deliverance*, these guys were pure cartel types. Their eyes were cold and their faces hard. They glanced over at me, their gazes taking me in from head to toe, and it made my flesh crawl.

"Flynn, it's about time you showed up," one of them said as Flynn slid into the booth. He was dark, from his hair to his skin to his eyes, and the clothes he wore were casual but expensive. I knew clothes, and he certainly hadn't gotten his off the rack. He was handsome but exuded menace.

Flynn grabbed my elbow and tugged me in with him. "We've had some heat from the cops," he said. "Had to change plans tonight."

The man looked at me. "And is this your new plan?"

Flynn nodded. "She's new 'round these parts. Feds aren't looking for her."

Oh, if he only knew . . .

"Do you have the latest order?" the man asked. The guy sitting next to him remained silent, his gaze roaming from us to the rest of the bar and back. I assumed he was some kind of security.

"Freshly made," Flynn replied. "Do you have our payment?"

The head guy laid a thick envelope on the table and Flynn was quick to snatch it up. He thumbed through the contents, his expression turning to a grimace.

"This is only half of what we agreed upon," he said.

The man shrugged. "You were late with your delivery. I gave myself a discount."

"That wasn't part of the deal," Flynn retorted. His voice was raised and belligerent, and that's all it took for four men to surround our booth. Weapons of various sizes pointed at us, though I was positive they were all quite lethal regardless of size.

Flynn closed his mouth, his throat moving as he swallowed.

"You were saying?" the leader asked, but Flynn just gave a jerky shake of his head.

"Nothin'."

The man smiled. "I didn't think so." He waved his hand and the guards stood down, melting away back to their tables. Then he looked at me, his eyes calculating. "I'd like to get to know the newest member of your team."

I stiffened. "I'm not part of the deal," I said.

"Deals can be modified," he said, "as I've just demonstrated." He stood and took my hand. "Come with me."

Everything in me wanted to fight him, because I knew where this was going, but I was pathetically outnumbered.

However, I was also armed.

I let the man lead me away from the table and through a doorway into a back room that was apparently the game room, with two pool tables and a dartboard. A country tune was playing over the sound system, and I was taken aback when he pulled me into his arms and started dancing.

"What's your name?" he asked.

"Mac. What's yours?"

"My friends call me Luis."

"And what do your enemies call you?" I asked.

His smile was thin. "They don't."

He pulled me closer and I reacted too late to try and stop him.

His arm wrapped around my torso and his palm rested on the gun I'd hidden underneath my clothes. He froze.

"What do we have here?" he mused. In a flash, he'd shoved the vest I was wearing off my shoulders and lifted my shirt.

"Stop it!" I protested, pushing against him, but he was too strong.

"You're full of surprises, Mac," he said, letting my shirt drop. His hold on me didn't loosen. "So tell me, is the gun for me? Or for Flynn and Jeb?"

I'd expected him to take it from me, but he didn't. I hesitated before answering, deciding to go with my gut.

"Flynn and Jeb," I said.

"Thought so." He began dancing again and I had no choice but to move with him.

I swallowed. "They're planning to double-cross you, you know."

His eyes narrowed. "Is that so?"

I nodded. "I heard them talking about another buyer who was willing to pay more. But they didn't think they could get out of the deal with you, so they're planning on an ambush to take you out and make it look like a rival did it." I was making all this up, but I certainly had Luis's attention.

"And who is this other buyer? Is it the Chivas gang?"

I shrugged. "I don't know. They been keeping it real quiet. It was just a matter of luck that I heard that much."

"And why are you telling me this?" he asked.

"I want out," I said flatly. "And I've got no loyalty to them."

"So it would seem. When is this ambush supposed to take place?"

"Tonight, when you leave." I was thinking fast. "They're back at our place, waiting. We're supposed to call in when the deal is done and the boys will head out to intercept you."

"We'll see about that," he said, his voice as cold as ice. He released me. "I'll let you keep your gun, but if I find it pointing at me, it'll be the last thing you do, understood?"

I nodded, barely breathing, hardly able to believe my ploy might actually work.

He took my hand again and pulled me along with him to the other room. As he passed by one of the guards, Luis took the man's weapon from his hand, raised it, and fired a single shot into the middle of Flynn's forehead.

My steps faltered as Flynn's lifeless body flopped forward onto the table, blood and gore splattering the wall behind him.

Luis hadn't even paused as he strode purposefully toward the door. His men followed—the rest of the patrons in the bar didn't so much as twitch.

Luis headed toward the SUV and jerked open the door. "Lead us back to their base," he ordered me. "And don't double-cross me."

His gaze was hard on mine and I swallowed before giving him a nod. "Okay."

Four vehicles followed me back to the trailer park, and I was amazed I was able to find my way. My nerves were shot—*probably a poor word choice there*, I thought somewhat hysterically. But Devon needed me to get us out of this mess and that was enough to steady my hands and my resolve.

It was too bad about Flynn and what was about to happen to Jeb, but I hadn't made the decision for them to get involved with dangerous men like Luis. They'd done that all on their own. And if they'd let Devon and me alone, none of this would have happened.

Karma could be a real bitch.

Luis was definitely the type to shoot first and ask questions later, so when all the cars pulled up, guns started blazing. I drove straight through the yard around back, closest to the trees. I jumped out of the SUV . . . and right into Jeb.

"What the fuck did you do?" he snarled at me, grabbing both my arms and shaking me. "What happened?"

I could hear more gunfire and yelling as Jeb's men fought back, and they were better armed than I'd thought they'd be. Maybe they stood a fighting chance against Luis.

"They double-crossed you," I lied. "And he shot Flynn dead." That part was true at least.

Cooking meth is a dangerous business—the chemicals are extremely volatile and flammable. So I wasn't a bit surprised when the trailer four doors down suddenly blew up.

We both hit the deck as debris rained down. I covered my head with my arms and crawled forward a couple of feet until I was mostly under the SUV. After a moment, things settled and I opened my eyes, relieved I hadn't been hit.

Jeb wasn't so lucky.

A ten-inch piece of scrap metal—probably from the roof—had impaled his neck, nearly severing it from his body. Bile rose in my throat at the sight, but I swallowed it down. Flickering flames cast wildly dancing shadows in the dark. I could hear people yelling and the occasional bursts of gunfire.

Time to go.

I ran into the woods, following the trail to the shed. No one was guarding it but the padlock remained. Digging out my gun, I thumbed off the safety and aimed. It took three shots, but I was finally able to get the lock off.

When I got inside, I didn't dare turn on the light for fear of attracting attention. Devon was still on the floor but struggling to wake up. I dropped to my knees beside him.

"We've got to go," I said, taking his arm. "Now. Can you stand?"

"Ivy . . ." He blinked heavily, looking at me, then processed my words and gave a slow nod.

"Okay, good. I'll help you." It took more strength than I thought it would have to get him off the ground, and he leaned heavily on me once he was up. The walk to the car was a struggle, and several times I thought we'd topple to the ground.

Frenetic energy kept me going as well as the fear that we'd get caught at any moment. Luis would kill us both in a heartbeat if he realized I'd set this thing up. Panic tempted me, but I forced myself to stay calm. One foot in front of the other, stay standing, keep Devon upright.

Finally, we reached the SUV and I was able to get him inside. I paused to buckle him in—God only knew what kind of ride it would be to get out of here—when he suddenly snatched my gun from my side and fired over my shoulder.

I jerked around in time to see a man holding a rifle crumple to the ground. It had been the guy guarding the shed earlier.

"Nice shot," I said, then slammed the door closed and ran to the driver's side. I wasted no time gunning it out of the trailer park, having to go between two parked sedans and scraping them both in order to clear a path. I winced at the sound of metal on metal.

A couple more gunshots rang out and the glass in the rear window broke.

"Get your head down!" Devon shouted at me, and I did the best I could while still being able to see the road.

I held my breath, pressing hard on the gas pedal, and whipped the SUV around onto the main road. It fishtailed, but I worked it out, then punched it. Tires squealed as we tore off down the road.

I watched the rearview mirror as I drove like a bat out of hell, glad I'd grown up on two-lane country roads like this one with all their curves and bad asphalt. No one followed us, thank God. The sky was an amber glow behind us, and I wondered how long it would take the police and firemen to come—or if they even would.

CHAPTER FIVE

I didn't know how far I drove or where I was going. I just drove. Devon had passed out again and I worried about him, wondering if I should take him to the hospital. But then they'd ask questions and what would I say? It wasn't like I could use my identification, or his, for that matter.

The sun came up and still I drove, my eyelids drooping more with each passing mile, until I finally pulled off at a rest area. My shakes had subsided, but I'd still feel better the sooner we could put this state behind us. The more space between me and Luis, the better.

There was a tickle underneath my nose and I swiped at it, surprised when my hand came away with blood. I flipped down the visor mirror and saw I had a bloody nose. I didn't usually get them and nothing had hit me last night that might've caused it. Maybe it had been from the meth fumes that had permeated the trailer park. I patted the blood with a tissue and tipped my head back for a few minutes until it stopped.

I thought back to the dog, Maisie, and what Liza had said. Could it be true? Was there something wrong with me? Maybe this was a side effect of the vaccine. But even if there was something wrong, there was nothing I could do about it. Whatever it was would just have to take its course. Quite a depressing thought.

I left the engine running to keep the A/C on, then laid my seat back and closed my eyes. I'd just sleep for a few minutes, then continue on. I'd have to stop for gas soon, and some food. Maybe by then, Devon would be awake.

It was scary being without him, though he was right next to me. I missed his strength, his decisiveness. I was stronger, more capable, than I felt I'd ever been before, but I needed Devon, too, no matter how adept I'd become at outwitting dangerous men.

On that troubled note, I drifted to sleep.

I woke with a start, my dreams yanking me from slumber.

"Shh, it's all right, darling."

Devon was awake and leaning over me, his eyes clear from the drug, and without thinking about it, I flung my arms around his neck to hold him tight.

"Thank God you're okay," I mumbled against his shirt. Tears stung my eyes, the relief overwhelming me.

"I'd be better if I remembered something from the past few hours other than shooting someone," he said, his lips brushing my hair. "What happened?"

I swallowed down tears and blinked my eyes a few times. Reaching to move my seat upright, I said, "You got in a fight with a bobcat. The people who stole our car found you and put something on it, then gave you morphine for the pain."

"That explains the smell," he said, frowning with distaste as he tugged his shirt away from his body to look down at his chest. "I'm afraid to ask what's in it."

I shrugged, the nerves and relief of getting away still washing over me. "I wouldn't know anyway. They didn't say." I flipped down the visor and started finger-combing my hair. God, I really wanted a shower after last night.

"And what did they do to you?" Devon asked. "I doubt they just let us leave. And there's the matter of me shooting someone."

"It was a good thing you did," I said, "or else we'd likely be dead, too." I gave him a quick rundown on what had happened from the time he left me until now, leaving out the weird thing with the dog that still sat in the back of my mind. ". . . and I have no idea where we are," I said. "I was just driving. I'm so tired." I rubbed a hand across my forehead, behind which throbbed a nasty headache. I needed food and sleep, in that order.

Devon grasped my hand, gently tugging it from my face. I turned to look at him.

"I am literally in awe of what you've done," he said. "And I feel like a prize idiot for getting myself hurt and leaving you to deal with that alone."

I shook my head, my cheeks heating in embarrassment at his praise. "It's fine. It's not as though you intended to get hurt. And I just did what had to be done." I was anxious to change the subject. The way he was looking at me made me flush even more, a softness and admiration in his eyes that I wasn't sure I deserved. Yes, I'd gotten us out alive, but lots of people were now dead. Even if they had been bad men, I'd brought death to them.

"How about we switch places?" he asked. "And I'll get us somewhere we can rest and clean up?"

"And get food?" I asked hopefully.

He smiled. "Absolutely."

It felt wonderful to climb out of that driver's seat and let Devon take over. I didn't normally view myself as a Lara Croft type, and even now I just looked at what had happened as what had needed to be done. Devon and I needed to be free—the rest had been collateral damage. Perhaps I was getting to be as cynical as Devon.

He figured out where we were and got us back on the road. I'd driven in the right direction at least, so that was good. And about thirty minutes later, he was pulling up to a motel that was much nicer than the one we'd tried to stay in the night before.

"Moving up?" I joked half heartedly. My head was killing me.

"I think we've learned our lesson about staying in local dives," he said.

I couldn't agree more.

He made me wait in the car while he checked us in, and I didn't protest. I was just too tired. I was dozing when he returned, and we leaned on each other as we made our way to our room. Thankfully, Jeb & Co. hadn't removed our luggage so we still had our things. I barely made it through a shower before collapsing into bed. And though the sun was bright in the morning sky and I was still hungry, I was out like a light.

I felt so much better the next morning. Something had woken me and after taking another deep breath, I realized what it was.

"Fried chicken," I said, sitting straight up in bed, which I immediately regretted as my head swam. Ugh. My blood sugar was obviously too low. I took a breath and closed my eyes, and after a moment, it passed.

"Thought you had to be famished," Devon said, continuing to unpack several plastic bags onto the table. "This is one of your favorites, is it not? Chicken that has been fried in the quintessential American tradition?" His eyes twinkled at me.

"Omigod, yes," I said, bounding up from the bed and over to the table. I had on a T-shirt and panties, but wasn't cold. All I could think about was the wonderful aroma of fried chicken and . . . "Did you get biscuits, too?"

He chuckled. "What's fried chicken without the biscuits?"

I grinned at him. "Indeed," I said, affecting a British accent. Then I was digging in and squealed with delight to find a chicken leg, which I quickly snatched up. I sank my teeth in, my eyes fluttering shut as I moaned in appreciation. Piping hot and juicy. Perfect.

Devon just smiled indulgently at me as I plopped down with my prize and chowed down. I cleared out three pieces of chicken and two biscuits in no time flat, then sat back in the chair, groaning.

"I ate too much, too fast," I complained, watching as Devon ate much more slowly and deliberately.

"I've found your weakness," he teased. "Deep-fried poultry."

I laughed. "That, and incredibly hot British men."

"Have you spotted one of those recently?" he asked. "Because all I've seen is an incredibly pathetic British man who let his girlfriend haul his arse out of trouble."

Uh oh. It seemed Devon's pride had taken a beating.

"And what could you have done?" I asked. "Logically speaking. You'd been attacked by a bobcat and then drugged. There seemed to be little point in me playing the damsel in distress, waiting for you to come around, when I could do what I could to get us out."

"True," he said at last, his blue gaze shrewd on mine. "But still . . . they could've hurt you. Hurt you more than either of us could handle."

I knew what he was talking about, of course. Having been sexually abused as a child left its scars. I'd been terrified that's what Luis wanted, and I'd do anything not to let that happen to me again.

Though Devon's words threw me slightly. *More than either of us could handle.*

"Either of us?" I asked.

"You're mine to protect," he said. "Do you think it wouldn't grieve me deeply to know I'd failed in such a horrific manner?"

His tone had changed to serious, his expression grave.

"I love you," he said. "That's a commitment. All I have and am, I devote to you. Including protecting you from any harm."

Tears sprang to my eyes. I got up and went to him, sitting myself on his lap and pressing my lips to his. He'd showered, too, but hadn't yet shaved. The whiskers on his skin gently abraded my palm as I cupped his jaw.

The sweet kiss quickly turned into more, his arms tightening around me as he deepened the kiss, his tongue sliding alongside mine. I made a noise of protest.

"I need to brush," I said, twisting away slightly. His mouth moved to my neck.

"Do you think I care?" he murmured against my skin. He turned my face so our lips met again. "Tastes like chicken . . ."

I giggled at that, but my chuckles quickly subsided when he tugged my shirt over my head and his mouth closed over my nipple. A flash of heat went through me, and my nails dug into his shoulders.

He picked me up like I weighed nothing at all, and my legs wrapped around his hips. His hands cupped my bottom through the thin layer of cotton I wore, the heat of his palms branding my skin.

He still kissed me, even as he walked to the bed and gently lay me down on the sheets. It took only a moment for him to drag my panties down and off my legs, then he was spreading my knees apart.

Devon's mouth settled between my thighs and I gasped at the sensation. Heat from his mouth sent my pulse into overdrive and my eyes slammed shut. Devon was a talented man, and his tongue parted my folds to slide against the most intimate part of me. I whimpered at the sensation, my toes curling as he pushed a finger inside while his tongue continued to torment me.

I forced my eyes open so I could watch him. His eyes were already on mine, watching me. This connection between us was more than sex, and it sent me over the edge. I was never quiet when I came and tonight was no exception. But Devon didn't seem to mind.

My fingers were threaded through his hair, clutching him to my body. He brushed a kiss on my inner thigh and climbed up my body, while he was still fully clothed. My chest was heaving and heart pounding as I reached for the buttons on his shirt. I fumbled with them and heard him chuckle softly as he nuzzled my neck.

"Need some assistance, darling?" he asked.

"Mmmm," was the most I could manage.

I finally got the garment undone and shoved it off his shoulders. The muscles in his arms were hard as rocks, the definition between his biceps and triceps a magnet for my fingers. As always, the size and breadth of him overwhelmed me. I made a noise of appreciation deep in my throat as his skin touched mine. He was always warm, which was nice for times like now when I was getting chilly.

"Covers," I murmured.

He obliged, tugging the blankets down and rearranging us until we were underneath them. Taking advantage of the situation, I pushed him onto his back and attacked his belt. His pants were much easier to remove than his shirt, probably because he was helping more with this part, urgency striking him, too. But I'd had an orgasm so now I was in less of a hurry.

With a wicked smile, I pushed him down again and settled between his thighs. His cock was standing at proud attention and I kept my gaze on his the same way he'd done to me as I took him in my mouth. His hands sifted through my hair and a groan left his throat as I slid further down on him, my tongue pressing lightly against the sensitive underside of his cock.

"Christ, Ivy, that feels amazing," he said, his voice a roughened whisper.

I smiled, my hand closing around the base of him. Nothing like a little praise to let a girl know she was doing it right.

I didn't want to end it like this, so when he began groaning and fisting my hair, his hips lifting up from the mattress to push himself deeper inside my mouth, I pulled back.

It wasn't necessary to say what I wanted because in a flash, he had me flat on my back and thrust into me. I let out a small cry as sensation overwhelmed me. He wasn't going slow or gentle, but that was fine with me. It was impossible to keep up with him, and I could feel myself hovering on the brink of another orgasm. Wordless gasps and moans fell from my lips, and my nails dug into his sweat-slickened shoulders.

He lifted my legs to his shoulders and shifted positions, sliding deeper inside me. I cried out, my body spasming around his. I could hear him gasp my name, his body slamming into mine, then jerking as he emptied himself inside me.

We were both sweating and gulping down air as he collapsed beside me and pulled me into his arms.

"Christ," he said. A hint of something in his voice made me smile. "Drape yourself on me, darling."

I obliged, nestling against him and sliding one bare leg over his. After a few minutes, I got my breath back. His hand was lazily trailing up my back to my shoulder, then down again to my hip. He'd drawn the sheet over us, but sat against the headboard with one leg exposed, his knee bent. Devon's thighs were just as muscled as the rest of him and I rested my hand on him, drawing my palm down to his hip and up his chest, then returning on the same path. His skin was still damp, but I didn't mind.

"You and me," he said quietly. "We're a good fit."

I turned my head to look up at him. "A good fit?"

He nodded. "Some couples can be the best of friends, agree on ideas, politics, religion, all that stuff. Raise a family, pay the bills, go to Disneyworld, have a fucking minivan. But they're not a good *fit*." He pulled me tighter against him to emphasize his point. "And if that one thing doesn't work, it doesn't matter a shite about the rest."

I thought for a moment. "Were you and Kira a good fit?"

Maybe mentioning his deceased wife might not be the best idea, but I also didn't want the topic to be off-limits. He stilled, his palm resting on my bare shoulder.

"Kira was a sweet girl, and I was attracted more to being her savior than to her. She was an orphan, like me. Only she was alone, whereas I had Vega and the Shadow. I cared for her, loved her even, but no, we weren't a good fit. Not really. If Vega hadn't interfered, I'm sure at some point it would have fallen apart on its own."

I rested my cheek against his chest and listened to his heart beating.

"Tell me a story," I said.

He pressed a gentle kiss to my forehead. "What kind of story?"

"Something good," I said. "Something that makes you smile."

Devon was quiet for a minute or two, thinking, I supposed. Then he spoke.

"Shall I tell you of when I lost my virginity? Disastrous, embarrassing catastrophe."

I laughed. "Yes, that I'd like to hear."

"I was sixteen, she was twenty-one—"

"Isn't that illegal?" I asked, looking up at him.

"Only if you tell," he replied. "Now don't interrupt."

I grinned and settled back against him. "I apologize. Do go on."

"As I was saying, I was sixteen and she twenty-one. A pretty girl, long legs, enormous breasts. The perfect schoolboy fantasy."

"I hate her already," I interrupted again.

"Shh. I knew she fancied me, but I hadn't got up the nerve to ask her out. Well, I decided a little liquid courage would help. So I nicked a bottle of whiskey from a shop."

"You stole something?"

He looked down at me. "Are you really surprised?"

I shrugged. "Kinda. But go on."

"So anyway, I had this whiskey, which I'd never drunk, and I took three shots of it before I went round to where she worked."

I smiled, picturing a younger, less confident Devon inside my head. His accent was stronger now, when he was relaxed and reminiscing, and I loved hearing him talk.

"She was just getting off and I asked if she'd like to take a walk with me," he continued. "Brandishing my bottle of confiscated booze, and of course she readily agreed. It was warm out and we walked a ways and sat underneath the stars, which I thought unbearably romantic. We proceeded to finish off that bottle of whiskey—"

"Wow," I interrupted again. "You drank an entire bottle?"

"See you know immediately what a mistake that was. However, I, in my naïve and untested youth, did not."

I laughed again. I could so see where this was going.

"Well, things got a bit hot and heavy and there it was . . . The Moment. When I was to become a man. I can still see her, naked on the grass, reaching for me. And just at the precise second things were coming to a head—so to speak—I vomited all over her."

Even though I'd suspected that's what he'd been going to say, I still gasped. "Oh no!" I tried not to laugh, but it really couldn't be helped. "What did she do?"

"It was awful. My being sick prompted a reciprocal nausea from her until we were both dry heaving. I managed to get her home as gallantly as I could, stopping several times along the way to heave into the bushes, but needless to say, we never went out again." He frowned. "Actually, I don't believe we ever even made eye contact again."

I was still giggling, which prompted a soft smile from him. His hand cupped my cheek and he looked in my eyes before kissing my forehead again.

"Well that's certainly a story," I said, letting him tuck me in closer against his side.

"Possibly the worst first-time story ever," he said.

Both of us thought it at the same time—*no, mine was worse*—but neither mentioned it. Instead, his arms tightened around me in an unspoken acknowledgment. It struck me then that my pain, the pain from my past, was now a shared one with Devon, just because he loved me. What happened to me, happened to him, and vice versa.

Yes, we were a good fit, in all the ways that counted most.

A drop fell to Devon's chest and I realized it was blood. My nose was bleeding again. Embarrassed, I swiped at it, then hurried to get up.

"Bathroom," I said, keeping my face averted from Devon's as I scurried into the restroom and shut the door.

I looked in the mirror. "Damn," I muttered, grabbing some tissues from the box on the counter. It was a darker blood, thicker than before, and I tipped my head back to stop the flow.

What did this mean? What was happening to me? I was terrified, but more afraid of Devon finding out. What would he do if I were sick? He was putting everything on the line for me, giving up his entire world to be with me. Would it devastate him if I were ill? I didn't want to leave him alone if something should happen to me.

"Darling, are you all right?" Devon spoke through the door.

I checked the tissue, then the mirror. It looked like the nosebleed had stopped, but I still needed to clean the blood from my face.

"I'm fine. I'll be right out," I said, wetting a washcloth and dabbing at my skin.

I brushed my teeth and hair before opening the door. Devon had put on his jeans and was looking at a map. Taking a deep breath, I smiled and headed toward him.

"So where are we?" I asked, pulling my T-shirt back over my head.

"Just outside Nashville," he replied.

"The Country Music Capital of the World," I quipped, deliberately pushing thoughts of my two nosebleeds to the back of my mind. Worrying about it would get me nowhere. Not to mention that Devon was so in tune to my moods, he would notice and ask questions.

Devon's face scrunched in distaste.

"Hey, don't be knocking country music," I said, elbowing him in the ribs, which probably hurt me more than it did him. "I love my Garth and Keith Urban."

"You do know that Keith Urban is Australian," he said dryly. "He's no more country than I am."

"I didn't say I liked him for his *music*," I teased. "He's pretty easy on the eyes. And I love that Australian accent."

He swatted my bare backside and I yelped, but before I could get away he'd wrapped an arm around my waist and jerked me to him. I giggled as he nuzzled my ear.

"Though not as much as you love mine, correct?"

"Mmmhmm." His breath in my ear and lips on my neck made it difficult to concentrate. "So how much further?" I asked. I didn't know what was wrong with me, but I had a gut feeling that I didn't have much time.

"Another couple of days should get us in to Key West," he said, loosening his hold enough for me to step away. I searched for my panties and pulled them on. "Barring any further difficulties with the natives." His dry sarcasm made me smile.

"Not all the natives are that nasty," I said. "Most of us are decent people. I think so, anyway." I shrugged.

Devon glanced at me, his expression a bit sad. "I'm glad you're still able to see the world that way," he said, pulling on his shirt and buttoning it. "It says more about you than it does them."

"What do you mean?"

"It means that even after all you've been through, from the time you were small until just last night, you have every reason to hate the world and believe the worst of everyone. Yet you don't. Because inside here," he pressed a finger between my breasts, "you're pure and good. So you can't believe others aren't the same."

I didn't feel pure and good. I was keeping something from Devon and it made me feel guilty inside. So I gave him a weak smile.

"I'm glad you think so," I said, reaching up on my toes so I could press a kiss to his mouth. He kissed me back and for a moment, I clung to him, then we parted.

"Let's get going," he said. "Driving at night and sleeping during the day will be better anyway. If anyone sees you, they're far less likely to be as switched on as during the daylight hours."

Oh yes, that one small detail of the FBI broadcasting my picture all over the place. Couldn't forget that . . . I sighed.

Physically, I was feeling better after sleeping all day and then eating enough food for three people. I'd showered and was in clean clothes, all set for a long night of riding in the car.

We settled in and Devon got us on the road, still sticking to the back roads rather than the highways, and after a while, I noticed that neither of us had really said anything for nearly an hour. Surely we weren't already out of conversation this early in our relationship? What if Devon grew bored with me? It wasn't like I was an international spy, like him. The most exciting thing I could contribute to a conversation was talking about the time a twister passed so close to our house, it took the roof off the shed.

"So . . ." I began with no idea what I was going to say. "It's chilly tonight, right?" I winced. Dear lord, was I really going to chat with Devon about *the weather*?

He glanced at me, a smile playing about his lips. "A bit. I didn't particularly notice. Are you cold?" He reached for the heat controls.

"No, no, I'm fine."

Silence again. I wracked my brain for something to say. Why was it that now that I had Devon all to myself, I couldn't think of a single thing to say? And trying to think of something only seemed to make it worse, my mind going blank.

"What's the matter?" he asked.

I faked a smile. "Nothing. Nothing's the matter." *Except I'm a dull, boring person who can't think of anything to say and that you'll probably tire of almost immediately*, I thought.

He reached over and took my hand, his palm warm against mine. "Tell me."

How to say what I was thinking? I didn't know. So I just blurted, "I'm afraid I'll bore you."

Devon frowned, glancing at me before looking back at the road. "You're afraid you'll bore me," he repeated. "Why on earth would you bore me?"

"Because you've led this exciting life and met all kinds of interesting people and been to exotic places." I waved my hand around. "Once this is over—the people chasing us, Vega after you—won't you find us, our relationship, to be a bit . . . boring? Too *normal* for what you're used to?" The life of a spy was vastly different from that of a teller from Middle-Of-Nowhere, Kansas.

He sighed. "I think you've been watching too many James Bond movies. What I do—what I *did*—for a living was exciting, I suppose, if you call knowing that each morning when you woke up it might be your last 'exciting.'

"And the people I met were by and large the worst human beings on the planet," he continued. "Many of the places were shitholes I can still smell in my nightmares. The prospect of being with you, building a real life—a normal life—with you, is the most exciting thing I can possibly imagine."

His words, so sincere and earnest, curled around me like a warm blanket. I blinked back tears and squeezed his hand.

"I hope we get that," I said. "I really do."

Devon just smiled. "Of course we will, my darling. I've no doubt."

I relaxed a little and he began telling me of some of the places he'd been. Some of them did sound exotic, but he didn't speak of them with any fondness. ("Iraq is a beautiful country, but the whole place smells like shite.") I asked him questions and before I knew it, we'd crossed into Georgia.

Devon and I arrived at another motel around five in the morning. I'd been dozing, but I woke when we stopped. It wasn't a dive, thank goodness, and I recognized the name of the hotel chain.

There was an all-night diner next door, which was awesome because I was starving.

"I'm sorry I fell asleep," I said, yawning as he turned off the engine.

"You're fine," he said. "Obviously, you needed your rest after all you've been through the past few days."

Inwardly, I agreed. Even after sleeping all day and dozing in the car, I was still tired. My dreams had been chaotic, preventing me from really relaxing. Images of Devon, unconscious in that shed, and Jeb with the metal through his neck, haunted me.

The diner was nearly empty save for a middle-aged man sitting at the counter, drinking coffee. The waitress saw us and approached with two menus. She led us to a booth and I gratefully slid into it.

We ordered some food, though I barely glanced at the menu. Anything sounded good.

"Are you sure you feel all right, darling?" Devon asked as the waitress walked away. "You look a bit tired."

"I think it's just stress and exhaustion," I said with a shrug. "Maybe we should take another vacation after this." If we got the chance and were still alive.

"Where would you like to go?" he asked.

"Someplace remote, with no people," I said without even having to think about it. "The mountains or someplace like that."

"That can be arranged," he said with a smile. He took my hand in his and pressed his lips to my knuckles. It was such a sweet gesture and I couldn't help but smile back.

The waitress brought our food and I devoured mine, glad that Devon didn't mind a girl with a healthy appetite. Pancakes dripping in syrup with a side of bacon went down way too easy. I'd finished and was sitting in the booth, sleepily looking out the window while Devon looked at the map on his phone of where we were going tomorrow.

Abruptly, my stomach gave a lurch. I frowned, pressing a hand to my abdomen. To my horror, nausea bubbled fast inside me.

"Excuse me," I mumbled, launching myself out of the booth.

I barely made it to the bathroom in time.

I threw up all my pancakes and bacon, which totally sucked, the heaves wearing me out until I had to rest my head against the wall of the stall. I closed my eyes and just tried to breathe.

"Ivy, are you all right?"

Devon's anxious voice from outside the single-stall bathroom.

"I'm okay," I replied, my voice weak. "Just not feeling well."

"Let me in."

I flushed the toilet and wiped my mouth before getting laboriously to my feet. I unlatched the door and Devon came in immediately.

"Ivy, good lord." The stricken look on his face had me glancing in the mirror and that's when I saw the blood coating the skin beneath my nose.

"Crap." I grabbed some paper towels and wiped my face.

"What happened?" he asked, turning me around to face him. He grabbed some more paper towels and wet them beneath the faucet, pushing aside my hand to swipe gently at the bloody streaks himself.

"I was just sick, that's all," I said. "It was probably throwing up that caused the nosebleed."

"You're ill?" he asked. "Where do you feel bad?"

"It was just too many carbs," I said. I didn't really think that was the case, but I didn't want to worry him.

"We need to get you to a doctor," he said.

I took the paper towels from him and turned to look back at the mirror. "And how could we possibly do that? In case you've forgotten, I have no ID. I'm wanted by the FBI, and you're a spy."

"There are always ways."

I shook my head. "I'll be fine. I'm just tired. Let's go, okay?"

"Ivy—"

"I don't want to talk about it," I said. Leaning over the sink, I ran the water and washed my mouth out and splashed water on my face. When I stood back up and dried off, Devon was studying me in the mirror, his expression shrewd.

"What aren't you telling me?" he asked.

I grimaced. "Nothing." I passed him and went out the door. The waitress had left water along with my decaf coffee and I took a tentative sip. Devon tossed some cash down on the table, then took my elbow and led me outside.

I was weak and shaky, but I hid it the best I could, forcing myself to act normal as Devon rented us a room and we took the elevator upstairs. By the time we'd made it to our room, I nearly collapsed onto the bed, too tired to change into pajamas. I toed off my shoes and pulled the quilt up over me, then I was out.

I didn't wake until Devon shook me.

"Ivy! Wake up, darling."

I mumbled something, turning away from where he sat next to me. In a flash, I was hauled upright in his arms.

"Thank God," he mumbled into my neck. "I was about to call an ambulance."

That helped wake me up in a hurry. I forced my heavy eyelids open. "What're you talking about?" I asked. "Why would you do that? Because I was sleeping?"

Devon pulled back to look at me. His arm still supported me or I would've flopped back onto the mattress, which sounded like a really good idea.

"You've not been 'just sleeping,'" he said. "You've been out for nearly fourteen hours."

Fourteen hours? Wow.

I glanced behind him at the windows. Yeah, the last rays of sunshine were disappearing over the horizon. I guess I had slept for a while. You'd think I'd feel more rested.

"No need to worry," I said. "I was just sleeping heavy."

"Bollocks," he retorted. "I've been trying to wake you for thirty minutes. Only the fact that you were still breathing kept me from calling for assistance."

"I'm sorry—"

"I don't want you to be sorry," he said, his voice gentling. "I want you to tell me what's going on."

I shrugged. "There's not much to tell. I've had a couple of nosebleeds and I feel tired. A headache yesterday morning, but that was because we'd been up for almost twenty-four hours straight. Then I got nauseous last night."

"How many nosebleeds?" he asked.

"Three, I think."

"Does it hurt when you get them?"

I shook my head.

"I'll find you a doctor," he said. "Today. Right now. And bring him here."

"How in the world are you going to do that?" I asked. "They don't make house calls. Not in this country."

"Don't worry about it. I'll take care of it," he said, settling me back down on the bed. "I just hate to leave you alone."

"I'll be all right," I assured him. If he really thought he could find a doctor to come back here, I didn't want to dissuade him. What was happening to me was a bit unnerving, and having a medical professional tell me it was nothing and would pass would greatly ease my mind.

"Are you sure? I swear I'll be as quick as I can."

I nodded. "I'll be fine. But where are you going to find a doctor? We're in the middle of nowhere."

"No, we're on the outskirts of Atlanta," he corrected me. "And there's a hospital about ten miles away."

Oh. I'd missed that somehow last night.

"Do you need anything before I go?" he asked. "Something to eat or drink?"

My stomach rolled at the thought and I shook my head. "No. I'm just going to rest." I squeezed his hand. "I'll be fine until you return."

He looked skeptical, but got up from the bed. I watched him change into slacks and tuck his wallet into the back pocket. He grabbed the car keys, then pressed a kiss to my forehead.

"Take care, darling."

I dredged up a smile for him, then watched as he walked out the door.

Ugh. I felt like crap and my mouth tasted gross.

Getting up, I made my way to the bathroom where I brushed my teeth and took care of business. A bath sounded great, but no way was I taking a bath in a motel tub, so I took a shower instead. I had to sit down on the edge of the tub several times because I got light-headed, but I figured it was from low blood sugar. Maybe I should've had Devon get something for me before he left.

I decided to try and fend for myself once I'd pulled on some clothes. My hair was wet and tangled, but I just pushed my fingers through it. I didn't have the energy to mess with it. Grabbing a couple of bills from some money Devon had left, I shoved them and the room key in my pocket. Maybe they had a vending machine with some juice or candy bars or something.

I wandered down the hall, following the sound of the ice machine. I felt like I had the flu. My hands were shaky and I wasn't that steady on my feet, but I kept going. If I could just get some food in me, I was sure I'd feel better.

The image of the dog Maisie whining at my feet flitted through my head, sending a chill down my spine. I shook it off the best I could.

Jackpot! Vending machines fully stocked with every kind of junk food imaginable. I took my time, trying to see if one thing seemed more appetizing than another. And which was more nutritious? Doritos? Or potato chips? Corn versus potato? Neither really, though maybe Snickers was better since there were nuts in it . . .

I was just putting money in the slot when something reflected in the glass of the machine caught my eye. A man was standing right behind me.

CHAPTER SIX

Devon paused for a moment in the hallway. He hated leaving Ivy alone but had no choice. It was painfully clear she couldn't continue without medical care.

Sickness. A complication he hadn't foreseen, and one he could do very little about. If someone was threatening Ivy, he could kill them. But an illness . . . that he was powerless against. A doctor would be able to take care of her, and Devon could provide one of those. He prayed they'd be able to help her. He didn't want to consider the consequences if they could not.

He drove to the largest hospital in Atlanta, which took longer than he wanted. The traffic was grueling. He parked in the lot reserved for emergency-room patients. Devon eyed the entrance to the ER, noting the busy flow of people in and out of the building. An ambulance had just pulled up, and paramedics jumped out to open the back as a male doctor and two female nurses hurried toward it. A stretcher was lowered, carrying an elderly woman, and then she was obscured from his view by the medical team surrounding her.

Devon got out of the car and strolled inside, following them.

The cacophony inside assaulted his ears, and the smell of antiseptic and bodies that had been sitting for too long in a too-warm environment affected his nose. He grabbed a seat and pretended to be amongst those waiting either for treatment or for a loved one.

Devon kept an eye out for the old woman, making note of a little old man who came rushing into the ER, the wispy white hairs on his head swaying in the breeze as he hurried to the desk.

"My wife," he said, out of breath. "They brought my wife in here—"

The rest of what he said was lost as a man hauled a woman past Devon, arguing loudly with her. The nurse led the old man back toward the patients, and Devon lost sight of him.

A few doctors caught Devon's eye and he rose, wandering to the back of the ER. Picking up a clipboard from a desk, he snagged a dangling stethoscope as well. With the scope around his neck and the clipboard in his hands, he was able to pass through the ER without arousing concern. It was a lesson Devon had learned a long time ago: look like you belong and nine times out of ten, no one will question you. People didn't like confrontation and always believed what they wanted to believe, no matter evidence to the contrary. Those human traits had served him well.

A female doctor caught his eye, her professionalism and speed struck Devon as more top-notch than some of the others, and he watched her. Others deferred to her opinion, which meant she knew what she was doing. Then he noticed the ring on her left hand and a handmade pasta necklace tucked beneath her physician's coat. Married with children. No, that wouldn't do.

Devon moved on.

The doctor who'd been tending the old woman stepped out of a curtained alcove, issuing orders rapid-fire to a nurse taking notes as he marked items on a chart. Devon sidled closer, flipping through the pages on the clipboard he'd nicked as he listened.

"—and make sure we have a comfortable place for her husband," he was saying. "He's about to lose his wife. The least we can do is make sure he spends his last few hours with her in something other than a plastic chair. Have someone move one of those old La-Z-Boys from the lounge into her room for now. And if you can't find someone, come get me. I'll move it myself."

"Yes, doctor," the nurse said, still taking notes as she went one way and he another. Devon kept the doctor in his sight and earshot. He glanced at his name badge.

Dr. J. Matthews, MD.

Next Dr. Matthews went into an alcove containing a woman and a child—a little girl about four with brown hair and huge, terrified blue eyes. She clutched her mother's hand and hugged a ragged stuffed bunny to her chest.

Dr. Matthews glanced at her chart, flipping through it quickly, then set it aside.

"Hi. I'm Dr. John," he said, pulling up a chair to the side of the bed and sitting down so that he was lower than the little girl and had to look up at her.

A perfect example of trying to set her at ease, making him seem less threatening and putting her in a stronger position than him, Devon thought. Instinctive on the doctor's part or had he been taught that?

"You must be Molly," he continued. "Who is your friend?" He gestured to the rabbit.

The little girl hesitated, glancing at her mother, who nodded in encouragement. The mother looked drawn and weary, dressed in a well-worn uniform from a local shop.

"Ruffles," she said in a voice barely audible to Devon.

"And Ruffles has a tummy ache, is that right?"

Molly nodded.

"Can you show me where Ruffles hurts?"

Molly pointed to the rabbit's side, down low.

"May I touch Ruffles?" Dr. John asked. The girl tentatively nodded and he pressed a couple of fingers into the stuffed animal's fur. "Hmm," he said. "I had better check that same spot on you to make sure I'm hitting the right spot. Can I do that, just like I'm doing to Ruffles?"

Another glance to her mom, another encouraging nod. A nurse stepped up to help and soon they had the little girl lying down as Dr. John carefully probed her belly.

"Does it hurt here?" he asked, moving his fingers and repeating the question several times. She nodded and winced at one point, her pale face going whiter.

"Let's get her in for an MRI stat," he said in an undertone. "Possible case of appendicitis." He spoke in a normal tone again for the benefit of Molly and her mother. "Looks like we need to take a picture of Ruffle's insides. Do you know how we do that?" She shook her head. "It's super quick and easy. We just lay Ruffles down, and this really big camera moves around his belly. Do you think you can hold him while we do that?"

"Does it hurt?"

"He won't feel a thing. I promise."

Dr. John spoke with the mother while the nurse took care of Molly, who was smiling and touching the rabbit Ruffles on one of the bedraggled ears. After a few minutes, he stepped into the hallway, glancing curiously at Devon who returned his attention to the clipboard in his hand.

"She needs to be moved to the front of the line," the doctor said to the nurse. "Her appendix appears swollen and symptoms point to a problem if she's not in surgery pretty damn quick."

"I'll do my best, but two surgeons are gone today and there are three procedures ahead of her," she replied.

"Do what you have to do. I'll get ahold of Pierson. Get her moved up."

"Got it."

They parted and the doctor went for one of the phones sitting behind the nurse's station. Devon didn't have to listen to know he'd found his guy. Good bedside manner, genuinely cared about his patients, took steps to do what needed to be done no matter the rules or red tape. No wedding ring either. Perfect.

The fact that the doctor was a young man in pretty good shape didn't deter him. It wouldn't take much effort to subdue him, not with the proper incentive.

Devon waited until the doctor saw two more patients and checked again on Molly, then followed him down the corridor. There were fewer people around, which suited his purposes.

"Pardon me, Dr. Matthews," Devon said, coming up behind him. The doctor turned.

"Yes? Can I help you?"

He surveyed Devon suspiciously. Not a fool, then.

"I'm Dr. Clay." Devon held out his hand, which the doctor automatically shook. "I need a consultation, if you have a moment. A very ill woman's life is at stake."

Suspicion was replaced by concern as the doctor's brow furrowed. "Of course. Where is she?"

"That's part of the problem," Devon said. "She's off-site and unable to come in."

"We can send an ambulance for her," Dr. Matthews said, taking three steps to a phone hanging on the wall. "What's the address?"

"Don't touch the phone," Devon said, his tone was such that Matthews stopped in surprise. "Come with me now and I won't hurt anyone."

"Hurt anyone? What the hell are you talking about?"

"I have a bomb set. And I'll be quite happy to detonate it, unless you come with me." Devon palmed his cell phone and flashed it at the doctor. "It's amazing what a cell phone can do, is it not?"

Devon guessed that this doctor would be more concerned about threats to others than to himself, given his age and obvious sense of right and wrong, fairness, and ethics.

Matthews swallowed, his gaze darting around, and Devon knew the thought processes going through his head. Denial first, which would be overtaken by the doctor's logical mind and deductive capacity. Then he'd deal with the problem, coming up with scenarios to get himself and others out of danger, each discarded in turn.

"Nothing you do is going to help, and will likely only get you and a lot of other innocent people hurt," Devon warned. He didn't have time for heroics. Ivy was waiting. What if she'd gotten worse since he'd been gone? "So get a bag of your medical supplies and come with me."

"And if I do that, if I come with you, what then?" he asked. "Is there really a sick woman?"

"Of course there is," Devon scoffed. "I wouldn't be going to all this bother if there weren't. Now come along. We're running out of time."

He could tell when Matthews made the decision to cooperate. There was always a resignation that came into their eyes and in their body language.

"This way," Matthews said. "I have to get my bag."

"Excellent."

They got a large black duffel, to which Matthews added more supplies. Devon had been right that he'd be concerned for the mystery patient, no matter the circumstances—and wouldn't try to make a break for it until they were in the parking lot. Honestly, he'd lasted longer than Devon thought he would.

Popping the boot on the SUV, Devon motioned for the doctor to climb inside. It wasn't a proper boot, but was far enough away from the driver's seat to not present a problem. A few zip ties, and he'd be trussed, alleviating any threat.

But Matthews didn't climb in. Instead, he shoved the duffel at Devon and started running. Devon was on him in seconds, taking a flying leap and sending both of them crashing to the ground. He landed on top of Matthews, who let out a grunt at the weight crushing him.

"Serves you right, mate."

Devon hauled Matthews to his feet, his hand fisting the man's collar. But then Matthews locked his hands around the top bar of the fence surrounding the lot.

Bloody hell, Devon thought. He knew it was next to impossible to break that particular hold, not without turning the man upside down, which would certainly attract unwanted attention.

Getting in close, he pried a thumb off and isolated the joint, bending and pushing hard in just the right way—

"Ow! Shit!" Matthews let go.

Devon shot two quick punches to his gut, catching him against his shoulder as the man began to double over. He slapped him on the back as though they were sharing a friendly man-hug, then hissed in his ear.

"I won't hesitate to leave your dead body in the street if you cause me trouble again. The woman waiting for me is worth anything I have to do to get her the help she needs. Now get your arse in the boot before I break something you'd prefer remain intact."

The doctor was smart enough to accept defeat, climbing painfully into the boot, an arm held tight against his abdomen. A few zip ties later, he was secure, to Devon's satisfaction.

"Hold this and don't try anything stupid." Devon tossed the duffel onto his lap, then closed him in.

It again took too long to get back to Ivy and frustration dogged Devon while worry gnawed at his gut. Being without Ivy wasn't an option. She would get better. She just had an illness, like a strain of flu. The doctor could diagnose her properly, give her something to alleviate the nausea, then she'd be able to keep food down and would be better soon, perhaps even by morning.

But Devon's hopeful optimism burst into panic the moment he pushed Matthews into the room ahead of him and saw Ivy was gone.

༃

There was a man standing right behind me. I gasped and spun around.

It was Scott.

How he'd found us, I had no idea, but he was blocking me in to the little room with the vending machines and ice maker. I had no weapon on me, nothing to fight with. Just my fists.

"No—!" I threw myself at him, hoping to knock him aside, and it didn't seem like he'd been expecting that because it worked. In the next instant, I was sprinting down the hall.

"Ivy! Wait!"

Like hell, I'd wait.

I hit the stairwell door and burst through it. I didn't know where I was going, I just knew I couldn't stop. We were on the fifth floor and I took the stairs at a run, hearing Scott enter just feet behind me.

Panic coursed through me. I couldn't let him get me. He'd take me back to them and the needles and the poking and prodding . . .

I was gasping for air as I rounded another flight, and the room spun. I stumbled, my hand reflexively reaching out to grab the handrail, and I missed.

"Ivy!"

Scott's cry echoed around me as I fell, the edge of the stairs catching me in the ribs and tossing me down further. My head cracked against concrete and everything swam in my vision. Finally, I came to a stop, but couldn't move. I was hurting and it was difficult to breathe, my lungs squeezed tight with the effort.

"Ivy, holy shit, talk to me," Scott said, bending over me.

I blinked slowly up at him, but couldn't speak. I felt a trickle of blood from my nose.

Scott muttered a curse, then slid an arm under my knees and another behind my back before lifting me up. He carried me up a flight and through a door, then down the hallway to another door. I heard him kick the door a couple of times, then it opened.

Taking me inside, he said, "Found her. And you were right." I didn't see who he was talking to as he laid me on the bed. "The nosebleed started a couple of minutes ago."

Too weak and disoriented to do anything but lie there, I saw Scott move away and another man take his place at my side.

Dr. Nayar. The man who'd been in charge of me in the facility. The man I'd walloped upside the head when I escaped.

I really hoped he didn't hold a grudge.

"It's worse than I thought," he said to Scott, his face grave. "I just hope you found her in time."

He messed with something I couldn't see, then I felt the prick of a needle in my arm. Tears of helpless frustration stung my eyes and I whimpered. Scott reappeared and brushed my hair back from my face as he dabbed at the blood above my lip. I stared at him, accusing him with my eyes, until I couldn't keep them open anymore and the lethargy overtook me.

The first thing I noticed when I woke was how much better I felt. I could breathe again, and though my body ached, I no longer felt as though I didn't even have the strength to lift my head.

"Ivy, how are you feeling?"

My eyes popped open. Scott was here, as was Dr. Nayar, sitting in a chair in the corner, observing me intently.

"What did you do to me?" I asked the doctor as I sat up, choosing to ignore Scott for the moment.

"I gave you medication that you desperately needed," he said.

"What kind of medication?"

"Ivy, listen to me—" Scott began.

"Don't talk to me," I hissed, anger filling me. "You betrayed me. They locked me up because I was *stupid* and trusted you."

He actually had the gall to look hurt.

I made a noise of disgust and climbed off the bed, which wasn't that brilliant of an idea as the blood rushed from my head and darkness crowded my vision. I swayed on my feet.

"Take it easy," Scott said, suddenly right next to me. His arm curved around my back to support me.

"Stop touching me." I pushed him away as my vision cleared. "You're a lying snake."

The doctor interrupted. "The medication was to try and stop the virus from killing you."

That got my attention. "What are you talking about? I'm vaccinated." I'd been given the only known vaccine by Dr. Galler himself.

"We saw it in the blood samples we took from you," the doctor explained. "A mutated form of the virus. We've been trying to find you to give you medication that will help alleviate your symptoms."

"But . . . but how?" I couldn't wrap my head around what he was telling me. Or maybe I didn't want to.

"We don't know," the doctor said. "You've probably noticed flu-like symptoms as well as nosebleeds."

"So what happens now?" I asked.

Dr. Nayar looked grim. "You need to come back with us," he said. "I don't know how long the medication I gave you will last."

"What do you mean you don't know?" I asked, a cold feeling spreading through my chest.

"The virus was mutated, so I made a guess, an on-the-fly estimate of what would counter it. I'm gratified to see that it's working, but it is only temporary. I wasn't able to create something that would rectify it completely."

"So I'm *temporarily* okay? But I'll probably get sick again? Will I die?"

He hesitated. "Yes, I think so."

Okay, that took a moment to process.

"You need to come with us, Ivy," Scott said.

"I'm not going back," I said.

"If you don't, you'll die."

I looked at the doctor. "Am I contagious?"

He shook his head. "No, I don't believe so."

"Can you cure me if I come with you?"

"I can help you," the doctor replied. "Help ease the symptoms. But I just don't know." He shrugged. "I can't promise anything."

Well at least he was honest. And by glancing outside at the dark sky, I knew I had an even bigger problem.

Devon.

If he was back by now and found me gone, he was going to freak.

"I have to go," I said. "Devon is going to be looking for me." I headed for the door, bypassing Scott, who grabbed my arm and pulled me to a halt.

"You can't just go, not when you're going to get sick again," he said.

I yanked my arm out of his grip. "I said don't touch me."

"Listen," he said, his voice now tinged with anger. "If it weren't for me, you'd be dead right now."

"Oh, so I'm supposed to *thank* you?" I sneered, getting in his face. "I trusted you. How would *you* like to be a human guinea pig in a lab? Did you even think about that? I'd still be there if I hadn't escaped. Which reminds me, how exactly did you find us? That part I definitely need to know."

"Why? So you can have Devon kill me?" he snapped. "Because that's exactly what will happen. If you tell him I'm here, he'll hunt me down and kill me. Is that what you want?"

That stopped me in my tracks and took the heat from my snit, because it was absolutely true. Devon would shoot first and ask questions later.

"Fine, I won't tell him, but I'm not leaving him. If I'm going to die anyway, it certainly won't be in some government lab. Unless you're telling me you're not going to *allow* me to leave." I glared at him. "Are there FBI goons outside waiting to cart me away again, Scott?"

"It's just me and the doctor," he answered. "I'm not here to take you prisoner again, though I probably should. I'm trying to keep you alive." He paused. "I care about you, Ivy. I really do."

I didn't trust him, but neither could I deny that whatever the doctor had given me had made me feel better. If I got too sick, I'd have no choice but to return to their lab.

"So you're just going to let me walk out of here?" I asked.

"If that's what you want. But take this." He handed me a cell phone. "It has one number programmed in," he said. "Mine. Just call me if you need me. If you get sick again and want to come in."

I slipped the phone in my pocket, still wondering if I was doing the right thing. But for now, I'd do what he said and see how things played out. I could always "lose" the cell phone if I had to.

"C'mon," he said. "I'll walk you up to your room."

"Thank you," I said to Dr. Nayar, and he nodded at me as I followed Scott out the hotel room door. We headed for the stairwell.

"Aren't you worried Devon will see you?" I asked.

"It's more important to me to make sure you get back to your room okay," he said.

Neither of us looked at each other, our words stiff and not at all like the last time I'd seen him. It bothered me that I'd thought we'd been close friends—possibly more if Devon hadn't returned—and he'd so quickly turned me over to the FBI. I didn't trust him, but neither did I want Devon to kill him. And not just for Scott's sake, but Devon's, too. He'd killed enough people. He didn't need to add to his tally.

"So where did you go after you turned me in?" I asked. "I didn't exactly see you on visitors' day." Okay, so maybe there was more than a little bitterness in my voice.

"I wasn't allowed in to see you," he said. "Believe me, I tried."

"And your solution was just to . . . what? Leave me there to rot?"

Scott didn't answer, his lips pressed into a thin line. I held my peace, feeling slightly guilty for being so hard on him.

When we were a few doors away from the motel room, I turned to him. "Far enough," I said quietly.

He stopped, but didn't look happy about it. "He hasn't hurt you, has he?"

I sighed. "Of course not. He's probably out of his mind with worry."

Scott nodded, shoving his hands in his pockets. "All right then. Call me. Keep me in the loop. In case you go downhill again."

"Okay." I shifted awkwardly and he turned away.

"Scott," I said, and he stopped to glance back. "Thanks."

He acknowledged my reluctant gratitude with a slight nod, then disappeared into the stairwell.

Digging my key card from my pocket, I opened the hotel room door . . . and found myself staring down the barrel of a gun.

"Bloody hell," Devon cursed, immediately lowering the weapon and pulling me into his arms. "Where the hell have you been? I've been worried sick." His hold was so tight on me, I could hardly breathe.

"I'm okay, I'm okay," I said, squirming a little. His arms loosened and he pulled me in front of him, looking me over from head to foot. "What's this?"

I panicked for a split second, thinking he'd seen a needle mark or something, but he was pointing to my temple where I'd hit the stairs when I'd fallen, which gave me the perfect excuse. I knew

I needed to tell him about the virus mutation, I just had to give myself a little time to process the repercussions first.

I was likely going to die. And sooner rather than later. That wasn't information you just dumped on somebody, especially the man you loved.

"I was hungry and went to find a vending machine," I said. "I must have gotten confused, or turned around, or something because I ended up in the stairwell. I think I passed out and fell, because the next thing I remember is waking up on the floor."

Suddenly, Devon swiveled, his arm coming up fast to point his gun at the far corner.

"You. Don't move," he commanded, his voice ice-cold and not to be disobeyed.

That's when I noticed someone else was in the room. He'd been sitting and had just stood up.

"Who's that?" I asked Devon, indicating the man who couldn't have been much older than me.

"The doctor," he said curtly.

"He's too young to be a doctor." And he looked quite uncomfortable with Devon's gun pointed at him. "Put that down," I said. "You're scaring him."

Devon looked at me like I'd sprouted two heads. "That is rather the point."

"Where's he gonna go?"

Logic seemed to get through to him, and he reluctantly holstered his weapon, his gaze hardening as he glanced back at the doctor.

"Don't think I need this to keep you in line," he warned.

"Yeah, I get that," the doctor said.

"I need you to look at her, find out what's wrong, and fix it," Devon said, taking my arm and leading me over to him.

"Because it's just that easy?" I asked Devon. I knew the poor guy didn't have a shot at figuring out what was wrong with me, much less "fixing" it. I turned to the captive doctor. "Hi, I'm Ivy," I said. "I'm guessing you're not here of your own free will."

"A moot point," Devon said with a shrug, completely unconcerned that he'd kidnapped a medical professional at gunpoint to force him to perform a house call.

"It hasn't been a . . . usual . . . evening, no," the doctor said. He held a hand out to me. "I'm Dr. Matthews."

I took his hand and shook it. "Thanks for coming. My boyfriend is just really worried, that's all."

"You've been bleeding from your nose, can't keep down any food, and were unconscious for hours," Devon interrupted, sounding irritated. "Of course I've been bloody worried."

Dr. Matthews looked concerned. "Here, have a seat," he said, taking my elbow and tugging me gently toward the chair he'd just vacated. He had a large duffel bag with him and he began digging in it as I sat down. "Bloody nose? Nausea? What else?"

I figured I'd try to make it sound like the flu as best I could. "Oh you know, the usual stuff. Body aches, tired, that sort of thing. I feel better now. I think it was just a twelve-hour bug."

"Maybe," he said, pulling out the requisite blood pressure cuff and stethoscope.

I endured the usual exam stuff as he listened to my lungs and my heart and took my blood pressure and looked in my eyes and ears. I stayed quiet and hoped he'd finish quickly.

"Your lungs have a slight crackle when you breathe," he said, "which concerns me as it could be pneumonia. And your blood pressure is low. Have you been coughing? Having any trouble breathing or shortness of breath?"

I shook my head. "No. Really, I think it was just a weird bug. I feel fine now." I turned to Devon. "I'm fine." Now wasn't the time for me to tell him the truth. Not when we had an audience.

"I can't diagnose anything without getting her to a hospital," the doctor said. "I'd need to run blood tests to see if she is actually suffering from pneumonia or something else. And I'm guessing there's a reason you didn't do that in the first place."

"How ever did you work that out?" Devon's dry sarcasm prompted a small smile from me. I did so love his British humor.

"We need to get going," I said to Devon, getting up from the chair. If my time was limited, I wanted as much time with Devon as possible. "I want to shower, okay? And you need to take this poor man back."

"I can't possibly take him back," he replied. "He's seen you. He'll tell the authorities."

His matter-of-fact tone had me stopping in my tracks. I glanced at the doctor, then got close to Devon. "You're not going to kill him, are you?" I asked in a low whisper.

Devon just looked at me. "I won't compromise your safety."

"No." My voice was implacable. "Absolutely not," I said. "He's done nothing to deserve that."

There was a battle of wills between Devon and me as we stared each other down.

"Do I get a say?" the doctor asked. "Because I'd really like not to die today."

I raised an eyebrow at Devon. "Well? If you hurt him . . ." I let the warning stand on its own.

"Fine." Devon's capitulation was given with ill grace. "But then he's coming with us."

"I'm what?"

"He's what?"

The doctor's and my questions overlapped each other.

Devon turned away and casually began sorting through his bag, carefully setting another weapon and several magazines on the table. "I want to make sure you're well, and he can help if you get sick again," he said. He glanced at me. "I'm compromising. Thought you'd like that."

I was too dumbfounded to know how to respond, but what could I say? I didn't want him to kill the doctor and if his answer was to take him with us and leave him in Key West when we left, I guessed that was the better alternative of the two.

"Fine," I said. "We'll . . . compromise."

"Hey, I don't want to go—" the doctor began. I shot him a look that clearly said *Shut up now.* He shut up.

I figured the display of weapons was to intimidate the doctor, and it appeared to work. I saw his eyes taking in the ease with which Devon handled the small armory, and his Adam's apple bobbed in his throat as he swallowed.

Grabbing my bag, I left them to it and went into the bathroom. I didn't think Devon would go back on his word to me and I just hoped the doctor didn't try something stupid. Devon would have no problem hurting him if that happened, I was sure.

The phone felt like it was burning a hole in my back pocket. I hid it in my clothes as I took a quick shower. The hair dye was washing out a tiny bit at a time, but would still hold up for quite a while. It was like looking at a stranger in the mirror, though a stranger who was becoming more familiar. The blonde hair was gone, and with it a kind of old version of me had been sloughed away, too. Unfortunately, the new me had an expiration date.

The thought made my gut ache. Devon had given up everything for me. What would he do if he knew that I was literally dying? That the virus was killing me inch by inch? He'd lost Kira and was probably going to lose me, too. The fear of dying was second only to my despair at leaving Devon alone. I had to do something, but had no idea what.

I was rapidly running out of clean clothes, and I thought we were going to have to stop at another thrift store or a Laundromat at some point. I pulled on the same jeans, but was out of clean panties. Okay, definitely going to have to stop at a store for that. Denim against bare skin? Um, no thank you.

When I came out of the bathroom, Devon and the doctor seemed to have reached an uneasy standoff. Well, it seemed uneasy from the doctor's point of view, his body language screaming tension. Devon looked as relaxed as ever.

"You need to shower and clean that wound," I said to Devon, gesturing to his chest. Whatever backcountry goo they'd put on him had done a remarkable job with the bobcat marks, but it still needed to be cleaned and rebandaged. "Maybe the doc will have something you can put on it. Ointment or something." I glanced at the doctor. "Do you have anything for an animal bite?"

"An animal bite? What kind of animal?" he asked.

"A bobcat," I said. "One got a chunk out of Devon."

"I'm fine. It's mostly healed," Devon said. He handed me a gun. "Watch the good doctor while I clean up, darling."

"You really expect me to shoot him if he tries to escape?" I asked.

Devon looked at me. "You're right. You wouldn't, would you." He sighed. "Fine." He picked up a knife from the table.

"Hey, what're you doing?" the doctor asked, scrambling up from his seat and backing away.

"Relax," Devon said. "You're quite jumpy."

He picked up the phone and unplugged the cord from the wall. Then he sliced off the cord at the phone's base. It was quite long, longer than needed for its intended use, but long enough for what I guessed was Devon's purpose.

"Don't tie me up," the doctor said. "I swear I won't try to leave."

"Yes, well, too bad I don't believe you," Devon retorted. "It won't be for long, so stop fussing about it. Now behave and this'll go a lot easier. On your stomach."

"No."

"Don't test me." Devon's voice was hard, the two of them locked in a staring contest.

"You're not going to kill me, and hurting me will only draw attention," the doctor said. "I'm not going to let you tie me up."

Devon moved fast, faster than I could track, and before I knew it, the doctor was on his knees and Devon had ahold of his hand, twisting his arm up behind his back. He was doing something to his fingers.

"How many fingers does a doctor need, really?" Devon asked. "You're not looking into being a surgeon, are you? I do think you'd need all ten for that, but as an average ER doctor, nine would be plenty."

"Devon . . ." I warned, but he ignored me.

The doctor's face was creased in a grimace of pain and he didn't reply to Devon.

"I think I've made my point," Devon said.

Devon hog-tied the doctor, first tying his hands behind his back, then his ankles, then the two together. It was sobering and a little frightening how quickly he was able to do that. When he was finished, he glanced at me.

"Better, darling?"

I gave him a look, not liking any of this one little bit. Devon's smile was thin as he took the gun from me.

"I'll be quick," he said, disappearing into the bathroom.

The doctor looked extremely uncomfortable. Feeling guilty, I got up and crouched down next to him. He turned his head to look at me the best he could.

"Let me turn you over," I said. "And you can sit up. I think." It took some maneuvering, but I managed to get him turned onto his back and propped him up so he wasn't lying flat.

"Your boyfriend's a real charmer," he said.

The doctor's brown hair had flopped down into his eyes so I pushed it back. He was an attractive guy, with brown eyes, high cheekbones, and a strong jaw.

"Sorry," I apologized. "He's just being protective."

"What'd you guys do? Rob a bank?"

"I wish that was it," I said with a sigh. "It'd be easier. What's your name anyway?" I didn't want to keep calling him *Doctor*.

"John," he said. "John Matthews."

"It's nice to meet you, John," I said. "And I'm sorry you got caught up in this."

"Me, too." He rested his head back against the wall where I'd propped him, his gaze drifting to the ceiling before he started looking around the room. His eyes fell on Devon's weapons again before quickly skittering away.

"You'll be okay," I said. "I promise. Devon won't hurt you. Not if I tell him not to, and you don't give him a reason, like what you did just now. So don't try anything else dumb, okay?"

John's laugh was bitter. "You think I'm not going to try and get away if I get the chance? You're crazy."

I looked at him, my expression serious. I wanted to get through to him. "Devon is a very dangerous man," I said. "Please trust me on this. You won't escape, and he'll hurt you. But if you just play it smart and wait, we'll let you go in a couple of days, completely unharmed. I promise."

"So what's he do anyway?" John asked, and it didn't escape my notice that he didn't agree to not try and escape. "Kill people for a living?"

Kinda. "Of course not," I lied. "He works for the British government."

"So he's . . . what? Like a spy?"

"You could say that."

"Then how do you fit in? He said they're after you. Who's after you and what did you do?"

I pondered lying, then thought *Hey, he's a doctor.* Maybe some of this would make sense to him.

"I escaped from an FBI facility," I said. "They were holding me because my blood carries a vaccine to a virus."

"What kind of virus?"

"It's man-made," I explained. "Derived from a strain of Ebola." Saying the word *Ebola* was like dropping a bomb in the room.

John looked stunned and was silent for a moment. Finally, he said, "If you have the vaccine, that means you're also a carrier."

"I'm not contagious," I said.

"I understand that, but maybe that's why you're sick," he persisted.

I hesitated. "Yeah. I think so." Just saying the words was like admitting to myself I had a death sentence. I got up off the floor before he could say anything more and before I fell apart in front of him. Pulling the cell from my pocket, I looked at the number programmed in, wondering if I should just go back to the facility with Scott.

As I was debating, Devon came out of the bathroom.

"Our guest survive all right?" he asked, toweling his hair dry.

He wasn't looking at me so I quickly slid the phone back in my pocket. "He's fine."

In short order, Devon had us packed up and made John walk in front of him down to the car, but when he went to get in, he turned to face Devon.

"Look," he said, "you don't have to tie me up. I'll come along voluntarily."

Devon's eyes narrowed. "Now why would you do that?"

"Because I think she needs medical care." He nodded toward me. "By all rights, she should probably be in a hospital. She's very likely patient zero of what could become an epidemic."

Devon turned to me. "You told him about the virus."

"And the FBI," I said. "I thought he should know what he's getting into."

"The virus isn't the problem," Devon said to John. "She's cured from that. It's something else, hopefully just a bug like she said. A hospital would be unwise at the moment, unless absolutely necessary."

My heart sank a little at Devon's words, the truth on the tip of my tongue. I couldn't imagine telling him that I wasn't cured at all, but instead was dying little by little. It seemed unreal. I had been fine just a few days ago.

"I'm not sure I agree with you," John said. "But regardless, she needs to be under some kind of medical supervision. So I'll come along voluntarily."

Devon looked at John as though he were measuring the truth of his words, but he seemed to be pretty sincere to me.

"All right," he said at last. "But if you do anything to try and injure Ivy or myself, you will regret it. Do I make myself clear?"

"Crystal."

John got in the back, Devon and I got in the front, and we were off. Nine hours later, we pulled in to Miami. I hadn't thought things could get worse, but that just goes to show—I never learn.

CHAPTER
SEVEN

The truth was burning a hole in my gut and with each passing mile, I cursed the fact that the doctor was in the backseat listening to every word we said. The poor man didn't need to get dragged into this any further, and exposing him to more information would no doubt only put him in danger. I stared out the window at the palm trees as Devon navigated Miami morning rush-hour traffic.

"How are you feeling, darling?" he asked, reaching out to take my hand. "You've been awfully quiet." His expression was concerned though his eyes were hidden behind sunglasses.

I forced a smile. "I'm all right. Just tired, I think. Though I shouldn't be since I slept so much yesterday."

"We'll stop soon," he said. "I have some things I need to do in Miami before we head on to Key West. You can rest then."

"Things you have to do?" I echoed. "What kind of things?"

"I have a contact here," he said, "someone I've worked with before. I think they could have information I need. About Vega."

Devon made a slight motion with his head toward the doctor and I could tell he didn't want to say more in front of him.

Like a little kid who'd overheard the one dirty word out of fifty, John piped up with, "Who's Vega?"

Devon sighed and didn't reply.

"Are we going to eat soon?" John asked. "Because I'm starving and Ivy should eat something, too."

"We just ate," I said, twisting in my seat to look at him.

"You may call a snack bag of pretzels a meal, but I certainly don't." He pointed out the windshield. "Cracker Barrel. Perfect. Breakfast is calling."

Devon didn't say anything, just pulled off the highway and into the crowded lot. I knew it wasn't because John was hungry, but because he was worried about me. I had to find a way to tell him what the doctor had said, even if it happened to be in the middle of a Cracker Barrel.

It felt good to stretch when I got out of the car, as I catalogued how I was feeling. I'd kept the pretzels down and they'd seemed to settle my stomach. My head ached a bit behind my eyes, but it wasn't anything I couldn't handle.

John was watching me as Devon got out and locked the car. "You're pale," John said.

I gave him a look as Devon slid an arm across my shoulders. "I avoid sunlight."

"Let's get you some breakfast," Devon said. "I want to see you put away a stack of pancakes drenched in syrup like I know you can."

John led the way and I followed, wincing a little at the too-bright sunlight. I had a knot in my chest, hating the thought of breaking the news to Devon, though I knew I had to. Keeping it to myself was no longer an option. If I could just find the right moment . . .

"Table for three, please," John told the hostess, who led us to a little table for four in the corner by the windows.

"Coffee, please, with cream," I ordered when the waitress asked. Looking over the menu, I tried to concentrate on anything but the impending doom of what I'd say that'd change everything for Devon.

"What sounds good?" Devon asked idly. "I must admit, I'm not familiar with some of the choices. I've heard of grits, but it doesn't sound like something one would want to ingest."

"They're good," John said. "I add some butter, a little salt, and a lot of pepper."

"Really? I'd think to add something sweet, like honey or jam."

"Real southerners don't sweeten their grits."

"What about cheese? Is that acceptable?"

"Depends on the cheese."

I looked at them perusing their paper Cracker Barrel menus, thinking I'd landed in bizarroland, with an abducted doctor discussing the proper way to eat grits with a man he'd been terrified of not ten hours ago.

"Stop!" I said. They both looked curiously at me. "I-I can't do this." Pushing away from the table, I got up and hurried toward the ladies' room. I could break down in there. But Devon caught up with me before I got there.

"What's wrong?" he asked, grabbing my arm and pulling me to a halt. "And don't give me any of that rubbish about being tired."

I stared at him as his image blurred from the tears in my eyes. "John's right," I said. "It is the virus that's making me sick. It's mutated inside me . . . and it's going to kill me."

Devon showed no reaction at first, he just stood there, staring at me. The same shock and denial I'd originally felt were no doubt going through him, too. Then he pulled me into his arms, wrapping me so tight, it hurt to breathe. But I didn't complain.

The noises of the restaurant went on around us, people chatting nearby about the weather, and the sunlight streamed through the windows. Our world, mine and Devon's, had paused in the midst of it all. It was one of those moments in life that you mark as a Before and After. Like being diagnosed with cancer. There was the time before, then everything after.

I squirmed, needing to breathe, and he released me. His hands settled on my arms and our eyes met.

"Tell me," he said.

"While you were gone," I explained, taking a deep breath, "Scott found me."

Devon's eyes narrowed. "The FBI agent?"

I nodded. "He'd brought along the doctor who was in the facility, overseeing my . . . treatment. He told me why I was sick. That my blood . . . they'd found the mutation."

Devon's face was expressionless, which I knew was how he dealt with anything that was hurting him. He'd once told me, "You learn to put things in boxes and put them away. Fear, pain, sorrow, and anger. It does make you a bit of a robot at times, but that's not bad. Sometimes you have to open one of the boxes, but you put it back when you're done." I knew he was doing that very thing right now. It was how he was able to function . . . whereas I was a complete basket case.

Tears slid down my cheeks, but Devon smiled a little and wiped them away. "Don't cry, darling," he said. "You were cured before. We just have to cure you again."

He made it sound like we were going to pick up a vaccine at Walmart. It wasn't that easy.

"The doctor, he said he didn't know if it was possible," I said, sniffing. "He gave me something he'd concocted to alleviate some of the symptoms. But it's just delaying the inevitable."

"I think we should get a second opinion."

Taking my hand, he led me back to the table. I swiped at my face and took a deep breath. I had to get a grip. Bawling about it wasn't going to help anything.

I was a little surprised to see John still at the table. I thought maybe he would've taken the opportunity to skedaddle out of there, but he was watching me as we returned.

"Is she not doing well?" he asked.

"*She's* fine," I said stiffly. "Just having a minor emotional breakdown. That's all."

A smile flickered across his lips, but he still looked concerned, sizing me up the way I discriminated whether something on the clearance rack would fit because hello . . . all sales are final.

We sat back down as the waitress came by, and I randomly selected something to order, barely listening as Devon and John ordered, too. The steaming cup of coffee in front of me beckoned and I went through the motions of adding sweetener and cream.

"Ivy's told you about her . . . infection, correct?" Devon asked John.

John nodded. "A man-made virus derived from Ebola. Not at all scary." He grimaced.

"Yes, but now the virus has mutated. And while she was immune, now she's not. What can you do to help her?"

John looked taken aback. "Well, I'm not a virologist," he said. "I just work in the ER. But I'd want to get some blood samples. She could use some steroids, help keep up her strength. Maybe an MRI."

"Where can we go to do that?"

"There's the University of Miami Hospital," John said. "They'd have everything we need."

"You can't just waltz into a hospital and demand to use their stuff," I said. "The FBI will be on me before I get past the doors and I'll be whisked off to a government facility to die." As opposed to what . . . dying in Miami?

"Not true," Devon said. "You can go anywhere, do anything, if you choose the right moment."

That was food for thought.

"We'll make a plan today, get some rest, and go tonight," Devon said.

Making a plan consisted of Devon and John dropping me off at a hotel with dual lectures on resting while they took off to get "supplies" and case the hospital for a while. I couldn't believe John was all in on this plan of Devon's, so I cornered him before they left.

"What are you doing?" I asked. "I thought you were just biding your time before you ran off at your first opportunity."

He gave me a sheepish grin and shrugged. "I don't know. It's kind of like a movie, you know? An adventure. When else am I going to have the chance to help a spy, save a damsel in distress, and play undercover agent? So long as Devon doesn't, you know, like *kill* anyone, I want to do what I can to help you."

I just shook my head. John was young and naïve, though he was older than me by a couple of years. He acted like this was a game, when I knew from hard experience it was anything but. I'd seen people die in horrible ways in the life Devon led. And people around him tended to end up hurt or dead, too. Even me.

I was tired so I didn't protest being left behind. The headache was throbbing again and I let Devon pull a blanket over me as I lay down on the hotel bed.

"We'll be back soon," he said, brushing a kiss to my forehead. He looked worried so I tried to reassure him.

"I'll be fine," I said. "A nap will do me a world of good, I'm sure."

Devon's smile looked forced, but at least he'd made the effort. I watched as he and John left the room.

I dozed for a while, on and off, as the morning sunlight streaming through the window gradually shifted into early evening shadows. Getting up, I brushed my teeth and hair before going to the windows to look at the setting sun. There was a terrace and a chair, so I grabbed my sunglasses and went to sit outside. Vitamin D could cure anything—that and hard work—or so my grandpa had always said.

A sedan pulled into the parking lot and I watched idly as it parked and two people got out—a man and a woman. The woman seemed vaguely familiar, which caught my attention even more. We weren't terribly high up, but too high for me to really see her properly.

She walked a few steps apart from the man, heading toward the entrance. Perhaps she felt my eyes on her because she glanced up.

Vega.

She was here, and somehow I doubted it was for a vacation.

Lifting her arm, she pointed at me, speaking to the man beside her, who looked up, too. I had no idea how she knew where we were, but there was no mistaking it. Vega had found me.

I wasted no time, jumping up from the chair and rushing into the room. I shoved my feet into my tennis shoes and hit the door running. But where to run?

The hotel wasn't big, but was rather one of those smaller boutique hotels. Which meant only two elevators and one set of stairs. If she knew I was running, she'd guess I'd take the stairs, so I went for the elevators.

Waiting was excruciating, and when the elevator finally *dinged*, I thought I might hyperventilate before the doors opened. I held my breath, and to my relief, the car was empty. I dashed inside and jabbed the button for the lobby. The ancient doors slid closed as though powered by glaciers, and I wanted to gnash my teeth in frustration.

It stopped at a lower floor and I had to wait as a family stepped on—a man, woman, and three children. The two youngest were fighting with each other and I moved over to make more room for them in the small space. The mom sent me an apologetic look that I didn't acknowledge.

The elevator lumbered on in its descent and I tried to calm down. My heart was racing and my headache pounding. When the doors slid open again on yet another floor, I bit back a scream of frustration. Then Vega stepped in.

Her eyes met mine immediately, then she glanced away, sidling alongside the man and woman who were still messing with their kids. I held my breath, waiting, as the door began to close. At the last second, I dashed through them and they closed behind me. I let out the air I was holding, relieved that the elevators were too old to have sensors that would've made the doors spring open again.

I was on the third floor, so I turned and ran for the stairwell. Panic dogged my heels. If they caught me, I had no doubts that I'd end up dead. Or worse.

My lungs were working overtime, sucking in air and making my chest hurt. I wasn't in the best of shape, true, but it was unusual. Ignoring the pain, I shoved open the door and hit the stairs at a dead run.

There were only three flights but they felt like twenty, and when I turned the last corner for the final flight, I skidded to a halt, nearly tripping over the top step.

Vega's partner stood waiting at the foot of the stairs. He smiled up at me.

"Going somewhere?"

Instinctively, I turned and started climbing. I could hear his steps hitting the stairs behind me, taking them two at a time, but I was struggling to breathe and knew I wouldn't be fast enough. Not this time.

He grabbed my arm just as I pulled open the door to the second floor . . . and looked right up into Devon's face.

"Duck."

I obeyed immediately, feeling the rush of air above my head and hearing the crunch of bone on bone as Devon's fist shot out, taking the man by surprise. It knocked him backward and he stumbled, losing his footing, and crashed down the stairs. He slid to a stop on the landing, but didn't get up.

Devon pulled me up and into his arms, the door swinging shut behind me. "Are you hurt?"

I shook my head, too out of breath and wheezing to actually speak.

"Devon!"

We both turned at the call from down the hallway. It was Vega, standing maybe fifty feet away, pointing a gun at us.

Everything froze in that moment. She had a clear shot at us both. Devon's arms were around me, helping to keep me upright when my legs felt like Jell-O. I felt Devon's entire body stiffen and curve around me, as though to protect me from a blow. But nothing happened. Vega didn't pull the trigger as we stood, waiting for the hammer to fall. She stared at Devon, unblinking, with an expression on her face I couldn't decipher.

Then the moment was over and Devon was shoving me through the stairwell doorway and half carrying me down the stairs. We stepped over the man, still unconscious, and faster than I could've gone myself, we were into the lobby and striding across the marble entry. Well, Devon was striding. My feet barely touched the floor as he carried most of my weight.

I clung to him the best I could, saw him nod at the doorman, and he didn't even break stride as John pulled to a halt in the SUV right in front of us. He had the back door open, stuffed me inside, and followed me before the vehicle had come to a complete halt.

"Go!"

He pulled the door shut as John stepped on the gas and I heard the sound of the tires squealing on the pavement.

"Just breathe, darling," Devon said, pulling me across his lap. "Look at me, and just breathe."

I focused on his eyes, so clear a blue they rivaled the sky on a midsummer's day. My lungs felt constricted, as though I wore a band wrapped around my middle. Air strangled in my throat.

Devon smoothed my hair back from my forehead and the touch of his skin against mine helped to calm me.

"Shh," he said softly. "Just breathe. In . . . and out."

It took a few minutes of desperate focus, but finally I was able to catch my breath. It was a relief not to be gasping for air any longer.

"Is she all right?" John asked from the front seat.

"I think so," Devon replied.

"Help me up," I said, struggling to sit up from his lap.

"Take it easy." But he helped me anyway, until I sat with my back against the seat. I felt as though I'd run a marathon.

"I'm okay," I said, my voice a weak rasp in my chest. "What happened? How did you know they were there?"

"I saw Wesley go into the stairwell," he said.

"You saw who?"

"Wesley," Devon repeated. "He's a Shadow agent. Rather new, actually. I saw him and knew Vega had to be here. I was heading for the stairs to get to you when you so opportunistically showed up."

"I was lucky enough to see them arrive," I said. "But that still doesn't explain how they found us."

Devon's face clouded. "You're right. It doesn't."

I was shaky and weak from the unexpected run for my life. The adrenaline was all used up, leaving me a wreck in its aftermath. My hands shook and I didn't want to talk anymore, still focusing on breathing in and out and how close of a call we'd just had.

John drove us to another hotel, and I was glad to be able to lie down again. Devon joined me in one of the two beds, pulling me into his arms. His expression was hard to read, but the way he touched me was infinitely gentle.

John took the other bed and was out in minutes. I could feel when Devon's body relaxed into slumber, too, though I remained awake, trying to figure out how Vega had known exactly where to find me.

Devon had an internal alarm clock that would wake him up at whatever time he chose. It was an amazing ability and it didn't fail no matter how tired he was. Tonight, he woke at ten o'clock, rousing me as well, as he stirred and sat up.

John was still snoring and I tugged at Devon's shirt with a slight pout. I didn't want to wake up and face the horrible reality. It was preferable to remain asleep, locked in his arms. But Devon didn't acquiesce. He took my hand, kissed the knuckles, and stood before heading into the bathroom.

I felt better and could breathe easier, but the headache still throbbed. I heard the shower start and glanced at John, still snoring like there was no tomorrow. Sliding out of bed, I went to the bathroom and eased the door open. Devon was already in the shower so I went inside the bathroom and quietly shut the door.

Shucking my clothes, I pulled back the curtain and stepped in behind Devon. He turned his head, water dripping from his hair into his eyes, and his gaze pierced me.

He'd been thinking about me, I could tell. His eyes were somewhat bloodshot and for this brief moment, naked pain was written on his face.

I stepped forward, my hand resting on his shoulder. He slid his arms around my waist and pulled me into him. Skin against skin, we stood there under the warm spray of water. I rested my head against his chest and listened to the beat of his heart. The feel of his arms surrounding me gave me the strength to breathe deep and relax. If my time was as limited as I believed it was, then this was exactly where I wanted to be.

We didn't speak, but then again, we didn't have to. Devon wasn't a man who said a lot of flowery things. He was much more a man of action. So I wasn't waiting for declarations of love or devotion. It was enough to feel the tight way he held me, his breath against my skin, and the touch of his lips to my forehead.

Naked bodies sliding together is sure to elicit a response from any man, and Devon was no exception. His erection pressed against my stomach, prompting heat to bloom between my legs. I lifted my face toward his, an unspoken request for a kiss. He obliged, his lips sweetly brushing mine.

I deepened the kiss, moving even closer. I needed to feel the way only Devon could make me feel: wanted and alive. Reaching down, I grasped the hard length of him.

"No," he murmured, brushing my hand aside. "You're ill."

Grabbing his hand, I spread my legs and pressed his palm to the heat between my thighs. "I'm fine at the moment, and I need you."

He needed no further encouragement to slip his fingers between my folds. My body was hotter than the water sluicing over us and he groaned, sliding a thick finger inside me. I clung to him, our mouths colliding in a fierce hunger that I felt down to my toes.

Suddenly he was gone. My eyes flew open to see he'd dropped to his knees in front of me, the spray from the water hitting his back. I had the brief thought that the hard surface of the tub could not possibly feel good on his knees, but then his mouth was between my legs and my brain shut down.

His hands palmed my ass, pulling me closer and helping hold me upright as my knees weakened. The hot slide of his tongue made me gasp, my nails digging into his shoulders. He played with my clit, lightly stroking the flesh before sucking it into his mouth.

I bit my lip to keep from groaning aloud, viscerally aware that we weren't alone in the hotel room. Then he added a finger inside me and I gave up trying to be quiet.

Devon knew my body better than I did and he took me to the brink and kept me there until I was begging him in gasps and pleas. He sucked hard at my clit, his finger curved inside me, pressing, and I came in a blinding rush of spasms that left me boneless. My heart was pounding as I finally pried open my eyes, aftershocks still washing over me.

He slowly lifted me off my feet. I arched against him, sighing when his cock pushed inside, stretching and filling me. My legs went around his waist and my back pressed against the wall. I squeaked as the cold tile touched my skin.

He froze. "Did I hurt you?" he asked, slightly anxious.

"No," I said with a little laugh. "It's just cold."

He relaxed. "Ah, the complexities of making love in the shower," he said, his lips curving in a soft smile. "I'd take you to bed, but I doubt you'd enjoy an audience."

"Not really, no," I said. "It's fine. Just don't slip."

His lips met mine. "No worries, darling," he murmured. "I've got you."

The water had steamed and heated the room to such an extent that although none of the spray reached me, I wasn't shivering. And with Devon pressed against me, I was plenty warm.

His arms supported my weight easily as he began to move. We kissed, lips and tongues meeting in a wet heat, then he pulled back and gazed into my eyes. Devon liked to watch me when he made love to me, his eyes seemed to see right through to my soul. His body claimed mine, possessing me completely.

The friction of his cock had my body coiling inside for another release. I threaded my fingers through his hair, curving my hand around the back of his neck and pulling him down to kiss me. His fingers bit into my flesh, but I didn't care. Cries erupted from the back of my throat as my orgasm overtook me. Devon's body rocked hard into mine, his cock emptying inside me as I held on, my legs locked around him.

Devon pulled back slightly as he sucked in air. His forehead rested against mine and the warmth of his breath brushed my cheek. Our hearts beat nearly in sync and I stretched up to hold him as close as I possibly could. Tears stung my eyes, but I blinked them away, determined not to ruin this moment.

He took a step, separating his body from mine, and I mourned the loss. My legs felt rubbery when I put my feet on the floor, but other than that, I felt pretty darn good.

Devon washed my body with leisurely ease, massaging my shoulders and back, and caressing every inch of me. It was one of those things—actions, not words—that told me what he was feeling. It was in the gentleness of his touch, the care he took with every movement. He even washed my hair, his hands sifting through the now-shortened strands.

Finally, we emerged from the bathroom. I was wrapped in a towel and another was tied around Devon's hips. He shook John awake.

"Time to get up, mate."

John was immediately alert, which struck me as odd until I remembered he was an ER doctor. They notoriously had to sleep while on the run, then be up at a moment's notice for a life-and-death situation. He got up and disappeared into the bathroom without a word.

I took the opportunity to get dressed. Devon and I didn't speak. The pall over us was almost tangible.

"John may find something that will help," I said. "Scott could be wrong." It was a long shot, but I felt like I had to hold on to some kind of hope.

"Perhaps," was all Devon said.

Both Devon and John dressed in scrubs and I didn't ask where they'd gotten them. It was after midnight when we went out to the car.

"It'll be easier to sneak in for what we need at this hour," John explained. "Radiology should be deserted."

"Why do we need to go to radiology?" I asked. "Why is an MRI so important? The virus is in my blood."

"The nosebleeds worry me," John said. "There's not a lot of reasons your nose would bleed, and none of them are good."

Devon's hands tightened on the steering wheel and I winced at John's bluntness. But I'd rather know the truth than have it sugar-coated for me. And there was only one way to know the truth.

CHAPTER EIGHT

Miami was a busy city no matter the time of day or night and the hospital was no exception, though the type of patients we saw as we passed through the ER were perhaps a bit more unusual than what I'd seen in Kansas. I saw a man dressed as a woman, and not doing a very convincing job of it; two men sitting side by side, each nursing bruised and bloodied faces; a woman with a baby and a toddler, the toddler running around the room while the mom just looked tired and resigned. There were more people there, but Devon and John walked through the waiting room pretty quickly, and I didn't make eye contact with any of the prospective patients.

"This way," John said, sliding through a swinging doorway that led into the bowels of the hospital. In minutes, we'd left most of the crowd behind and the hallways grew emptier. We were following the signs to Radiology.

I was tense, wondering how this was going to go down. In a hospital this size, I imagined someone would still be working in the department even at this hour. And I was right.

John drew to a halt a few yards away from an open doorway. I could hear someone moving about inside the room and the quiet whir of machines.

"You promised no casualties," John said, in an undertone to Devon.

"I know what I said," Devon replied. "Though I didn't promise. I don't make promises I may not be able to keep."

John's lips pressed together in a thin line. "We're here to help Ivy. Killing the radiologist would be a bad idea."

"I'll keep that in mind."

Devon's dry reply had a ghost of a smile flit across my lips.

"Give me thirty seconds," he said to John before walking down the hall and into the room.

John and I stood, silent and tense, waiting. He glanced down at me.

"Thirty seconds? Really?" he asked me. "He seems pretty confident." He was teasing, and I could tell he wanted to ease my fear and worry. It didn't work, but I appreciated the effort.

"He won't hurt them," I assured him. "Not permanently anyway."

John acknowledged that with a nod. "Okay. Let's go."

I followed him into the room, unsurprised to see a woman sitting in a chair in the corner. Her expression was grim, but she appeared unhurt. John didn't say anything to her. Instead he immediately set me up on the MRI table.

"Are you claustrophobic?" he asked.

"I don't think so." I'd never had an MRI before, but knew the procedure. Lay on the table—they slide you into a tube and could magically see inside. It sounded pretty straightforward.

"Once you're inside, you'll be able to hear me talk to you," he said. "So if you should become uncomfortable, just tell me and I'll move you out."

"Okay."

"You want to come with me?" he asked Devon, who shook his head.

"I'll stay with Ivy."

I flashed him a wan smile. He took my hand and held it. The table was narrow and hard and I could feel nausea churning in my stomach.

John disappeared behind another door that took him into the control room. I tried to concentrate on my breathing as I waited, my thoughts going back to what he'd said about things that could cause a nosebleed. My imagination was going crazy thinking of what those things could be, and I was terrified in the way you get when the inevitable is something too awful to consider.

The table began slowly moving me into the tube. Devon held my hand for as long as he could, then I felt his palm on my thigh, then my calf before I stopped moving. I stared up at the inside of the tube, unprepared for exactly how small it was. No wonder John had asked if I was claustrophobic. I'd never considered myself such, but as I lay there, I could feel a creeping unease. I tried to relax.

"You all right?" I heard John's voice over a tinny speaker.

"Yes."

"Just relax and lie very still. This won't take long."

The table hummed, then the sudden sound of jackhammers nearly startled a squeak from me. I tried not to think about how I was in a tiny metal cylinder and couldn't get out. The metal above me was scant inches from my nose and I stared at it. I thought I should close my eyes, but I couldn't bring myself to. The nausea and panic notched upward and I broke out in a cold sweat.

I felt Devon squeeze my leg. "It's all right, my darling. You're doing beautifully."

His voice and touch soothed me and I took another deep breath. Then another. I wasn't going to panic and screw this up. It wasn't like we had much time or that we'd get a second chance.

After what felt like an eternity, John said, "Great job, Ivy. We're all done."

Immediately, the table began sliding out of the machine. Cooler air touched my skin and the hard knot in my chest eased as I was finally out. Devon helped me sit up as John emerged from the control room.

"How are you doing?" he asked me. "Feel okay?"

I nodded. "I'm tired and have a headache, but that's all."

"Good. I'm going to nicely ask the radiologist over there to help me go over your scan."

"I'm not going to help you," the woman said stiffly, speaking for the first time. "You're not authorized to be here or use this equipment. Not to mention threatening me."

"I apologize for my friend," John said. "I am a doctor and circumstances required us to be a little . . . creative in accessing the imaging equipment." He indicated me. "This woman is very ill. Deathly ill. I need some help in correctly diagnosing her scan. Please. Will you help us?"

The woman's gaze swerved to me. She was a petite lady of Asian descent, maybe in her mid-forties. The ID tag attached to her clothing read "Sonya." I waited, unblinking and unflinching as she surveyed me.

"Fine," she said at last, the word curt. "But I will be reporting all of this to the police."

"We aren't asking you not to," John said, using what I was sure was his "doctor voice." The calm, reasoned, and reassuring tone that all doctors at some point or another had to cultivate, especially for delivering bad news. "Just take a look at the scans."

Sonya glanced warily at Devon, who remained quiet, though that didn't lessen the edge to him that anyone with half a brain could instinctively sense. She got up and John let her precede him into the control room. He closed the door behind them.

Devon slid his arm around my shoulders and I leaned into him, waiting. It took the better part of ten minutes, but then John and Sonya emerged.

Surprisingly, it was Sonya who approached me rather than John.

"Your scan was inconclusive," she said. "You don't have a tumor, but neither did I see a cause for your nosebleeds or headaches."

Devon's hand squeezed my shoulder tight, and I was grateful he was helping to keep me upright. My knees were shaking.

"We'd need to do more tests to determine the cause. Starting with blood tests in the lab."

Blood tests. But they couldn't have my blood. They'd know something was different. Would they lock me up again if they knew about the virus?

"It's come on very quickly, correct?" she asked. "And gotten worse?"

I nodded. "Just in the last few days."

"Then we really don't have much time," she said. "You need to be admitted right away."

I didn't know what to say and a heavy silence fell.

"I'm sorry," she said, and the compassion in her voice and pity in her eyes nearly broke me.

"Thank you," I managed to get out. I looked up at Devon. "I want to leave now."

"Of course, darling." He turned to John. "Is there anything you can do for her?"

He nodded. "Yeah. Let's go. Thank you, Sonya."

"Wait," she said, holding up a hand and stepping in front of me. "You can't just leave and take her. She needs to be admitted. She needs more tests."

"I'll do what I can," John said.

Sonya's jaw tightened and she straightened her spine to her full five feet. "You're not removing her from this facility. She obviously needs care and a physician who can diagnose her symptoms. I won't let you take her."

I stared at her in awed surprise. She was a stranger to me, standing in front of two men—one of whom had already threatened her and who she had to know was extremely dangerous—yet she was demanding I stay, putting her own safety on the line for a woman she didn't even know.

"You don't have a choice," Devon said, and his tone was such that there was no arguing.

"Thank you," I said to her. "I'll be okay." A blatant lie, but what else could I say?

Sonya watched us leave and I wanted to reassure her further, but I couldn't find the words. My thoughts were a bit preoccupied, to say the least.

"I want to put Ivy in a room," John said. "That'll draw less attention, then I can get her some medication."

"What kind of medication?" Devon asked.

"Stimulants. Steroids. Things that will help her body fight back and keep going. It won't cure her, but can't hurt either. I've seen it help terminal patients."

Terminal. The word gave me a jolt. Was I terminal? The MRI showed no tumor, but it was almost worse not knowing the reason for the headaches and nosebleeds.

John again looked like he knew exactly where he was going, leading me to an empty exam room.

"Stay here. I'll be back."

"Should we let him go on his own?" I asked Devon as John left us alone in the room. "Don't you think he'll escape or something?"

"He's not going to try and escape," Devon said. "I doubt he even views himself as a prisoner anymore."

We waited—Devon with a relaxed patience, and me barely able

to sit still. I was acutely conscious of our vulnerability here inside the hospital.

The minutes ticked by with excruciating slowness, until even Devon began to show signs of tensing, then John suddenly burst back into the room.

"Give me your arm, Ivy," he said. He was carrying a needle and he reached for me, yanking the cap off the syringe with his teeth and spitting it out onto the floor.

Before I could reply, he'd pushed the needle into my upper arm and injected me. I hissed—the medicine burned something fierce—then he was repeating the procedure with another syringe.

"These are extremely expensive injections," he said as he finished. "And I think I just outed us when I took them. So we should really haul ass now."

I had no idea what he'd given me, but I felt an immediate reaction. A surge of warmth in my veins with a pleasing numbness spreading in its wake. The pain became muted, dulled, and my muscles relaxed.

"Wow, that's some amazing stuff," I said.

"Watch out," he said to Devon. "Its effects are almost like getting high. She may be prone to paranoia or feelings of indestructibility. And you should probably get rid of those scrubs."

Devon hurriedly complied, stowing the scrubs in the trash bin. Underneath, he wore jeans and a white button-down shirt, complete with holster and gun. Only now he'd added an official-looking badge hanging from the front pocket of his jeans.

"Where'd you get that?" I asked.

"Our recce last night. Thought it might come in handy."

Taking my hand, we followed John out into the hallway. Moving his grip to my elbow, he propelled me forward.

"You're my prisoner," he said. "Do come quietly."

John led us into the ER and we began wading through the people. Three uniformed policemen were gathered around the admitting desk. The nurse was talking to them animatedly, gesticulating with her hands.

". . . Sonya said they're still here," she said. "Random people who threatened her and used the radiology equipment. And she said the girl may be kidnapped."

One of the cops glanced at us as we walked by, and his gaze dropped to the badge hanging from Devon's pocket. He frowned and a sense of foreboding crept in to my chest.

"Hey, hold up," he said, jogging up to us. We'd been feet from the door and I stared longingly at it, the darkness outside beckoning.

We had no choice but to halt.

"Who're you?" the cop asked Devon. "What are you doing?"

"I'm Detective Clay, MPD, Vice Squad," Devon said, British accent nowhere in evidence. "This woman is an informant, and I'm taking her into protective custody."

"Informant for what?"

"That's not your jurisdiction, officer," Devon said coolly. "Now, let us pass." He moved us around the cop.

"Wait a second," the man said, blocking our path again. "We've got a situation here and I can't just let people come and go—I don't care who she is or who you are."

John stepped in. "I'm her attending physician and I say she needs to leave for her own health. If you keep her here, you'll be responsible should anything happen to her." He paused, then added, "How's your professional liability insurance, officer? All paid up on your premiums?"

The belligerent look on the man's face changed to one of uncertainty, then resignation. "Fine," he said. "No need to be an asshole about it. Go."

Devon steered me forward and I looked back at John. He and Devon exchanged glances.

"What about John?" I asked.

"He has to stay for our cover," he replied, hustling me out the exit. "It would look suspicious if he came along, too, and they're watching everyone."

"We can't leave without him," I said once he had me inside the SUV.

"Wasn't planning on it," he said. He drove around the hospital to the front, and that's when we saw the police cars. More of them than even in the back. I counted six. We pulled into an empty space and Devon killed the headlights.

"They're putting the hospital on lockdown," he said. "We can't wait much longer."

Anxiously, I watched the entrance, hoping John would emerge. He'd already put himself out on a limb for us and I didn't want him to get into trouble, but neither did I want to lose him.

We finally did see John emerge . . . in handcuffs.

Devon let out a vicious curse and I wanted to cry as they put John in the back of a police cruiser. Without a word, Devon flipped the lights back on and pulled out of the lot.

"What do we do now?" I asked.

Devon was driving, but I didn't know to where. And it seemed he didn't either because he swerved into a gas station lot and threw the gear into park.

"I need to think," he said.

The phone Scott had given me was burning a hole in my pocket. The urge to call was strong and I wanted to give in to the temptation to go back to the FBI facility. I was scared. My body was turning against me and I had no clue what to do.

But better to die with Devon by my side than amongst strangers as a lab rat. And yet I was a burden to Devon, sick as I was. Was it fair to him for me to stay? The answer to that was obvious. It would be selfish of me to stay.

"I'll call Scott," I said to Devon, digging out the cell phone. "Maybe he and that doctor are still here. I'll go with them, back to the FBI facility."

Devon snatched the phone from me. "Where did you get this?"

"Scott gave it to me," I said. "It has his number programmed in."

In a flash, Devon rolled down the window and tossed the phone, then threw the SUV into drive and took off from the lot. I stared at him in open-mouthed surprise.

"What did you do that for?" I asked. "Now I have no way to reach him!"

"Scott works for Vega," he said. "She told me as much."

Shock warred with dismay. It couldn't be true. Yes, Scott had turned me in to the FBI, but at least that I could sort of understand— he felt like he was doing his job. But for him to be working for Vega . . . Yeah, he hadn't mentioned *that* in the hotel room.

"How long?" I asked, my voice sounding strange in my ears.

"Since the beginning."

My eyes slipped closed. God, what a fool I was! To think that I'd thought him a friend, had confided in him, trusted him. And all that time he'd been paid to do a job for Vega. It was horrible and demoralizing. I felt his betrayal all the way to the bone.

"So you think that's how she found us," I said, pulling myself out of my shock. "At the hotel. Because of the phone."

"It would be the logical conclusion, yes."

I winced. Again, my naïveté and trust had nearly undone everything Devon was trying to do. Devon wasn't going to get himself killed—I'd no doubt manage that as well.

"Forget it," I said abruptly. "I'm done."

Devon glanced quizzically at me. "What?"

"I'm done. It's over. Before, it was just a price on my head. Now? It's a death sentence. I need to go back to the facility and give them what they want. Sticking with you is only going to get you killed. At the moment, it's me they want."

"Bollocks," he said. "There's no bloody way you're giving yourself up to them, regardless of your health. We'll find a cure. We'll find another vaccine, just like before."

"You can't vaccinate whatever it is that's killing me, Devon!" I cried, anguish and frustration bringing tears to my eyes, "It's done. I'm not going to have you wait until I die before you realize that. I'm leaving."

Devon swerved to the side of the road and jerked the car to a stop. He turned to me, one arm resting on top of the steering wheel, the other on the back of his seat.

"Listen closely, my darling," he said. "You will not be sauntering off on your own like some martyr waiting to die. That is not the Ivy I know, and I won't allow it."

"You won't allow it?" I asked, my temper rising. "It's my life, Devon—"

"No it bloody well isn't!" he exploded. "It's my life, too. Do you think you're disposable to me? That I can replace you as easily as I could a shirt?" He looked livid, angrier than I'd ever seen him, and it rendered me speechless.

Pressing his lips closed, he turned back to the road, staring out the windshield and gripping the wheel tightly. I stared, then jumped when he slammed his palm against the dash. He clenched and unclenched his fists.

"We're in this together," he said at last, his gaze locking on mine. "And I don't know what else I can say or do to convince you of that. Live or die, we're together. I will not desert you, and neither will I allow you to separate from me out of some misguided attempt to spare my emotions."

Tears filled my eyes, spilling over and tracing down my cheeks. Devon reached out, tenderly swiping them away, and when he spoke again his voice was gentle.

"When I say I love you," he said, "they are more than just words. I want you to hear them, hear me, and understand." His fingers beneath my chin prodded my gaze upward until our eyes met. "Love is not what you've known," he said. "Love is not pain, and betrayal, and subjugation. It is whole, and selfless, and unconditional. Sometimes there's sadness and loss, but in love there is always hope. I won't stop hoping, just like I won't stop loving you."

Tears fell even faster and I threw my arms around his neck. He pulled me close as I cried on his shoulder. His hand sifted through my hair and down my back, soothing me. I was grateful, too grateful for words about how incredibly lucky I was to have him, to have the love we shared.

"I love you, too," I managed at last, once I could speak. My voice was thick with tears.

"I know you do, darling," he said, brushing a kiss to my forehead. "Now let's work together on getting you well and no more talk of leaving, all right?"

I nodded. "Okay."

I scooted to my side of the car as Devon put it into gear and swung back out onto the road. Reaching across the seat, he took my hand and we held tightly to each other.

Another hotel, the desk clerk unsurprised at our very late check-in. Devon paid in cash, signing in as Jim Dale and wife. When we got to the room, I was more than ready to lie down.

"No one will know you're here," he said, slipping off my shoes for me and covering me with a blanket. "You'll be safe."

I frowned. "Where are you going?"

"I need to run an errand and call an old friend I'm hoping will help us," he said. "I shan't be long, I promise."

I believed him. "Okay. Be careful."

"Always, darling." The door closed quietly behind him, leaving me alone. I was asleep in seconds and didn't wake for hours. When I did, I felt marginally better. The ever-present headache was still there, but it was now more of a dull throb that I could handle.

Devon had returned at some point as he lay next to me, obviously not wanting to wake me. He was sound asleep and I arranged the blanket over him, then eased out of bed.

It was after noon, and as I dug through our duffel bag to get my toothbrush, my stomach growled. I took that as a good sign. An appetite signaled that my body was doing okay.

After cleaning up, I took a few bills from Devon's wallet along with the room key. I left a note telling him I was getting some food and would be back soon. After last night, I could visualize him waking up, seeing I wasn't there, and thinking the worst.

The hotel was a discount one that saw a lot of turnover and didn't remember names, so it wasn't surprising to me that there wasn't a restaurant inside. The sun was shining outside, beckoning. Thinking I could use the exercise and fresh air, I went out.

I walked for a short while, the sun warm on my shoulders and hair, until I found a small Cuban restaurant. The menu looked good, so I ordered myself and Devon something to go. He had to be starving, too. It felt good to be taking care of this one small task: lunch. I wasn't helpless and we were a team, just like he'd said.

The waitress who took my order looked at me kind of oddly. She didn't speak much English and my Spanish was nonexistent. I ordered from the menu based on numbers and slid onto one of the stools in their small bar to wait. It wasn't until I saw her talking to a man and both of them looking at me that my instincts kicked in.

I couldn't forget—my face was all over the news. Even with the hair redo, people could still recognize me, if they were aware enough. It seemed this unlikely place and this too-observant person was just that.

Shit.

I slid off the stool and headed for the door, but the man the waitress had been talking to intercepted me.

"Excuse me," he said, his accent thick. "Your order has been delayed a few more minutes. The cook misread the ticket and has to remake it."

I gave him a fake smile. "That's fine. I'm just going to step outside and tell my girlfriend." If they reported this to the FBI, I wanted them to think I was traveling with a woman, not Devon.

"Please, have a seat, and a drink. On the house." He took my arm, propelling me back toward the bar.

"No, thanks. I don't drink." I tried to pull out of his grip, but he only held me tighter. "Let me go," I said, giving up all pretense and yanking my arm away.

He lunged for me but I sidestepped him. I had a split second to decide what to do, and I went on the offense.

Rushing forward, I got up in his space and grabbed his shoulders. He reared back in surprise, then my knee caught him square in the crotch. I was out the door before he'd even collapsed to the floor, moaning in pain and holding himself.

The temptation to run was strong, but that would catch the eye of anyone following me, so I made myself walk. Luckily, the sidewalk was crowded with tourists. An outdoor flea market was set up in the adjacent parking lot, and I walked through the vendors, looking for an opportunity. I saw my chance when a woman selling scarves and purses began haggling with a tourist over the price of a quilted clutch bag. As I brushed past, my fingers caught at a fluttering scarf. Two tables later, I wrapped it over my hair and tied it. Someone else had set down their sunglasses to look at a hand-made clock. I picked them up as I walked by, not even pausing in my stride, and slipped them on. Two minutes after I'd escaped the Cuban restaurant, I was somewhat disguised and headed back to the hotel, hidden amongst a throng of people in a tour group.

My heart was pounding, but I was relieved I'd made it out of there. Deciding that ethnic food was going to have to be for another time, I popped in to the McDonalds next to the hotel. No one there noticed a thing as I ordered a Big Mac and chicken nuggets, extra fries, a couple of Cokes, and a shake just for the hell of it. If I was going to die, might as well get the ice cream, too.

I was waiting for the elevator in the hotel when it happened.

A blinding flash of pain in my head that had me reeling. My vision clouded and the bag and cups fell from my hands. I clutched my head, feeling the warm trickle of blood ooze from my nose. The pain was excruciating and I squeezed my eyes shut as nausea climbed into my throat. Tears leaked from my eyes and I heard someone talking to me, but couldn't concentrate on what they were saying.

My knees gave out and I hit the floor hard as the pain spiked once again. This time I couldn't handle it, and everything went dark.

CHAPTER NINE

The first thing I became aware of when I opened my eyes was that the blinding pain had receded into the dull, aching throb I was growing too accustomed to. I could taste blood on my lip as I looked around, realizing I'd created quite a scene.

"She's awake," someone called out.

A group of people surrounded me. A woman knelt by my side, her expression concerned as she asked, "Are you all right?"

I nodded and sat up, which produced a wave of light-headedness, and I had to sit still for a moment and wait for it to pass. Everyone was watching me. What if someone else recognized me? A knot of panic grew in my gut.

"I'm so sorry," I said, swiping at the blood under my nose. Someone thrust a handful of tissues at me, which I gratefully took. "I made an awful mess."

"Don't worry about that," the woman said. "We were about to call an ambulance."

Panic struck. "No!" I said, too loudly. I dialed it back. "I mean, no, I don't need an ambulance. I'm fine. Really." I struggled to my feet and the crowd around me began to drift away.

The woman looked puzzled. "I really think you need to go to the hospital," she said.

"I will," I lied. "Just not in an ambulance. I'll get my friend to take me."

"Are you sure?"

"Absolutely. But thank you for helping me." The elevator doors opened just then, and I gave her a wan smile before darting inside, grimacing at the puddle of Coke and ice cream on the lobby floor. I punched the button for the correct floor and breathed a sigh of relief when the door slid shut. Unlike the restaurant, I didn't think anyone had recognized me, or at least they hadn't shown any sign of it.

I wiped off the blood the best I could, but had to clean up and change my shirt when I got back into the room. Devon was still asleep, thank God. I knew he'd want me to tell him what happened, and I would tell him about the waitress, but I hesitated when I thought of how I'd collapsed in the lobby. There wasn't a thing he could do about my health and it would only worry him. It wasn't like pain and nosebleeds were a new thing at this point. The medicine John had given me had helped, but hadn't lasted very long.

I'd just finished tucking a fresh tank top into my jeans—black this time, so if there was more blood, at least it wouldn't be so obvious—when Devon stirred.

"Hallo, my darling," he said, beckoning me. I willingly climbed onto the bed and into his arms. "How are you feeling?"

"Better," I said, which was true. I felt way better than I had in the lobby. That had been awful.

His hand curved around my shoulder, pressing me a little closer. "I'm delighted to hear that."

I was glad I'd decided not to say anything. The relief and hope in Devon's voice made my heart hurt.

"Where did you go?"

I twisted to look up at him. His gaze was steady. "You heard me? I tried to be quiet."

"Of course I heard you," he said. "I thought you might need some time alone. I trust you didn't go far?"

I shook my head. "No. Not far. Though my disguise isn't working very well." I explained what had happened in the restaurant.

He squeezed my shoulder hard when I spoke about getting away from the man, and I felt his lips brush the top of my head. He didn't speak for a moment, and when he did, he had to clear his throat first.

"I'd like to take you shopping today," he said. "Buy you something pretty."

Devon knew how much I liked clothes. They were a passion and obsession of mine. He'd indulged me many times, but shopping didn't hold the same appeal it used to. Not now. Not anymore.

"I really don't care what we do," I said, nestling my head against his chest. "So long as I'm with you."

"That's very sweet, my dear, but I know how your face lights up when you find the perfect skinny jean, or a strappy sandal that makes me glad I'm quite a bit taller than you."

I couldn't help but smile at that. "I do love a strappy sandal," I agreed. "Especially if they're sparkly." I was still worried about being recognized, but I trusted Devon. If he said it'd be okay, then it would.

I heard his laugh rumble in his chest. "Sparkles are always a plus, I agree," he said with mock seriousness.

Devon changed into light khaki pants and a striped blue button-up shirt, which he left untucked. In deference to the heat, he folded back the cuffs and the top two buttons remained undone.

We strolled hand in hand along the high-end shopping district in downtown Miami. I wore the scarf I'd purloined, and the sunglasses. Though I was supposed to be shopping, all we did was walk and talk.

"Tell me a story," I said. I loved hearing Devon talk, not only because of his accent, which I found particularly appealing, but because of his word choice and dry humor.

"I'm to entertain you, is that it?" he teased.

"Absolutely." I smiled at him, enjoying the way the sunlight made highlights in his hair shine like gold.

"All right then." He thought for a minute as we strolled. "I suppose I could tell you about the time I met the Queen."

I stopped in my tracks, gaping at him. "You met the Queen?" I asked.

He nodded. "And Prince Charles."

"Bullshit."

He laughed. "Darling, would I lie to you?" He tugged me forward and we resumed our stroll. "Now pay attention and I'll relate the tale. It was many years ago, and I was but a new lad in the service. It's not often Shadow agents interact with the royals—we're usually tasked for other things—but on this particular occasion, I was assisting with security for an event due to a credible IRA threat. Normally, even that wouldn't get me much closer than twenty meters of their actual person, but there was a slight incident."

I was enthralled. Devon had played bodyguard to the Queen of England? Just . . . wow.

"What kind of incident?" I asked.

He grimaced. "A man—obviously a bit bonkers—thought it'd be jolly good fun to run about naked as some kind of political statement. The only statement it really made was how unimpressive the size of his manhood was."

I laughed as he continued. "So this naked bloke is cavorting about, holding up some sort of sign with a rubbish motto written on it, and of course everything goes into lockdown mode as a matter of procedure. Though he had no weapon and no place to hide any sort of weapon, protocol must be followed. The royals were sent through an alternate exit and I was charged with being the primary on that detail. We rushed them into their waiting sedan, but the Queen gave me a smile and nod before she got in."

I could visualize it, the tiny woman acknowledging the service of her subject.

"That is so cool," I said. "Did you say anything?"

He shook his head. "I'm not a huge fan of the royals, but I admire the Queen. She's an extraordinary woman. I must admit, I do hold that memory quite dear, much to my surprise."

"Did Charles say anything? Did he nod at you, too?"

Devon shook his head. "No. He's a bit of a sod, actually. Not very fond of him."

I laughed at the grimace on Devon's face. He smiled and pulled me closer as we walked.

"What about you, my darling? Shall I prod you for a story of your own?"

I shrugged. "My life is boring in comparison. Growing up on a farm in Kansas isn't exactly the stuff movies are made of."

"Dorothy and Toto would disagree, I'm sure," he said, and I laughed. "A farm in Kansas sounds lovely. I particularly enjoyed meeting your grandparents. Your grandfather was quite vehement in letting me know he had a shotgun and wasn't afraid to use it should I behave with any impropriety toward you."

I laughed. "That sounds like grandpa. I wondered if he did anything like that while we were there. I suppose I should apologize for that."

"Not at all," he said. "That's his job and his duty, to make sure nefarious creatures like myself don't take advantage of his young, beautiful granddaughter."

I shook my head, marveling that even now, Devon's compliments could make me blush.

"You're not shopping," he said, tugging me to a halt outside a designer store. "Let's go in."

I allowed him to pull me inside, though I didn't see the point. Why spend a bunch of money on some outrageously expensive outfit that I'd die before I got to wear? Though I supposed Devon could always return it . . .

I sighed at the morbid thought as a shop girl saw us and walked over, a welcoming smile on her face. "How can I help you today?" she asked.

I searched her face for any sign of recognition as she looked at me, but there was only the friendly open expression of an employee working on commission.

"We're looking for a dress," Devon said. "I highly doubt you'll have one as beautiful as my lovely lady, but perhaps one near to it."

The girl's smile widened. "I think we can find a few options. Come with me."

I rolled my eyes at Devon, but couldn't suppress a smile as I followed the girl to the dressing rooms. She asked me my name and chitchatted about Miami while I undressed. Sizing me up with a practiced eye, she said she'd be right back with some dresses.

I spent the next hour or so trying on clothes and I had to admit, it did cheer me up. The fabrics were so silky with beautiful, bold colors. The lines of the dresses draped perfectly on me, making me feel as though I were the old me—the healthy me.

"That's the one," Devon said when I came out of the dressing room for the eighth time. "We'll have that one," he told the girl. "And don't forget the shoes."

It was an Oscar de la Renta dress, the hem hitting just below my knee. Sleeveless with a scoop neck, it was a soft aqua, the entire front embroidered in an elaborate design with flowers, butterflies, and ivy. It was exquisite. The shoes were a matching aqua sandal with a low heel.

I turned my back so he could unzip me, but he said, "No. Wear it."

I looked at him. "But it'll get dirty."

"Doesn't matter. I want to wine and dine you, and that is what I want you to wear. Be a dear and oblige me?"

Well, when he said that, who was I to say no? "You're too good to me," I said, not even wanting to know what an original Oscar de la Renta cost.

"You mean I'm not nearly good enough for you," he said, taking my hand and raising it to his mouth to press a kiss to my knuckles. "But I am ever so fortunate you love me despite my many faults."

"Aw, that's so sweet!"

We both turned to see the shop girl watching us dreamily. I laughed a bit self-consciously, but Devon merely slipped an arm over my shoulders and followed the girl to the front.

I tensed when I saw Devon give the girl a black credit card. "I thought we didn't want to be tracked," I said in an undertone to him.

"They already know we're in the city," Devon said. "Besides, I want them to know."

I couldn't question him further, not with the girl trying hard to pretend she wasn't listening to us, but I gave him the look that said he'd be explaining further once we got somewhere private.

"We'll have that, too," Devon said, pointing to a wide, floppy straw hat. It was gorgeous and combined with my stolen black, over-sized sunglasses, I felt a bit like Audrey Hepburn when we walked out.

"I know a wonderful place for dinner," Devon said. "It's right along the beach. Fancy some seafood, darling? How does that sound?"

I loved fresh seafood, but rarely got it. In the Midwest, that was about the most expensive thing you'd find on the menu and even then, it was hardly ever fresh unless you went to really nice places. On my salary, those hadn't been in the cards, so I eagerly agreed.

The restaurant was indeed right on the beach, and the waiter took us outside to a cozy table for two on the deck. A small candle was lit and I absorbed the incredible view while the waiter draped the linen napkin in my lap. The sun was going down and the light glistened off the water like diamonds had been tossed into the waves.

"It's beautiful," I said with a sigh. I took a deep lungful of the sea air, listening to the crash of the waves and the seagulls' cries. This was a good place to be. A good place to—

Die was the word that came to mind, though I didn't want to think about it. I wanted to make it to London with Devon, but after the episode this afternoon, I wasn't sure that was going to happen.

Devon was watching me rather than looking at the menu, and I was suddenly self-conscious.

"What?" I asked with a smile. "Does the hat look silly?" I reached up and took off the hat, smoothing my hair down even as the ocean breeze tousled it.

"You look beautiful," he said.

"My hair has been chopped in a cheap motel, then given a bad dye job," I said. "Beautiful isn't really the right word."

"You're right," he said. "Stunning is more appropriate. I look at you and see the love of my life."

My heart skipped a beat as I stared at him, my jaw agape. He was serious, I could see it in his eyes, and it made mine fill with tears.

"Oh, Devon . . ." But I couldn't continue, my throat thickening too much to speak.

He reached across the table and took my hand, bending to brush a kiss to my knuckles. Then he pressed my palm to his cheek.

"It's quite true," he said. "I am in awe that I found you. And I will not give you up so easily."

I sniffed and used the corner of my napkin to dab my eyes under the sunglasses. Devon needed to see that things weren't going to end well, not for me anyway. I didn't want him to continue to be in denial.

"Devon, please try to understand," I said. "I know you're used to saving the day, to being the hero. But this time . . . this time it's just not going to work out. It's not an enemy you can shoot or kill or thwart. It's inside me. And there's nothing you can do about it."

He didn't say anything, just looked at me, his jaw set in a hard line.

"Let's not dwell on it," I said, squeezing his hand. "I'm wearing a lovely dress, having dinner with the man of my dreams, in one of the most beautiful places I've ever been. It can't possibly get better than this."

"We'll see about that," Devon said.

I just smiled. Things would be okay. In the end, if I was with Devon, then I could die content. Sometimes life was like that. It didn't turn out like you'd planned and you had to make it up as you went along, grabbing the moments of true happiness when and where you could. I was just grateful I'd had those moments, that I was having one now, and that I was wise enough to appreciate it and not take it for granted.

The waiter came back and Devon ordered for us, the special entrée, which was fresh tilapia with a citrus glaze and risotto. He also ordered a bottle of champagne.

"Champagne?" I asked. "Are we celebrating?"

"I don't see any reason not to have champagne, no matter what," he said, making me smile again. I couldn't agree more.

The sun had dropped below the horizon so we both discarded our sunglasses, talking about unimportant things and enjoying the scenery. The waiter brought an appetizer Devon had requested: fried fresh calamari that seemed to melt in my mouth.

It was an amazing dinner and I was able to see the ocean for quite a while until it got too dark. By then, I was stuffed full of calamari, tilapia, crème brûlée, and enough champagne to make me smile for no reason at all. Just because.

"Let's take a walk, shall we?" Devon asked after he'd paid the bill.

Him paying reminded me about him using a credit card and what he'd said in the shop, but I'd had enough to drink that I decided I didn't care to bring up Vega and Bad Things. I trusted Devon to know what he was doing. If he thought it was okay, then it was.

I took off my sandals and Devon carried them, the delicate leather straps caught around two of his fingers. His other hand folded around mine and we stepped down from the restaurant's deck onto the soft sand.

I wiggled my toes with a sigh and Devon chuckled at me.

"Best exfoliator ever," I said. "My feet will be as soft as a baby's bottom after walking on this stuff."

"I can't say I've ever touched a baby's bottom," he said. "I'll have to take your word for it."

I glanced at him as we walked toward the water. "Really? You've never been around babies?"

"When would I possibly have been around babies? Or children at all, for that matter?" he teased me. "It's not as though one sees a lot of them dealing in international intrigue and espionage."

I shrugged. "I don't know. I guess it's hard for me to imagine the life you've led. Mine has been so different."

"True," he said. "But neither can I imagine yours."

"Mine is boring," I interrupted. "Trust me."

He laughed softly. "To you it may be boring, true. To me, it sounds like a foreign adventure. I'd quite like to touch a baby's bottom." He glanced at me. "In a non-weird way, of course, which is not at all how that sounded."

I laughed outright. Who would've known Devon was a funny guy?

By now we'd reached the water and Devon paused, looking up. I followed his gaze and saw the moon was half full in the night sky. Too many city lights prevented viewing a lot of stars, but it was still beautiful. Down by the water, it was quieter. There were fewer sounds of the people and city. If I closed my eyes, I could almost pretend we were the only ones around.

"Ivy," Devon began, turning me toward him. "I have something I want to ask you. Something quite important, as it happens."

I opened my mouth to ask what it was, when he lowered himself to one knee in the sand, kneeling in front of me. Then my mouth dropped open in shock.

"Ivy Mason," he began, still holding my hand.

I started to cry.

"Ivy Mason," he continued, his thumb gently rubbing the back of my hand. "I've been waiting my entire life for you. In you, I've found my perfect match. To put it in the simplest terms, we fit. And I want to be with you, call you my own, for as long a time as we have on this earth together. My darling Ivy, will you do me the utmost honor of being my bride?"

Tears were streaming down my cheeks. I hadn't imagined this, had never thought Devon would propose, much less in such a romantic way. The waves were breaking mere yards from us. The sand was cooling underneath my feet. And the man I loved still knelt in that sand, waiting for my answer.

"Yes," I choked out. "Yes, I'll marry you."

A blinding smile lit his face, then he was on his feet and picking me up in his arms. He spun me around once, twice, then kissed me. My arms circled his neck as I held on, hardly able to believe what had just happened.

Carefully, he set me on my feet, then produced a small velvet box from his pocket.

"This is for you," he said, bending back the lid.

I gasped. A perfect square-cut diamond ring sat inside. A platinum band with additional diamonds set into it glinted in the dim moonlight. It was too beautiful and looked too expensive for me to touch, much less actually wear.

He took the ring from the box and lifted my left hand. My hands were shaking as he slid it onto my finger, then he kissed my fingers.

"My love," he said, our eyes meeting. "I'd go to the ends of the earth, and beyond, for you."

I pressed against him, holding him tight. For a few blissful moments, I'd forgotten the death sentence I was under. I shoved the thoughts away. This was the best moment of my entire life, and I was going to live every second of it, no matter what the future held.

The pain came like before, out of nowhere and excruciating. I gasped, my eyes slamming shut as my knees faltered. If Devon hadn't been holding me, I'd have collapsed on the ground.

"What is it?" he asked anxiously, but I was in too much pain to answer.

I clutched my splitting head, moaning in pain, and felt the warm gush of blood from my nose.

Devon cursed, one arm supporting me while he dug for his pocket square to stem the flow. I barely noticed. It hurt so badly, more than it had before, and I could barely stand it. Tears leaked from the corners of my eyes, but these weren't from joy.

"Been looking for you, Devon."

That voice was familiar, and I pried open my eyes enough to see Scott. He stood about ten feet away and had a gun pointed at us.

"Agent Lane," Devon said. "I'm not at all surprised to see that Vega sent you."

"At this point, who else would she send? It's like rats deserting a sinking ship. Everyone knows the UK government wants the Shadow dismantled, and Vega's power along with it. The other Shadow agents have gone to ground, disavowing her."

"And you're the last rat standing?"

A shot rang out and I started, then realized he'd fired a warning at Devon, the bullet kicking up sand mere inches from him.

"Watch your mouth, Clay."

"You lying sonofabitch," I snarled. I went after him, determined to sink my claws into any part of his flesh I could reach, but I only made it one step before Devon snagged me around the waist and hauled me back.

"Oh please," Scott snorted in contempt. "Spare me the self-righteous betrayed outrage, Ivy. You saw what you wanted to see: another man so infatuated with you, he'd blindly do whatever you wanted."

"So it was all fake?" I spat, trying to push Devon's arms away. "You were never my friend? You were always working for her?"

Scott winced, but his voice was hard. "Don't try to pretend you felt anything for me, Ivy. You were using me. You used me in Paris when you had no one else to turn to and you used me ever since, whether to keep you safe or to soothe your bruised ego." He paused, then dropped the bomb. "You think I wouldn't find the pages you hid in my apartment?"

Devon stiffened next to me. I'd never told him I hadn't burned the entire journal or that I'd hidden the encrypted pages in Scott's apartment.

"I was just another pawn to you," Scott said bitterly. "I thought about denying Vega, but when it was obvious I meant nothing to you, I didn't think twice."

"That wasn't how it was, Scott. We were friends. I trusted you."

He was silent for a moment, staring at me. "It doesn't matter now anyway," he said.

"Please tell me you didn't give Vega the pages," I said, hoping beyond hope, but Scott just looked sad.

"I had to," he said. "She's always watching. She knows . . . everything." He shrugged, looking resigned. "I wasn't lying about the doctor, though. He was trying to help you. But it was Vega who gave you a mutated form of the virus. The one that's killing you. It didn't mutate on its own."

My eyes slipped closed and it felt as though lead filled my stomach. I should've known. I'd been unconscious for how long with her scientist? That was probably when they'd done it. I should've known Vega wouldn't let an opportunity like that pass her by.

"That's what was encoded on the pages, wasn't it," Devon said.

"Yeah. Along with the cure. The mutation is different than the original virus, which you can be vaccinated against. This one can reinfect unless you get the medicine."

"Are you going to help Ivy?" Devon bit out, interrupting him. "That is why you're here, correct? To kill me and take Ivy?"

"That's the mission, yeah," Scott said.

"Tell me you have the medicine," Devon demanded. "Because otherwise, she's not going anywhere with you."

"It's close by," Scott hedged. "Now put her down and step away."

"Did Vega really tell you to kill me?" Devon asked.

Scott hesitated. "I don't think she'll mind. One last loose end tied up. She knows there's a target on her back. All that's left is to play her last card so she can retire in peace and not in the grave."

"She's not going to take kindly to you killing her best agent, no matter her retirement plans."

"She'll get over it. Now put Ivy down."

Devon began lowering me to the sand and from somewhere, I dredged up the energy to fight.

"No," I said, holding on to his shoulders for dear life. "No, please Devon. Don't." If Scott wouldn't shoot Devon while I was in the way, then I'd just shield him with my body. We could die together, but I wasn't about to let him give up his life for mine.

But Devon was still lowering me inexorably toward the ground. I began to sob and knew I was near hysterics. Scott was going to kill

Devon right in front of me, and there wasn't anything I could do about it. I wasn't strong enough to stop Devon from unwrapping my arms from around his neck and the pain was sapping every last ounce of energy I had.

"No, please . . ." But my begging fell on deaf ears.

Devon kissed my cheek, then my forehead. "I love you, dearest Ivy," he said quietly.

He released my arms and stood, taking a large step away from me. I immediately forced myself to flip over onto my stomach and began clawing my way through the sand toward him, knowing my legs wouldn't hold me if I tried to stand.

The gunshot wasn't loud, but I cried out anyway, cringing into a ball and covering my head with my arms. Sobs wracked me as I heard a body fall to the sand. I decided right then, in that instant, that I would kill Scott. Even if it had to be with my bare hands, I'd find a way to kill him.

Grief turned to rage, pressing back even the pain knifing through my skull. I lifted my head and clenched my hands into fists, looking for Scott. I'd drag him into the ocean and drown us both.

But Scott wasn't there. Alarmed, I sat up, looking around wildly.

"Take it easy, darling. It's all right."

Devon crouched beside me. Whole and unharmed. I stared at him in shock. Then I threw my arms around his neck.

"Oh my God! How . . . ? I thought . . ." But I couldn't continue.

"Shh, it's all right. I'm all right."

"Where's Scott?"

"He's dead. I searched his body for the medicine. He was carrying a syringe with him. I'm afraid I have to stick a needle in you, darling. Hold still."

I barely noticed as he injected me in the arm with something, too busy was I memorizing every detail of his face. He'd nearly died mere moments ago, for me. I could barely comprehend what had happened. It had happened so fast.

The medicine felt like fire going in and as before when the doctor and then John had injected me, I felt better almost immediately. It was bizarre. The pain in my head receded, which was such a relief that I sagged against Devon.

"Everything all right? Is she good?"

I squeaked in alarm at yet another voice speaking in the darkness, trying to jerk back, but Devon held me. Twisting in his arms, I looked up to see a man looming over us, carrying a long rifle of some sort. It was hard to see him clearly in the dark, but he was tall and lean, with hair as inky black as the night sky. His eyes glittered in the pale moonlight, his face a cold mask of near indifference as he surveyed us. He looked vaguely familiar, but I couldn't place him.

"She's fine, thank you. And nice shot, by the way."

"No thanks required, and of course it was a nice shot. *I* was doing the shooting."

The man's lips twisted in a lopsided smirk, though his eyes remained serious. I noticed a trace of concern in his eyes as he looked me over, but then it was gone.

"So we're square now?" the man asked. "I don't want you coming back in another six months. I'm retired."

"Yes, we're square," Devon confirmed, getting to his feet. He helped me up, too, supporting most of my weight. The man's brow creased as he spotted the blood on my face, and he let out a sigh of long-suffering.

"Please tell me you didn't hit her," he said, his dry tone holding a note of warning. "I'm not usually one who'd give a shit, but I've grown a conscience lately, which totally sucks, because then I'd have to kick your ass."

"Devon didn't hit me," I said. "I've been . . . ill."

He eyed me, as though testing the veracity of my words "Good," he said at last. He glanced at the watch on his wrist. "Because I have a plane to catch."

"Thank you for coming," Devon said.

"Like I had much choice," the man groused, but he didn't seem actually upset about it. "By the way, the other thing you wanted me to check? I hacked into the Miami police department and cleared your guy of all charges and had him released. He caught a plane to Atlanta earlier this evening."

I looked quizzically at Devon. *Your guy?*

"Excellent. That was above and beyond, but I thank you."

"Yeah, I'm all good-hearted and shit now. Whatever. I'm out of here. Have a nice life, Clay."

"Same to you."

"I plan on it." The man walked away, melting into the darkness.

I turned to Devon. "Who was that?"

"He's called Tombstone," Devon said. "I don't know his real name. He's an assassin I've known for quite some time. He also has additional skills in the computer field which come in handy."

"And he just happened to be here?" I asked.

"Of course not. I coordinated with him last night. He's no longer in the business, but he owed me a favor. I thought Vega would try to kill me, but you needed the medicine and Scott was our best shot at getting some for you. He was my life insurance policy."

"What if he'd missed?" I asked. "Or hadn't been here? Scott would have killed you."

Devon shrugged. "It was a chance I was willing to take. You're worth it."

I wanted to scream in frustration and kiss him all at the same time. It was incredibly selfless what he'd done . . . and also infuriating. I didn't want the man I loved dying for me.

"How are you feeling, darling?" he asked, brushing my hair back from my face. "Better?"

I decided to save the lecture for another time. There was nothing I could do about it now anyway. I nodded.

"Yeah. It's better." I was still shaky, but thought that was the aftereffects of shock and pain. I looked beyond him to the dark lump in the sand. "Is Scott dead?"

Devon glanced over his shoulder. "Quite. Tombstone is very effective at his job. Shame he's retired, actually."

"What did he mean by *your guy*?"

"The doctor, of course. John. Looks like he's been released and is probably stepping off a plane in Atlanta at this very moment. Back to his normal life."

I relaxed. "Oh good. I was worried about him. I didn't want him to get in trouble just for helping us."

"He'll be fine," Devon said. "Let's worry about you, shall we?"

He helped me to my feet and started to walk us back the way we'd come, but I stopped him.

"Wait, I want to see Scott." I wanted to say goodbye, and mourn. He'd been yet another of Vega's casualties, forced into doing something and becoming someone he'd never intended.

Devon and I were silent as we stood over Scott's body. Tears leaked from my eyes. I hadn't wanted this, but neither had I wanted him to shoot Devon. It was another reason Vega had to be stopped. She'd hurt too many people and would only hurt more, especially now that she had a new biological weapon and the only cure for it.

"We can't just leave him here," I said, my voice thick. "It's not right."

"I'm sorry, darling, but we have no choice." Devon said gently. "We can't just turn up at the police station with a dead body."

Logically, that made sense, but I felt a guilty kind of horror at leaving Scott in the sand as Devon led me away.

I had to lean on him pretty heavily as we made our way back from the beach to the road. Devon flagged down a cab that took us back to our hotel, and I was never so glad to see a cheap motel room than when Devon unlocked the door and let me inside.

Looking in the bathroom mirror, I was relieved to see that somehow the dress had escaped unscathed. No blood marred the fabric, and while it needed to be cleaned, it was otherwise in pristine condition.

I grabbed a washcloth and began wiping the blood from my face. My head felt weird, like it was buzzing on the inside, but there was no pain and I was more grateful for that. The weight of the ring on my finger was new and unfamiliar and I paused, glancing down at my hand.

The lights made the diamond sparkle like fire and I lost my breath all over again staring at it. I was engaged. Devon had asked me to marry him. And maybe, just maybe, I wasn't going to die.

CHAPTER TEN

The next morning, Devon "traded in" our SUV for a convertible for the drive to Key West. I didn't ask where he'd gotten it and he didn't offer an explanation as he held the passenger door open for me. I tied the scarf I'd pilfered over my hair, slipped on my sunglasses, and enjoyed the warm sunshine and breeze as he drove.

I was wearing a cheap sundress I'd picked up at the same market where I'd snatched the scarf. Thin and light, it was perfect for the heat, the spaghetti straps leaving my arms bare, though Devon had insisted I put on sunscreen or he'd put the top up on the convertible.

I'd never driven over the Keys before, and the endless bridge over the sparkling water fascinated me. Traffic was light and we passed few cars. It was difficult to talk with the wind rushing by, but that was okay. It felt good just to be alive and pain free. Devon held my hand in the space between us, his thumb occasionally brushing over the ring on my finger, as though to reassure himself that it was still there. I didn't mind. I kept glancing down every once in a while too, just to admire it.

I couldn't wipe the stupid grin off my face. I knew the threat of Vega still loomed, but for the first time, I was hopeful. We'd made it this far, against impossible odds. Maybe God was finally smiling on me.

We stopped for lunch at this little hole in the wall on one of the Keys. They served fresh, fried grouper sandwiches that melted in my mouth. Devon and I sat at a dilapidated picnic table under the shade of a few palm trees, getting sauce on our hands and grease on our mouths.

He told me of a "chap I once knew" who was the "luckiest unlucky bloke on the planet" and that you "wouldn't want to be standing next to him in a firefight." I laughed at the absurd stories and sipped on the piña colada he'd insisted I have.

We talked for a while, not in any hurry, and I didn't mind. I was happier than I'd been in my entire life, and I was loath to end our journey and let the real world of Vega and the Shadow intrude.

But we couldn't tarry forever and soon we were back in the car. Devon felt I'd been in the sun enough so he closed the roof and turned on the air-conditioning for the rest of the drive. I was dozing in the seat when he pulled to a stop. Coming awake, I yawned behind my hand as I looked around.

We were in front of a really nice hotel, and I'd hardly gotten a glimpse at the "Casa Marina" sign before a valet was opening my door.

"Welcome," he said with a smile. I smiled back as I stepped out. Devon was handling the ticket for the car as another valet opened the trunk.

"I'll take that one," Devon said, grabbing the duffel that contained all his weapons.

We walked inside and I craned my neck, taking it all in. It was beautiful, with hardwood floors and expansive windows in the lobby. My gaze caught on the sight of the ocean outside. Palm trees flanked a paved path, which ran straight from the doors to the beach, lined on both sides with long, narrow pools of water. It was beautiful and the ocean was just yards away.

I drifted to the windows to see better while Devon checked in. Some workers outside were setting up a few white wooden folding chairs on one side of the beach, while others tied white organza and flowers to an iron arch. If I'd had to guess, I'd have assumed they were setting up for a wedding.

"Do you like it?" Devon asked. He'd come up behind me and slid his arms around my waist. I leaned back against him.

"It's beautiful," I said. It rivaled the hotel we'd stayed in while on Maui just a few months ago.

"Do you think you'd like to be married here? On the beach?"

Surprised, I twisted in his arms so I could look up at him. "Really? We could?"

He nodded toward the outside. "They're setting it up now. If that's what you want. If not, we can do it later or some other location. You'll probably want your grandparents there, and Logan—"

It seemed like nervous chatter, which was so unlike Devon that I smiled and cut him off.

"We'll have a party back home to celebrate. But if you're saying you want to marry me today, on a beautiful beach in Key West, I am not going to turn that down."

He let out a small sigh, his smile a bit relieved as he relaxed, and my heart melted. I found his nervousness sweet, especially for as confident and self-assured a man as he was. To think he was unsure of what my response would be to marrying him so quickly was endearing.

"Mr. Clay, your room is ready."

We followed the bellhop with our luggage to the tiny elevator, then down the hallway of the second floor to a room. I was delighted all over again to see we had a room with our own private lanai overlooking the same view I'd had in the lobby. Two chaise lounges were set up along with an umbrella for shade, so that's where I plopped down as Devon tipped the man and sent him away.

"I didn't bring a swim suit," I said as Devon sat down on the matching chair.

"There's a shop down below," he said. "You can buy what you need there."

"I can't believe this," I said. "How did you manage to pull all this together so quickly?"

"A couple of phone calls and money is all it takes to get most things done, darling."

I just shook my head. Devon was a force to be reckoned with. If he wanted something, there wasn't a lot that could thwart him.

"I already have the dress," I said. "It just needs to be cleaned. Do you think they could have it cleaned in time?"

"No need for that," he said. "I picked up another dress for you. I believe they hung it in the closet."

My ears perked up at that. "Another dress? How?" But even as I said it, I knew Devon could have easily bought another gown while I was busy trying things on at the shop. Flashing him a grin, I jumped up and dashed back inside. Devon followed me, chuckling.

It was another Oscar de la Renta. A column gown of tiered champagne-colored lace panels over soft silk, cap sleeves, and a sweetheart neckline. The detailing was exquisite, the color perfect since white had a tendency to wash me out.

"It's beautiful," I said, literally in awe. Once on, the dress would hit right at my ankles. Perfect for a barefoot beach wedding.

"Not nearly as beautiful as you, darling," he said, brushing my cheek with his lips.

"We won't have any guests," I said, carefully hanging the dress again. "That might be odd. We should tell them not to bother setting up chairs."

"Oh we'll have guests," he said.

I looked at him, eyebrow raised. "Please tell me you're not paying people to come to our wedding." *That* would be more than a little mortifying.

He laughed outright at the look on my face. "Of course not. I merely suggested that we'd have a lovely dinner and champagne for any of their suitable hotel guests who might enjoy a romantic beach wedding and celebration with us."

"So you *are* bribing them," I accused, but I couldn't help grinning. It really was quite absurd. We'd know not a single soul at our own wedding. And yet, it seemed to fit what had been an unconventional romance with Devon from the start.

"Harsh words, darling," he said dryly, making me laugh again.

"I want to go lay on the beach," I said, changing the subject. "Maybe I can get a little sun beforehand. Do we have time?"

"We have as much time as you'd like," he said. "A sunset wedding won't be for hours yet. Plenty of time to lie about in the sun."

It took me no time at all to run downstairs and find swimsuits for us both, then back up to change. Sooner than I'd hoped, we were having the beach boy set up a couple of chairs in the sunshine, mere yards from the ocean's edge.

We lay in companionable silence, sipping cocktails and listening to the seagulls and the sound of the ocean. It was calm here, and Devon explained it was because of the Keys and how big waves didn't really crash against the shore the way they did elsewhere, like when we were in Maui.

It was beautiful and perfect, and I had to keep pinching myself because I was in paradise, with my fiancé, and today was my wedding day. It was almost too fantastic to believe. I felt as though I were holding my breath, waiting for something awful to happen and ruin everything. Because it couldn't possibly be this easy, could it? Marrying Devon? Being happy hadn't ever really been in the cards for me and yet, here it was, enveloping me with warm arms.

Devon left first, saying he had to see about the tux fitting he'd set up for himself.

"You're not supposed to see me before the wedding," I said. "It's bad luck."

"All right," he said, indulging me. "Then I will meet you, right over there," he pointed to the now-finished archway, the flowers covering the iron framework and filling the air with their heady scent. "At sunset."

"It's a date."

He kissed me, a long, deep, slow kiss that made butterflies dance in my stomach. His skin was warm and he smelled of the sun.

When he pulled back, he brushed my lips with his, murmuring softly, "That, my love, is your last kiss as a single woman."

And the butterflies took flight.

"You are such a romantic," I teased him. "Who would've known?"

"I trust you won't tell," he said, kissing the tip of my nose.

"Your secret's safe with me." I watched as he rose and walked back to the hotel. His body looked mouth-watering and I wasn't the only woman who kept her gaze on him until he disappeared inside.

It was a little sad to think that my grandparents and friends wouldn't be here to see me marry Devon, but too much had happened to jeopardize our lives for me to consider waiting. It was carpe diem, seize the moment, because it might not come again.

Now I stood staring in the mirror, trying not to cry and ruin my makeup. The dress was perfect, amazing, and I couldn't believe I was wearing a designer gown for my wedding. *My wedding.* I was so excited and terrified at the same time. Would he show? *Of course he would.* But what if he didn't? *Don't be ridiculous. He'll show.*

And so it went, arguing with myself. Nerves defied logic, and as I made my way downstairs, the thought occurred to me, *Maybe he's also wondering if I'll show up?* And the idea of Devon being nervous, too, helped steady me.

The manager of the hotel was waiting in the lobby and his face lit up when he saw me emerge from the elevator. He hurried over.

"Good evening," he said with a slight bow. "May I say how beautiful you look? Congratulations on your wedding day."

"Thank you," I said, smiling at the compliment. "I think I need to head outside."

"May I be of service as your escort?" he asked, offering me his arm, which I took.

"Yes, thank you."

The sun was just edging to the horizon when we stepped outside. He'd taken me to the side of the building and we walked through a path edged with tropical plants that concealed me from view. As the end of the path neared, he paused.

"If you'll wait here, I'll get the coordinator and start the music," he said.

I nodded, too nervous to say anything. Sure enough, a few moments later, a woman came up to me and I heard the sound of a ukulele playing. It was a very "island" sound and it made me smile.

"You look wonderful!" the woman said, introducing herself as Bernice as she handed me a bouquet of pink orchids. She explained that I'd walk further down the path until I reached the sand, where I'd see Devon and the archway.

"Just follow the sand to your fiancé," she said. "Say 'I do,' repeat the vows, and you'll be married by the time the sun sets."

I heard someone singing now, along with the ukulele. "Somewhere Over the Rainbow."

"Who picked the music?" I asked.

"Your groom," she replied, a twinkle in her eye. "Do you like it?"

A nod to my home, to Kansas, and Devon had thought to do it. Too choked up to answer, I just nodded.

"Oh no, no tears yet!" she said, whipping out a tissue and dabbing the corners of my eyes. "You don't want to smear your makeup, dear."

That prompted a bit of a laugh from me. Wedding coordinator orders must be followed so I sniffed and blinked a few times. She was right. I didn't want Devon to see me all crying with a red nose and blotchy cheeks.

Bernice smiled and stepped aside. "Good luck, dear. Enjoy."

I took a deep breath, the scent of the orchids filling my nostrils, and started down the walkway. The man was singing the chorus now, the lyrics hopeful and sad at the same time. It was beautiful.

I took my time getting there. A girl only got married once . . . hopefully.

When I reached the end of the path, the foliage opened up and I could see the archway, covered in blooms. People I didn't know sat in every chair, all turning to watch me. But all I saw was Devon, breathtaking in an ink-black tuxedo. His eyes were so blue, I could see their piercing color even from where he stood, waiting for me.

I was captivated by him, as I'd been since the first time I saw him walk into the bank and lay eyes on me. I'd been afraid of him then, so much about him had screamed danger and warning to me. Now I knew that, though he was a dangerous man, he was also a good man, and he'd never hurt me. He'd protected me, many times, and had been willing to die to save me.

Everyone stood as my foot stepped into the sand, distracting me for a moment. I felt a blush creep up my cheeks and glanced down, but I couldn't keep my eyes off Devon for long, my gaze inexorably drawn back to his.

The way he was looking at me made me want to memorize it, to capture it forever in a mental photograph so I could relive it. As though he simultaneously wanted to strip the dress off me and worship the ground I walked on. I'd never seen him awestruck, but that's exactly how he looked. It made me smile, happiness bubbling up inside me. I'd never felt like this before, anticipation and so much joy, it was an amazing feeling that I never wanted to end.

I barely realized where I was as I reached the end of the aisle, my focus had been so much on Devon. But now I was finally there, in front of him.

"You are the most beautiful creature I've ever laid eyes on," he said softly, just for my ears. He took my hand in his. The man was still singing, the lyrics drifting over us as the guests resumed their seats.

"You're gorgeous, too," I said. "I can't believe you're mine."

"I'm all yours, darling."

His smile was the sweetest I'd ever seen as we stood there and the music drifted into silence.

The man officiating spoke for a brief time, but his speech was short and to the point, and before long, I was reciting vows in a voice that shook slightly with emotion. Devon's was strong and sure.

"I now pronounce you man and wife. You may kiss your bride."

I turned to Devon, the weight of the wedding band he'd placed on my finger new to me. He stepped closer and used both hands to cup my face before he kissed me.

I lost myself in the feel of him—his lips against mine, the press of his palms holding my jaw, the feel of his body so close. Then the kiss was over and he rested his forehead against mine.

"You're a dream come true, sweet Ivy."

I choked up and couldn't reply, could only look up at him and hope he saw in my eyes everything I was feeling. I was overwhelmed with emotion.

Then everyone was applauding and it broke the moment. Devon put his arm around me and turned us to face the small crowd. Everyone had smiles on their faces, and I heard the popping of champagne corks as the white-jacketed waiters began filling flutes and passing then around.

"To us, my darling," Devon said, clinking his glass against mine.

The bubbles tickled my nose as I drank, the liquid cool against my tongue.

Devon took my hand and led me to where a photographer stood waiting. I hadn't even noticed him taking pictures, but I guessed that was part of the package. We posed for so many pictures, it was dark and they'd lit tiki torches by the time dinner was served.

Many of the guests came by to congratulate us . . . and introduce themselves. I'd thought it might be awkward, but everyone was so nice and didn't seem to be surprised that we wouldn't have a lot of guests at what they kept calling a "destination wedding."

Devon had ordered surf and turf for dinner, and I didn't want to think of the cost as the champagne flowed. I ate, but was paying too much attention to Devon to really care much about the food. He seemed to feel the same. His arm was slung over the back of my chair, resting on my shoulders, as he kept whispering in my ear and pressing light kisses to my neck. His fingers lightly brushed the back of my neck.

"Let's take a walk," he said, drawing me to my feet. We left everyone else behind as he took my hand and led me down the beach. The moon was high in the sky, its pale light illuminating our path.

After a little ways, the noise of the party faded away and Devon pulled me into his arms. "Was your wedding day everything you hoped it'd be?" he asked.

"You mean *our* wedding day," I said, sliding my arms around his waist. "It was beautiful. But it was the man I married that made it everything I'd hoped it'd be. Not the setting."

His eyes searched mine, and it felt like he was more open and vulnerable at this moment than I'd ever seen him.

"You mean everything to me," he said. "I want you to know that. No matter what happens."

That dimmed my mood. "What do you mean?" I asked. "What's going to happen?" I'd survived the virus and sickness. What else was going to work against us?

"You know I still need to go to London and finish this mission," he said gently. "That hasn't changed."

My stomach clenched. "Let's just run away," I said, taking his hands tightly in mine. "We can leave, go somewhere Vega won't find us . . ."

But Devon was already shaking his head. "I won't do that. Not with you. We won't spend our lives running and always looking over our shoulder. I have to finish this." The ocean breeze stirred my hair and he brushed some stray tendrils back from my face. "And I want you to stay here."

I stared at him. "What? What do you mean?"

"It will be dangerous. I can have Beau protect you while I'm gone."

"What exactly did those vows mean to you, Devon? For better, for worse, and all that? Were they just words? Because I don't want to stay behind and wait to hear that my husband didn't make it. You don't have to take me everywhere with you, but don't leave me on another continent, for goodness sake."

He studied me, brushing my hair back again, his fingers caressing my ear and jaw. His brow was furrowed and I held my breath. I'd gone with him before on his missions. I didn't want to be left behind. Not now. Not when we were supposed to be in this together.

"All right," he said at last. "But I will leave you somewhere safe over there, and you mustn't argue."

"I won't. I swear."

He pulled me close and pressed his lips to my forehead. I nestled in his arms, inhaling deeply of his cologne mixed with the scent of the ocean.

"I saw a hammock back there, I believe," he said. "Care to join me?"

"I'll go wherever you lead."

Getting into the hammock was easier said than done, and I was laughing so hard by the time we both got settled, my stomach hurt. It had nearly dumped Devon on the ground, and then when I'd climbed in and he'd followed, it nearly sent both of us tumbling. He was laughing, too, as we both cautiously maneuvered until we were in each other's arms.

"The stars are out," I said, looking up at the night sky.

"They wouldn't dare not shine brightly, on tonight of all nights," he said. "I'd have to lodge a formal complaint."

"With who?" I asked, smiling at his playfulness.

"With God, of course." He snorted, as though it were obvious. "I would have several issues to take up with him, actually, but we'd start with the stars."

"Like what issues?" I asked, curious.

Devon got quiet, his hand tightening on my shoulder. I waited, wondering why he'd grown thoughtful.

"I'd like to know how someone as good as you had something so awful happen to you."

I wasn't sure what to say. I didn't view myself as particularly good, at least not any better than the next person. As for the "something awful," Devon had been through as much if not more than me. He wasn't the only one who had a few issues to take up with The Almighty.

"Did you ever think you'd be married again?" I asked.

"Never. I never thought I'd have the opportunity to meet someone again, much less fall in love enough to risk it."

"Me, neither."

Devon glanced down at me, frowning. "How could you possibly believe you wouldn't be married?"

I shrugged. "I just never thought I'd find anyone who'd be able to help me overcome my past." I smiled at him. "Then I met you."

"Not the whirlwind romance of every girl's fantasies, though, was I?" His tone was wry and tinged with regret.

"It wasn't a usual type of romance, but I'd like to think I'm not a usual kind of girl," I said.

"In that, you are correct."

We stayed there in companionable silence for a while, gazing up at the night sky and listening to the sound of the ocean. At last, Devon said, "Shall we check on our party, darling?"

"Sure." It was our wedding, after all. We should probably go see the guests . . . whom we didn't know from Adam.

It took some maneuvering, but we managed to escape the hammock without mishap, and I arranged my dress and hair. Devon had undone his bowtie and the top couple of buttons of his tuxedo shirt. He looked like he could step into a men's fashion magazine, and just the small amount of exposed skin at his throat was enough to draw my eye and send my pulse skittering.

The guests were enjoying the music, dancing, and champagne without us, half the party inside the small but resplendent ballroom complete with chandelier. The other half were still outside amongst the burning tiki torches.

Devon snagged a couple of champagne flutes from a passing waiter and handed me one.

"Is it my turn to dance with the bride?"

I squealed in surprised delight to see Beau striding toward us. He gave me a tight hug.

"Congratulations," he said.

"What are you doing here?" I asked. "How did you know?"

"I told him we'd arrived," Devon said with a sigh. "Though I'd hoped he'd at least give us the night." The last part sounded like a reprimand.

"Hey man, I totally would've, but we've got intel on Vega and a source we need you to verify."

"What kind of source?"

"A former Shadow agent. Popped back up on the grid unexpectedly, so we grabbed them."

Devon's eyes narrowed. "Where are they now?"

"We have them at a secure facility, not far from here. But I hate to wait. MI6 is itching to get their hands on her and we can delay them for only so long."

Wait a second . . . her? Had Beau said it was a woman?

"Then let's go," Devon said. Tipping up his champagne flute, he drained it.

"Let me go change first," I said. I wasn't saying that *every* dress I wore with Devon got ruined, I just wanted to be cautious.

"There's no sense in you going," he said. "You can stay here."

I gave him a look. "It's the CIA. How dangerous could it be? Plus, it's my wedding night and I'd prefer not to spend it alone."

"Woman's got a point," Beau said, and Devon fixed him with a glare.

"Fine." Devon's response was curt, but I didn't care. I was going.

Fifteen minutes later, I'd changed into dark denim shorts and a thin, ivory lace tank with spaghetti straps. Not exactly what I thought I'd be wearing on my wedding night, but hey, at least it was lace.

Beau was waiting out front of the hotel inside a car. Devon opened the door and I slid in the backseat. He got in the front with Beau. I leaned up between them, bracing my arms on the seats.

"So who is this former agent?" I asked. "And I thought no one left the Shadow?" I vividly remembered Vega having Clive murdered right in front of me, just to prove that very point.

"Her name is Alexa," Devon answered. "She's the only female agent the Shadow's ever recruited."

"And she's lethal," Beau piped in. "No one who's ever taken a contract to terminate her has ever returned. After the sixth one turned up floating facedown in the Seine, minus the rest of his body, Vega couldn't find anyone else who'd take the job."

"That's not precisely true," Devon said.

I looked at him. "Please tell me you didn't."

He looked slightly abashed. "I was intrigued by the challenge," he said with a shrug. "And at the time, thought she was a danger to the Shadow and Vega. I had no qualms about terminating her."

"So what happened?" I asked. "Because obviously you both are still alive."

"I caught up to her in a back-alley watering hole in Singapore," he said. "She knew I was coming, of course, was waiting for me. Just not in the manner I expected."

"Do tell." A female spy? I was both jealous and intrigued.

"She was at the bar, drinking," Devon said. "And had been there for a while. I sat down beside her. I had her bang to rights anyway. She wasn't getting away. But as a former agent, I thought she deserved the respect of my introducing myself."

"So what happened?" Both Beau and I were caught up in the tale, as he was hanging on every word, too.

"She knew who I was. Said she knew Vega would send me at some point, and that she'd been waiting for me."

"Waiting for you . . . but why?" I asked.

"Yes, intriguing, is it not? I ordered a drink and asked her. That's when she told me that Vega was hiding more than I knew, that she was manipulating me, and that if I didn't get out, I'd regret it. 'She'll never let you go, Devon,' she said. I thought she was being overly dramatic, of course. Now, in hindsight, I realize she was quite serious. Though how she determined this, I never found out."

"Why?"

"Oh, she had staged a backup fracas. It broke out shortly after I sat down and she managed to lose me in the chaos. The last thing she said to me was that she pitied me too much to kill me. But to tell Vega that if she ever saw me again, I wouldn't be allowed to return."

"And then what?"

"I related to Vega what had happened," Devon said. "To my surprise, she neglected to pursue Alexa. I thought it odd at the time, but chalked it up to her deciding to give Alexa a chance to repent and come back into the fold."

"But she never did," I said.

"No, she didn't."

I mulled all this over as we drove, picturing it inside my head. Devon, outwitted by this woman. And it seemed she knew more about Vega and Devon than she'd said outright.

I was pulled from my reverie by Beau parking the car. I glanced around, confused. We were in the heart of Duvall Street, party central for Key West, and nighttime revelers swarmed the sidewalks.

"This is where you put her?" I asked as we got out of the car.

Beau flashed a grin. "Easiest place to hide something is right out in the open."

Bemused, I followed him and Devon as we walked about a block, past bars and vendors hawking tourist trinkets made in China. My attention was caught by a beautiful two-story white home that looked like it had been converted into a bar. It was obviously old, with vines and heavy trees draping the front and side. But Beau didn't lead us inside, instead going down another block and into a little side alley.

A sign declared the establishment upstairs to be "Adam & Eve," and attire was optional. He headed right for the stairs.

"Really?" I asked.

"Not a lot of tourists come up here," he tossed over his shoulder. "And if they do, they don't stay long."

Good lord, I bet not. Attire optional? That sounded vaguely nauseating. And germy. And I wasn't wrong.

There was a four-man band playing covers of old seventies and eighties tunes, plus about two dozen customers who had taken the sign at its word. They were all as naked as the day they were born.

No wait, a few of the women wore pasties and thongs, though not the ones that should have.

"Oh my," I breathed, my eyes wide as I took in the scene. I winced at the sight of bare bottoms on barstools and chairs.

"This way," Beau said.

Devon took my hand, dragging me with them as I goggled like the naïve farm girl from Kansas that I was.

In the corner was a door, which Beau had to enter a code to get through. Once the door closed behind us, I realized it was no ordinary door, because it blocked the noise from the bar entirely. Beau flipped on the lights and the dimness was replaced with bright fluorescent illumination.

We followed Beau across the small space to another door, where he entered another code, then leaned down for it to scan his eye. Only then did it open. He held the door for us.

I'd never been in a secret CIA holding facility before, and I was watching avidly as he went through these security protocols. We were in a very narrow hallway that opened into a larger room than I'd expected. The only thing it held was a cell, and inside the cell was a woman.

She was sitting with her knees up on a bed that looked too comfortable to be inside a cell, and she looked too calm for a woman being held against her will, glancing up at us with an almost bored expression. But she perked up when she saw Devon, her body stiffening and her eyes narrowing.

"Well, I didn't expect Vega's lapdog to walk through that door," she said dryly.

"Nice to see you, too, Alexa," Devon replied. Beau stepped aside so Devon could approach the bars. I held back, too, watching.

"Are you here to kill me?" she asked. "The Americans don't have the balls for it." She sent Beau a scornful smile.

"That could be arranged," Devon said.

"Except if you kill me, then you'll never find out the truth about a lot of things I think you'll care about very much."

She looked quite smug and self-assured as she said this. I had trouble reconciling this petite blonde as a cold-blooded killer and spy. She was tiny and delicate, like a porcelain doll, but her eyes were cold and her tone bitter.

"The 'don't kill me, I know important things' cliché," Devon mocked. "Honestly, Alexa. I expected something better."

Her smirk faded at this and I saw her swallow. The first betrayal of any kind of disquiet or fear I'd seen. Her eyes flashed quickly to Devon's hands, as though expecting him to pull a weapon at any moment.

"Then try this," she said. "Your parents didn't die in that bombing because they were just in the wrong place at the wrong time. They were sent there to be murdered."

CHAPTER ELEVEN

Those words landed with the force of a small bomb, and I didn't know which of the three of us was more shocked.

For a moment, Devon didn't move, as though he were processing Alexa's statement. Then he was striding forward and grabbed the bars of the cell. It happened so fast, it startled me and I jumped. It must've had the same effect on Alexa because she flinched before she could stop herself.

"Tell me what you're talking about," Devon demanded, his voice like ice. "How could you possibly know anything about my parents?"

"I'll be glad to, but not from in here."

Devon glanced at Beau, who didn't look happy.

"I'm not authorized to let her go, Devon," he said. "She'll disappear on us and we'll never find her again."

"The only reason you found me in the first place was because I *wanted* to be found," Alexa interjected.

"Bullshit," Beau retorted.

She shrugged, which just seemed to irritate him more.

"Perhaps we can trade," Devon said. "You want Vega taken down. Alexa may be the one who can help me do it. But I need her."

"He most certainly does."

Devon didn't reply to Alexa's comment, his gaze on Beau. They stared at one another for a moment.

"I'm going to be in deep shit," Beau said.

"Not if I hand you Vega on a silver platter."

Beau glanced at Alexa, who was watching their interplay with interest. He let out a sigh.

"Fine. But if my ass ends up in a sling, you'd better come riding to my rescue."

"Consider it done."

Devon turned back to Alexa. "You are not free to leave. If you try, I will stop you. The agreement is you come with me, help me find Vega's weakness, and destroy her and the Shadow. If you do this, you'll have earned your freedom. If you flee and don't honor your agreement, I will hunt you down. Only I won't turn you over to the Americans, because the Russians want you, too."

Alexa paled slightly.

Devon's lips twisted. "Yes, I see you're quite aware of what you may have done to upset the Russians. And exactly what they'll do if you're handed over to them."

"I won't run," Alexa said. "I told you, I'm here of my own accord."

"What-the-fuck-ever," Beau mumbled under his breath.

"Good," Devon spoke over him, ignoring how pissed off Beau was obviously getting at Alexa.

Beau unlocked the cell and Alexa rolled to her feet. She moved with a lithe grace, like a cat, and I could see then how dangerous she might be.

"So who's she?" Alexa asked Devon, nodding toward me as though I couldn't hear perfectly well what she was saying.

"This is Ivy," Devon said. "And as of a few hours ago, my wife."

Alex's gaze swiveled from me to Devon and she grinned. "Seriously? You got married again? Good for you." Her smile turned grim. "Better make sure Vega doesn't find out. She'll kill her like she did Kira."

I was surprised she knew about that, as was Devon, because his eyes narrowed with suspicion.

"I just found out she had Kira murdered," Devon said. "How is it that you already know?"

"I made it my business to know exactly for whom I was working. Something you should have done a long time ago."

"Let's get out of here," Beau interrupted. "Before the people watching the security cameras figure out exactly what I'm doing."

He hustled us back out the way we'd come. I kept my eyes averted from the naked-as-jaybirds partiers in the bar, though I saw Alexa glancing curiously over at them as we passed by.

"I can have a transport to Gitmo waiting in the harbor by morning," Beau said. "We'll catch that, then a military flight to London from there."

"We'll go back to the hotel tonight," Devon said. "Get some rest."

"I'm coming with you," Beau said. "We can't afford to let her out of our sight." He nodded toward Alexa. "And I have a feeling you'll be otherwise occupied tonight."

"I'm not going anywhere," Alexa said. "I don't need you watching over me like a bloody babysitter."

"He may trust you," Beau retorted. "But I certainly don't. So you can just cope and deal, or I can take you back inside and stick you in that cell again."

Alexa looked pissed, but she stayed silent, her blue eyes shooting daggers at him.

"Let's go," Devon interrupted. "In case you've forgotten, it's our wedding night."

With that, he opened up the rear door and I climbed in, Alexa after me. Devon sat in front again with Beau.

"How old are you?" I asked Alexa. "You look really young."

She glanced at me, then back toward the front. "Age is just a number."

"If it's just a number, then what is yours?"

She turned to me again, her expression one of irritation. "Why do you care? You're barely into your twenties, no doubt as innocent and pure as the bloody snow. You don't need to know anything about me."

"Well excuse me if I was curious," I retorted, getting angry now. "There's no need to be a total bitch about it. It was just a question."

"A rude question."

We glared at each other. So much for us being friends. And here I'd been planning a sleepover.

"Ladies, please." Devon's tone was a little more patronizing than I would've liked and I sent him a glare.

"What?" My tone should've warned him.

"Let's not get into a catfight, shall we?"

My anger at Alexa suddenly found a new outlet.

"Did you just compare us to felines?" I asked.

"Because we're women, so our disagreement and dislike must be silly and belittled," Alexa chimed in, and it seemed she no more appreciated Devon's comments than I had. Well. At least we agreed on one thing.

"I meant no such thing," Devon said, having the gall to sound affronted.

"Bollocks," Alexa said. "That's exactly what you meant."

Devon turned back around, mumbling curses under his breath while Beau smothered a laugh.

It was slightly less uncomfortable in the backseat after that, though Alexa and I didn't talk.

At the hotel, Beau let the valet take the car, and he and Alexa followed us in to the lobby. I could practically feel the tension radiating from them, but Devon seemed oblivious. Or else he just didn't care, which was a very real possibility.

"Shall I see if they have an adjacent room?" Devon asked Beau.

"Just one?" Alexa cut in.

"Don't worry," Beau said to her. "Your virtue is safe with me."

Even I winced at his sarcasm.

"Yes, but aren't you afraid I might slit your throat in your sleep?" Alexa sneered.

"Oh, I'll be fine. Don't think for a minute that you won't be tied up."

"Like hell I will!"

"Enough!" Devon's command shut them both up. "There will be one room and you will not kill each other. Am I understood?"

Beau and Alexa looked like a couple of recalcitrant children taken to task, but they shut up.

Devon booked the room next to ours, though they didn't actually connect. We dropped them off and he gave them one last warning.

"We do not want to be disturbed tonight," he warned them. "I will not be pleased if I have to come in here to play referee."

I hid a grin at this.

"We'll meet you downstairs at 0700," Beau said. "The boat will be ready by 0730."

I winced. That was really early. But I didn't complain. At least I was getting to go along.

"Done. Now, good evening, to both of you."

Devon took my elbow and led me into our room, closing and locking the door behind him.

I was inexplicably nervous, which made no sense. Devon and I had made love many times—this was no different.

And yet, it was. Because we were married now.

The butterflies in my stomach increased tenfold.

Devon walked to the phone on the desk and dialed. "Yes, I'd like to order some champagne, please. For two." He listened for a moment. "Excellent. Thank you." Then he hung up.

He slid off his jacket, and his fingers began undoing the buttons of his shirt. I watched, mesmerized as his skin was revealed, inch by inch. It didn't matter how many times I saw him—he never failed to take my breath away.

The breadth of his shoulders and circumference of his arms made me weak in the knees. The scars on his back and chest only made him more appealing. A scattering of light hair covered his chest, thickening slightly into the line that went from his navel downward, disappearing underneath the band of his pants.

The low light from the lamp danced across the muscles of his back as he moved to the closet to hang his shirt. I watched him unabashedly, wanting him, and still unable to believe he was mine.

"You're looking at me as though you've never seen me before," he said, his back still to me.

My face warmed. "Should I stop?"

"No," he said, turning around. "I like it."

"I'm sure you've had many women stare at you over the years," I said. We'd rarely talked about the women he'd been with, but suddenly I was feeling insecure.

"I can't help if they stared," he said, leaning against the wall and crossing his arms over his chest. My eyes were immediately drawn to how that pumped up his biceps. "But it's not often that I noticed, or wanted them to."

I made my gaze return to his rather than drinking in the way he looked, so casually at ease in a body that was nothing less than perfection.

"You're talking in the past tense," I said. "Women still stare at you. Want you."

"And men don't stare at you?" he countered.

"It's not the same."

"Oh, it's not," he said with a small laugh. Now his hands were in his pockets. I may have made a slight sound at the view of his chest that afforded me. "Please explain that to me."

"I do notice—*did* notice," I said. "And I've never liked it. Never liked feeling conspicuous."

"And you think I have?"

I frowned at him. "Haven't you?"

"Darling, being conspicuous goes against my job description. Has it generally been a convenient thing that women find me attractive? Speaking generally as a bastard, absolutely. It's not as though I've had to work hard at having female companionship. But you and I, together, are completely different than anything I've ever had before."

That made me feel better. He was just so beautiful. My insecurities melted away at the look in his eyes as he stared at me. There was a little smile playing about his lips, and his eyes took a slow path down my body and back up to my face.

"How so?" I asked. Was it a shameless request for him to tell me how much he loved me and how special I was? Yes, indeed. But I didn't think he'd mind.

Devon pushed off the wall and sauntered toward me, hands still in his pockets. I couldn't take my eyes off his, so blue it was as though I was looking into the summer sky.

He stopped in front of me and I felt his hands settle on my hips, his fingers just brushing to touch my skin underneath the lace tank I wore.

"You are," he began, "my beautiful bride. A woman I've been entranced with since the moment I laid eyes on you." His fingers moved to my stomach and edged upward. I felt my knees begin to tremble. "You're the only woman I see now. The only woman I want in my bed. The only woman I'll allow in my heart."

I couldn't help the smile that seemed to come from deep inside me and spread across my face. Devon's lips curved in turn as he bent toward me.

Our lips met in a sweet kiss that made my bones melt. His hands went to my arms, sliding down to my wrists and lifting my arms to wrap them around his neck. The touch of my skin against his sent a shiver through me.

Air hit my stomach as Devon lifted my shirt, dragging it over my head and tossing it aside. It broke our kiss for just a moment, but then we were devouring each other again. His kiss was familiar, the cadence and rhythm one that I knew and loved.

Devon could take off my bra faster than even I could, and sure enough, it was undone in the blink of an eye. I smiled as he kissed me and he paused, lifting his face a bit so he could talk to me.

"What's so funny?" he murmured, his lips moving to my jaw.

"You're like the Bra Whisperer," I said. "You just have to look at them and they fall off me."

He muffled a chuckle against my skin and my smile faded as his hands found my breasts. I became lost in a pool of sensation as he kissed my neck and his thumbs brushed my nipples.

"I love how your skin tastes," he said. "Just like I love how you taste between your legs."

His hands moved to the button on my shorts, undoing it and sliding down the zipper. I sucked in a breath as his fingers brushed my panties. He was teasing me, barely touching me. My fingers pushed into his hair as I kissed him. His hands slipped down inside my shorts to cup my ass, squeezing, and the garment fell to my ankles.

In one smooth motion, he picked me up and carried me to the bed, laying me down on the cool sheets. I went for his pants, wanting them off, but he stepped back and did it himself. The lights were still on and I drank in the sight of him, naked.

I didn't get a whole lot of time to just look at him though, because he was already back on the bed, tugging down the sheets and bracing himself on his hands so he could kiss me.

Just then, there was a knock on the door.

"Shit," Devon muttered. "That's the champagne."

He vaulted off the bed and I grabbed the sheets, pulling them up to cover me as he headed for the door.

"Put something on!" I couldn't believe he was walking to the door naked. But he did as I asked, grabbing a towel from the bathroom to wrap around his hips. Of course that did nothing to hide the tent his erection made, but it was better than nothing.

The hotel worker discreetly averted his eyes as he carried the tray of champagne and glasses to the table and set it down, though I thought I saw his ears turn red. Devon gave him a tip and he was gone within seconds.

"Yeah, that wasn't awkward or anything," I grumbled.

"Don't be absurd," Devon said, unwrapping the foil from the top of the champagne bottle. "I'm quite sure he's seen worse."

"If that's supposed to make me feel less embarrassed, it's not working."

The champagne cork popped out with the distinctive cheerful sound that made me smile in spite of myself. Devon began pouring the sparkling golden liquid in the glasses.

"Then let's get tipsy, darling, and you'll forget all about it."

"There are lots of ways you can make me forget all about it," I teased.

"And I plan on doing them all to you." He handed me a glass. "To us, my darling."

"To us."

The glasses clinked and I drank the cold liquid, though my gaze was locked on Devon's. Anticipation shivered in my veins, dispelling the butterflies. From our first kiss, Devon had known how to touch me, our bodies so in synch and perfectly matched. My imagination was already conjuring up memories of us together.

And Devon was true to his word. He did all of them, and then some.

❦

Devon and I did finally get to sleep in the wee hours of the morning, but I was still exhausted when seven in the morning rolled around. Well, exhausted but satisfied.

As usual, you couldn't tell Devon had slept for a mere three hours, whereas I was piling concealer on the dark circles under my eyes.

We met Beau and Alexa in the lobby and they didn't seem worse for wear, though there was a strange tension between the two and they avoided looking directly at each other. Hmm . . . I wondered what exactly had happened last night in their room.

We reached the harbor and parked, Beau leading us out to the very last slip where a boat was waiting. It was a pretty big boat, thank goodness, plenty big enough for all of us and then some. I knew it was only ninety miles to Cuba, but hadn't wanted to make the trip in some little motorboat I'd been afraid to picture in my head.

Once we were onboard, the captain and crew lost no time in heading out to sea. Beau was talking to them as Alexa drifted toward the bow. Devon took my elbow and followed her.

"We have four hours to kill," he said to her, leaning on the railing next to her. "Let's hear your story."

"And why should I tell you that?" she countered.

"I bargained for your freedom. You owe me all the information I ask for."

"I'll tell you about Vega, but you don't need to know my life story," Alexa said. "I'm here because you need me to take her out. And she needs to be taken out."

"Fine." Devon's reply was curt. "Tell us about Vega."

"She was born Elizabeth Percy and grew up in the Scottish highlands. The only daughter of William and Annette Percy. Her mother died when she was three years old. Elizabeth—Vega—attended St. Mary's Catholic School until the age of fifteen."

"Why just fifteen?" Devon asked.

"She and her father left the area suddenly with no forwarding address," Alexa replied. "No one saw or heard from her again. Until years later when she turned up as Vega working inside the Shadow, and worked her way up the chain of command."

"How did you find all this out?"

"I followed the bread crumbs," Alexa said with a shrug. "Everyone comes from somewhere. Everyone has a past."

"And Vega allowed you to find all this out about her?"

"She tried to kill me," Alexa corrected.

"Only when you left her employment. And you haven't mentioned the reason you did that. I don't need your life story but that, I would think, seems pertinent."

Alexa considered Devon for a moment, the wind ruffling her hair such that she had to tuck it behind her ears. I eyed the blonde locks somewhat enviously. I missed my normal, blonde hair.

"She sent me on a mission guaranteed to fail."

My brows rose at this, but I didn't say anything, content to listen.

"There's never a certainty of success," Devon replied.

"I understand that," Alexa said, her voice tight. "There's a difference between something difficult and sending an operative on a suicide mission."

"And you're saying that's what she did."

"I was sent to assassinate the second-in-command of the Al Qaeda contingent in Islamabad."

There was a pause as Devon took that in, though it meant nothing to me. *Al Qaeda* was never exactly a good thing, though, was it?

"You know what that means," she said. Devon's expression was grim.

"Wait," I interrupted. "I don't know what that means. I mean, it sounds dangerous, but why do you say that it was a suicide mission?"

"Because she's a woman," Devon replied.

I looked at Devon, confused. "So? She certainly seems capable of killing someone." I shot Alexa a glance. "No offense."

"None taken."

"It's how they treat women that's the problem, not Alexa's capabilities," Devon said. "The odds of her getting close enough to do the job were slim. Getting out afterward, nearly non-existent. And what they'd do to her if caught . . . let's just say I wouldn't wish that on anyone."

"So you can see why I decided to get out. I didn't know why she wanted me dead or why she didn't just kill me herself, but I wasn't waiting around. I got out. Disappeared."

"And she's been trying to kill you ever since," Devon added.

"*Trying* being the operative word. You got the closest, but only because I let you."

"What did you mean that night?" Devon asked. "You said Vega was hiding something from me. That I should get out while I could or she'd never let me go."

"You wouldn't believe me." Alexa leaned on the rail as she gazed out over the dark ocean.

"Try me."

"You'll figure it out on your own," she said, "Once I take you there. You'll have what you need, and I doubt she'll try to kill me again. She and I called an uneasy truce."

"When did you do that?"

Alexa looked at Devon. "When I sent you back alive."

Her words, so simply stated, sent a chill down my spine.

A light off the port bow, low to the water and approaching fast, caught my attention.

"What's that?" I asked.

Both Devon and Alexa turned just as an alarm sounded on the boat. Alexa ran for the bunkhouse while Devon grabbed me around the waist, hauling me in front of him as he rushed from the bow. Wood splintered near our feet and then I heard the report of the rifle. Devon shoved me through the door ahead of him.

Beau and three members of the crew were donning bulletproof vests and holding rifles of their own. And they were moving fast.

"What's going on?" I asked. Who was shooting at us? Even now, I could hear the report of gunfire and the sharp smacks as bullets hit the hull.

"Drug traffickers," one of the men explained. "They patrol these waters to guard their routes. Shoot first, ask questions later."

"But you're the CIA," I said. "They'd have to be crazy to attack you."

"We're not the Coast Guard," one of the men said. "This boat isn't marked."

"They'll shoot us and dump us in the ocean, then take the boat," the other said.

"Not tonight, they're not," Devon said. He looked at Beau. "Give Alexa a weapon."

Beau glanced at Alexa, who was waiting expectantly. "You turn on us and you'll regret it," he said. "I'll hunt you down."

"Don't think so highly of yourself, cowboy," she sneered. "As if you're worth the effort."

"I ain't a fucking cowboy, princess."

"Don't call me princess, jackass."

I watched this exchange slightly open-mouthed. It seemed really odd and unnecessarily argumentative for the situation in which we found ourselves.

"Are you done with the foreplay?" Devon cut in, slamming the magazine home in his pistol. "Because I believe they're still shooting at us."

He grabbed another bulletproof vest and bundled me into it before I could say anything. Not that I was protesting. Being even partially bulletproof sounded pretty darn good.

"You two head aft," one of the crewmen said, pointing at Beau and Alexa. "We'll head forward and split up. They'll try to board from the side. You stay here, defend the captain upstairs driving the boat."

Devon didn't particularly like being left behind, but I was glad not be alone. Beau and Alex didn't look happy being stuck together, but they didn't protest, just followed orders. I watched them head out the back door.

The two crewmen went out the front, coordinating together and rushing out together amidst the gunfire. I winced, fearing the worst, but they seemed to make it without getting hit.

"What should I do?" I asked, feeling useless. I didn't have a weapon. If anything, I was just cannon fodder, which rankled, but I wasn't going to pretend I had any kind of training for something like this.

"You're going to go about the very important business of staying alive." Devon took up a position next to one of the small windows, his gun at the ready as he peered out.

"That doesn't seem very helpful," I groused.

"If someone makes it past me and gets upstairs, they can take control of the boat," he said. "I'd much rather not end up in a third-world shithole tonight."

"But aren't we headed for Cuba?"

He shot me a look, but his lips twitched at my joke.

Probably not the best time, but I was nervous and my filter was gone. I had every faith that the agents, Beau, Devon, and even Alexa, would keep us safe. But I didn't think it was going to be pretty and I didn't want anyone to get hurt. My stomach churned with dread and a sense of the inevitable.

The yelling and gunshots sounded much closer, which made me jump.

"Get down," Devon ordered.

I obeyed without question, not wanting to distract him by having him worry about me.

There was a weird thumping sound from both sides of the boat, and more yelling in Spanish.

"They're boarding from both sides," Devon said. "There must be more than one boat."

"More than one?" I squeaked. "We can't fight off so many."

"Of course we can," Devon said. He spied a fire extinguisher on the wall and ripped it off. "We just may need to be a bit creative."

"With a fire extinguisher?"

"Surprisingly effective, given the right preparation."

He began pulling open drawers in the console. He grabbed a box of something, then kept searching, finally pulling out a roll of duct tape. In seconds, he'd dumped the box, which contained nails, and taped a bunch of them to the outside of the fire extinguisher.

"What are you doing?" I asked.

"Causing more damage."

He grabbed the extinguisher and watched out the window again. "They're climbing over the side. Help me out, darling. When I count to three, you pull open the door."

I hurried to the door and grabbed the handle.

"Careful to stand behind it when you open it," he cautioned. I nodded. "Okay then. One . . . two . . . three!"

I yanked open the door, staying behind the thick wood as Devon tossed the fire extinguisher, sending it rolling right toward the men boarding. I saw one of the crewmen go down and prayed he wasn't dead.

Devon aimed, firing off two shots, and the fire extinguisher exploded. The force of it pushed two men overboard right away. The third was knocked to the ground and I saw his body jerk as the nails hit him. The fourth and last one was killed instantly with a well-placed nail that made nausea climb into my throat. Then Devon was back inside and slamming the door.

"We've betrayed our presence," he said way more calmly than I felt. "But it couldn't be helped. Do get down, darling."

I ducked behind the console again, my heart in my throat and my pulse racing. I wanted to cry but held back the tears. They were more of a reaction to the stress and fear than anything else.

More gunshots, and this time Devon said, "I'm afraid I'm going to have to go out there." He looked at me. "Stay put."

I kept my mouth shut, but wanted to scream in frustration as he headed out the door. I hated feeling so helpless. And now the man I loved—my *husband*—was heading straight into danger while I cowered, hiding.

I waited, heart in my throat, and prayed as gunshots sounded outside, and thumps, and yelling in English and Spanish in voices I couldn't distinguish. I searched for a weapon, opening the same drawers Devon had, and found a hammer. I grabbed it. It was heavy in my hand and a bit unwieldy, but certainly better than nothing.

The door flung open. My nerves flew into a panic as I stared at an unfamiliar man nearly twice my size. He was carrying an assault rifle and it was pointed directly at me.

I froze, my breath caught in my lungs, staring at the muzzle. But to my amazement, he didn't fire. He smiled in a slow, sneering way that made my skin crawl. He said something to me, but I'd only had freshman Spanish in Kansas, so it was completely lost on me. I could gather the meaning, though.

He saw the hammer I held and laughed outright.

I knew with a sick feeling in my stomach that he wouldn't be standing there if Devon had anything to say about it. I prayed my husband was only hurt and not dead. I couldn't think about that right now, though, because this guy was walking toward me, and whatever he had on his mind, I didn't want to have any part of.

My hand gripped the hammer. It was all I had. And by God I'd go down swinging.

I backed up as he approached, until I hit the wall. He laughed again, sure I was cornered. I waited until he was close enough that I could smell the sourness of his breath.

He reached for my hand holding the hammer, which I'd hoped he'd do. It distracted him from my other hand, which held the pair of scissors Devon had used to cut the duct tape. Gripping them tight, I struck, not stabbing overhead, which would only cause the point to hit his breastbone. No, instead I went down low on his side, aiming upward.

I wasn't prepared for what it felt like to actually stab someone. The resistance of the flesh and muscle made me falter, a mistake as it turned out. Only about an inch of the scissors made it in, which basically just served to piss him off.

He jerked around, cursing, his automatic response was to backhand me. My teeth rattled at the force of the hit and I slumped to the side. It hurt. It hurt a lot. And it made me angry. I channeled that rage and when he grabbed my hair and yanked me back, I came up swinging.

The heavy steel head of the hammer caught him right underneath the jaw with a sickening crack of bone breaking. Blood flowed from his mouth as he fell backward, his eyes wide in shock and pain.

Fury propelled me forward, hammer in both hands as he tried to get his rifle up. But we were too close for him to get a good angle and I swung again, using both hands. My teeth were gritted in a grimace of rage, and I felt an unholy satisfaction as the head of the hammer caught him at the side of the head.

He went down, and then I was on top of him, hitting him again and again, barely aware of what I was doing. He'd hurt Devon, I was sure of it, maybe even killed him. And he'd been going to hurt me, too, the same way I'd been hurt too many times before.

The hammer grew too slippery to hold and I dropped it before I realized blood covered the handle. His blood. I stared, aghast at what I'd done. He was dead. Very dead. I began to shake, but I didn't have time to fall apart.

How many of them were there still? How many of us were still standing?

Swallowing down my nausea, I leaned down and took his rifle. I didn't know anything about how to fire a rifle like that, and I prayed it was as easy as point and shoot.

The door was closed and it was quiet outside. I went to open it carefully, not flinging it open but just easing it a scant few inches.

The dead men from Devon's jury-rigged bomb were still on deck, as was one of the CIA crewmen. I hurried over to him, crouching down and praying he was all right. But to my dismay, he'd been shot in the head. His eyes stared sightlessly at me and the back of his head was gone.

I couldn't keep the nausea down and crawled to the railing, vomiting over the side into the ocean. All I could picture was Devon's face with sightless eyes. I didn't know if I'd find that or not if I kept looking, but I had no choice.

I'd just stood up when a noise made me turn. Devon stood a few yards away, having come around the gatehouse.

My relief was so overwhelming, I felt like I'd be sick all over again. Scrambling to my feet, I ran to him, throwing myself in his arms. He held me tight.

"Oh God, I thought you were dead," I managed to get out.

"Not today," Devon said, and I could hear pain in his voice. Hurriedly, I stepped back, my gaze surveying him for injuries.

"What's wrong? Did they shoot you?" I asked.

"It degenerated into a brawl," he said. "Think they broke a couple of ribs, dislocated a finger. But they're gone now."

I was relieved to hear he hadn't been shot, breathing out a sigh. "What about the others?"

"Only one casualty," he said, indicating the man on deck. "Though Alexa's been injured."

"What happened? Is she all right?"

"One of them had a knife, which she ended up using on him, but not before he sliced her. Beau is taking care of her now." His eyes narrowed as he looked at me, his expression turning anxious. "What happened to you? Why is there blood all over you? Are you hurt? Did someone get in? I left no one up here, or so I thought."

"A guy came in, but I took care of him," I said. "It's his blood. Not mine."

"His blood." Devon looked pained. "Darling, I didn't leave you with a weapon."

"I found a hammer."

I swear Devon grew pale.

"I left you alone and you had to defend yourself with a hammer," he said, his voice flat. "I'm the worst fucking husband on the planet."

"Stop," I said. "It's not your fault. You defended us, didn't you? They're gone. I'm fine. I did what I had to do."

He shook his head slightly, staring at me in something close to stunned disbelief. "You're amazing," he said. "And calm."

I didn't know how calm I was, not on the inside, though maybe outwardly I seemed that way. I was reminded of when I was a kid. *How do you keep going after a traumatic event?* The answer was: You just did. You do what you have to do . . . and that's what I'd done, before, during, and after the man had attacked me.

"Let's get you cleaned up," Devon said.

He took me back inside to what I called the bathroom and he called "the head," assiduously washing my hands, then taking a cloth and wiping splatters from my arms and face. I tried not to think of how all that blood had gotten there. We'd skirted the body coming in, Devon taking a long look while I averted my gaze.

"Wait outside," Devon said. "I'm going to run up and see the captain."

He waited until I was out the door before climbing the short set of stairs to the top. I gazed off into the blackness that was the ocean at night, listening to the sound of the engine and waves. I didn't look at the body of the crewman. I couldn't. Tonight had turned into a nightmare.

The boats were long gone, thank God. As I was waiting, Beau and Alexa came around the corner. The other crewman was walking behind them. He stopped when he saw his partner's body on the deck, but I couldn't tell what he thought by looking at his face, which remained blank.

"How are you?" I asked Alexa.

Her face was creased in a grimace and white with pain. "I'm fine," she said. "Just a scratch."

"Bullshit," Beau said. "You need stitches."

"I'm not going to bleed to death," she retorted. "Stitches are to prevent scarring, and I don't really care if it leaves a scar."

"You don't have to prove to me you're tough," Beau said. "You held your own tonight."

"Like I care what you think of me," she said. "And you can bet your sweet American ass I held my own. As if there were any doubt."

Beau grinned a little, not as much as he usually did, but it was enough for me to see that he liked Alexa. He liked her a lot.

The next couple of hours were spent with the men cleaning the deck while Alexa and I stayed in the gatehouse. She argued that she would help, but Devon told her in no uncertain terms that she was to stay with me. She opened her mouth to protest again, but then caught sight of the mangled body of the man I'd killed.

"Bloody hell, Devon," she said. "Did you run out of bullets?"

"Ivy took care of that one," Devon said.

She didn't say anything as Devon dragged the body out. We sat in silence for a few minutes.

"Ever killed anyone before?" she asked.

I shook my head.

"You'll get used to it."

I didn't know if that was sad or if it should make me feel better. Both, I thought.

"How many people have you killed?" I asked her.

"Too many."

That sounded ominous. "And was the first time hard?"

"Yes," she said. "It's like your first time having sex. You never forget even the smallest details." She paused, staring off into space as though she were remembering. "He was an informant. Within our own government. A citizen turned spy."

"That must've been hard," I said. "It being one of your own countrymen."

She turned to look at me. "Not just my countryman. My fiancé."

I stared at her, open-mouthed. She looked away again.

"I suspected something was amiss, but I didn't want to believe it. We were happy together, or so I thought. In the end, both of us were lying to each other. It was sad and tragic and all those adjectives they use in Nicholas Sparks novels. Only for us, there was no happy ending. He looked me in the eye when I shot him. He made his choice, and I had no alternative but to make mine."

It sounded awful and horrible, and though she talked about it so matter-of-factly, I couldn't imagine how an event like that had scarred her.

"Since you left the Shadow, have you just been running?" I asked. "Always looking over your shoulder in case Vega sends someone to kill you again?"

She shrugged. "It's not perfect, but I'm still alive. Perhaps once Devon has done what he needs to do, I can stop running."

"Will you help him?"

"I'll do what I can," she said. "But ultimately, only Devon has the power to take down Vega. No one else."

I frowned in confusion. "Why do you say that?"

She looked at me, studying me as though trying to decide whether I could be trusted. She opened her mouth—

"All done," Beau said, walking in the door. "And we're almost there. Another ten minutes and we'll meet our escort that'll take us into Gitmo." He walked up to Alexa. "How're you doing?"

"I'm fine, I said." She huffed in exasperation. "For a CIA spook, you sure worry like an old woman."

"I just don't want British MI6 crawling up my ass because you got yourself killed. They want you to work for them."

Alexa snorted in disgust. "Like I want to sacrifice any more of my life for the noble cause. I'm through. I just want to live my life."

"The CIA could help with that."

"I'm sure they could." The disbelief in her tone was obvious. "But I prefer my freedom. I answer to no one."

"And there's no one to know or care if you live or die."

I wondered at the worry on Beau's face and the stubborn set of Alexa's delicate jaw as they stared each other down. Devon was taking it in, too, but where I was fascinated, he was impatient. Our gazes caught and he rolled his eyes. I hid a grin.

The military escort got us in to Gitmo and I was sorry it was still dark as it was hard to see much of anything. I was nearly dead on my feet from exhaustion and the adrenaline, not to mention the mental shock that still hovered on the edge of my mind from killing someone.

Little was said to us as Beau spoke with the guards who met us at the gate. We were taken to some kind of bunkhouse where I promptly flopped down on a semi-comfortable bed. I was out in minutes.

CHAPTER TWELVE

We left around mid-afternoon the next day, flying out on a private military plane, which bordered on luxurious. One of the men acting as a flight attendant said the plane had been confiscated from a drug lord, which explained the plush leather furniture. I felt better after some sleep and put what had happened on the boat from Key West to Cuba out of my mind.

Alexa was with us, after having been sewn up and given antibiotics by the medical officer on the base. And to my surprise, Beau came with us, too.

"I didn't realize you were coming along," Devon said to him. "Is this a recent development?"

It didn't take a genius to hear how sardonic his tone was as he eyed Beau, then Alexa, who'd elected to sit in the last of the seats.

"Thought you could use another set of hands," Beau said with a careless shrug. "I got authorization, and my boss wouldn't mind a set of American eyes on events over there as they unfold."

"I see. All very valid indeed."

"Yes."

The two men stared at each other, but neither one broke. It was interesting to watch Devon interact with another man, a friend. I hadn't seen that before. Devon's lips twitched slightly and he gave Beau a nod, then took the seat next to me. Beau hesitated a moment, then went back and sat in one of the two seats facing the rear directly in front of Alexa. I saw her raise an eyebrow.

"Don't stare. It's not polite," Devon said mildly.

"I think they like each other," I said.

"Of course they do, but they haven't decided to admit it." One of the two military stewards came by, offering us water.

"I think they'd make a good couple," I mused. "I like her."

"She's dangerous and a bit unpredictable," Devon said. "Perhaps a bit too emotional."

I rolled my eyes. "Isn't that a typical man? Anything a woman does means she's 'too emotional.'"

His brows lifted. "It's true," he said. "Men can put emotion aside much more easily than women."

"And who decided that's a *good* thing?" I asked. "Men did, that's who."

"It's obvious it's a good thing," he countered. "Decisions must be made on facts and logic. Not feelings."

"So you coming back for me, quitting the Shadow, that was logical?"

"Of course not, but then again, I never said it was."

"So you *are* saying it was *ill*ogical."

Devon eyed me. "I'm not going to get into a semantics argument with you, darling. Love isn't logical. It just is. It happens, sometimes in spite of all the many reasons why it shouldn't. And there are many, many reasons why you and I should never be together. But despite them all, I wanted you. And you wanted me."

I couldn't argue with that, not when every word of it was true.

"So where are we going?" I asked. "London?"

But Devon shook his head. "No. Edinburgh, actually."

I frowned. "Scotland? Why?"

"Because that's where Vega's from," Alexa interrupted. She'd walked over to us, sitting down in the row facing us. The leather chairs were plush and comfortable, though I saw her wince slightly as she sat down. She'd refused pain medication other than a local anesthetic for the stitches and some over-the-counter pills.

"How do you know where she's from?" I asked. Beau followed Alexa, looking slightly disgruntled, and settled in beside her.

"It comes out in her accent," Alexa said. "When she's angry."

"And you've heard this?" Devon asked.

"Oh, she's been angry with me a lot. Usually, her accent is posh. But when she's upset, when she's absolutely livid, you can hear it. It's indigenous to certain parts of Scotland the way a southern American accent can tell you if someone is from Alabama or the Carolinas. I knocked on a lot of doors, spoke to a lot of people, and eventually, I tracked her down to a small village in northern Scotland called Inverbervie."

"After we land in Edinburgh, we'll drive there," Devon said, his gaze on Alexa. "And you'll show me what you won't tell me."

"Yes, I will."

I didn't understand what it was that she was so adamant Devon see, but I had a gut feeling that I wouldn't like it.

The drive from Edinburgh to Inverbervie was more boring than I thought it'd be. I was in Scotland, of all places, and the scenery looked exactly like Middle America. The only exception was that the cars drove on the opposite side of the road.

"Stop here." Alexa's order to Devon took me by surprise. We were in the middle of a small village and I could see the ocean from where we'd parked.

I got out of the car and followed Alexa to the top of the small hill. Tombstones marked our path and I lingered, reading the inscriptions.

Cemeteries intrigued me, to read of men, women, and especially children, dead often before their time. The words of love and loss carved in stone were bittersweet and poignant.

It was chilly and I wrapped my cardigan around me, wondering how I'd come to this place from where I'd been. A farm girl, born and raised in Kansas, meeting and falling in love with a man no woman should. A life filled with danger and uncertainty. Who wanted that? And yet, I couldn't turn my back on Devon.

"Here," Alexa said. I glanced over at her, silhouetted against the setting sun.

It was a beautiful cemetery, set high on a hill overlooking the water. The grass was green and the grounds well tended. It was peaceful and serene, though that's not how I felt at the moment.

Devon and I clasped hands, as though we knew something bad was coming.

"This is what I wanted you to see," Alexa said, pointing at a tombstone carved in granite.

The words were hard to make out, the weather having worn some of the letters away. *Dillon Clay McGewan. Beloved Son. b. Feb. 22, 1956 d. August 15, 1985.*

I stared, wondering at the name. I looked at Devon, who was also staring at the headstone.

"What is this?" I asked Alexa. "Who is this?"

"Dillon McGewan was my father," Devon answered instead. "Vega thought it would be best to use my middle name—the same as my father's—as my surname rather than McGewan. August 15th, 1985 . . . it was the day of the bombing." He looked at Alexa. "How did you find this? Vega claimed she never knew where my parents were buried. And where is my mother's headstone?"

"Vega didn't care about your mother," she said. "Just your father."

"Why? Is this some kind of trick?"

"No trick," Alexa said, a little sadly. "I came here and found this grave. Then I went searching for exactly who Vega was. I think you should find out, too. Come with me."

Devon and I glanced at each other as Alexa walked away. His hand tightened on mine. Even if we were heading into the unknown, we were doing it together.

We followed Alexa down the walkway to the sidewalk, then down the street. Beau followed at a discreet distance, but it felt surreal, as though our every move was preordained.

Alexa finally came to a stop in front of a small home along King Street. She rapped her knuckles sharply against the door.

"What are you doing?" I hissed. "Who are these people?"

"Someone Devon needs to meet," was Alexa's cryptic reply.

A woman answered the door, and she was as old and gray as I'd expect from someone who most likely lived in the same village from the day they were born until the day they died.

"Yes?" she asked as she answered the door. "Can I dae somethin' for ye?"

Her accent was so thick, I had trouble understanding her. But Alexa didn't seem to have the same issue.

"Elva, it's me. Alexa," she said. "It's been a while, do you remember?"

The woman peered at her, then her face cleared. "Och aye, Alexa dear! It's been a fair while. Whit are ye dain' here?"

"I brought some friends to meet you," Alexa said. "This is Devon. He has some questions I thought you could answer."

"Hello," Elva said, giving Devon a sweet smile. "I'd be fair chuffed to help if I can, though my mind is no' as fleet as it used to be."

"I'm looking for some information," Devon said. "About a woman named Vega. Would you happen to know anything about her?"

"Vega?" the woman asked. "No, I'm sorry. I dinny ken anybody ca'ad that."

"He means Elizabeth Percy," Alexa said. "Do you remember her family?"

Elva's face cleared at that. "Och, aye," she said. "Elizabeth Percy. Such a sad tale. Aye, I ken the story well."

"Who are you again?" Elva asked Devon.

"He's a distant relation," Alexa said. "He'd like to know what happened to the Percys. Elizabeth grew up here, remember?"

I could see why Alexa might need to jog her memory. Elva had to be in her eighties.

"Aye, aye she did," Elva said. Whereas before she'd been eyeing Devon warily, now she seemed relieved to have something in common to talk about. "She was a sweet girl. It's too bad how things turned out."

∽

"What do you mean?" Devon asked.

"Och it's a long tale," she said. "Come away in and I'll pit on some tea. It'll take a while to tell ye properly."

We followed her inside the tiny house and into a painstakingly neat parlor. Two cats lounged on a sofa covered in a busy floral upholstery.

"Hae a seat and I'll put the kettle on," she said, bustling out of the room.

Devon shooed the cats off the sofa, who didn't look happy about that, then sat. I took the spot next to him with Alexa at my side. Beau sat in one of the two matching pink wingback chairs.

"I'm going to have cat hair all over me," Beau muttered.

"Really, that should be the least of your worries," Alexa said with a snort.

"What do you know of my worries?" he snapped back.

"I don't. Nor do I care."

They continued to bicker, and after a while, seemed to notice we were staring at them.

"What?" Beau asked.

"Really?" Devon replied.

Beau's face flushed, but he didn't argue further with Alexa.

Elva returned, bustling about with a tea tray and table, setting out cups and saucers. It was obvious she'd gotten out her best, the delicate china probably a family heirloom. I wanted to help, but I knew nothing about how to properly pour tea from an English tea service.

"Here, let me help you," Alexa said, jumping to her feet.

"Thank you, deary." Elva handed her a cup.

Before long, we all had matching cups and saucers. A platter of cookies sat in the center of the coffee table. Shortbread. Yum. I tried not to eye them too closely.

"So you were going to tell us about the Percys," Alexa prodded, taking a tiny sip of her tea.

"Och aye, right enough." Elva settled back in her chair. "They fowk have bin in the same hoose in the village fur as lang as ourselves. I used to see Elizabeth when she wis just a bairn. A sweet wee thing. I wis devastated when her dear mither passed."

"How did she die?" Devon asked.

"Cancer," Elva said. "Took her right quick. Neither Elizabeth nor her faether, William, e'er got ower it. Yid think faether and dauchter wid hiv foond comfort in one anither, but William changed whin dear Annette died. He drank mair than a Scotsman shid, which is a fair bit.

"Elizabeth wis a proud wee girl, and though I think he might've beat her, she ne'er breathed a wird. She endured. Went to school and grew up. William kept a tight leash on her, sendin' her tae St. Mary's, though they could'ney afford it. Rarely let her hae friends as he thoucht most of 'em were scunners . . . Malarkey o'course.

"Then one day, a new family moved to the village," Elva continued. "And that's when the trouble started . . ."

⌒

Elizabeth watched through the break in the hedgerow as the truck was unloaded, several men carrying furniture into the small house next door. A woman was hurrying from inside to outside, looking harried as she directed them.

New people in the neighborhood. That hadn't happened since she'd been ten and the widower two streets over had passed away. It had taken six months for someone new to buy his house and move in, and they hadn't been nearly as interesting as the people moving in next. Especially one particular lad . . .

He was young, maybe only a year or two older than Elizabeth's fifteen years, but he was extraordinarily handsome. The wind tousled his light brown hair and the smile he gave the other men as he chatted with them was a mixture of sheepish young boy and mischievous man. He was entrancing and Elizabeth couldn't take her eyes off him.

It wasn't as though she'd never seen boys before. Certainly not at St. Mary's, which was an all-girls school. But there were boys in the village, several of whom she'd grown up with. However, none of them looked like this particular boy.

She watched until she heard her da calling.

"Lizzie! Where are you?"

To her mortification, the new neighbor boy heard and glanced to where she stood behind the hedge. Then he smiled.

Elizabeth jumped back, a blush climbing in her cheeks. Turning, she ran up the small hill and around to her front door where her da stood waiting. She could feel the boy's eyes on her the entire way.

His name turned out to be Mark Clay and he was seventeen. Elizabeth found out that much just from the village gossip. His father was in the military and his mother stayed at home. She'd seen Mark outside occasionally when she walked home from the shop where she worked part-time, but had hurried by without saying anything. She wondered what he'd do if she stopped and said hello . . .

"Is dinner done yet?"

Elizabeth pulled herself out of her daydreaming to answer her da. He'd been drinking again, but when didn't he?

"It's finished," she said, hurriedly shoving the food onto two plates. Her father was in no mood to wait and she grabbed some silverware and set the plates on the table, sliding one in front of him.

"What the hell is this?" he asked. "It's burned."

"It's not," she said. "Just a little crispy perhaps." She hadn't been paying enough attention, instead watching out the window for Mark.

"Bollocks," he spat, shoving the plate onto the floor. "Lazy bitch. Don't know why I put up with you."

Elizabeth knew what was coming, but wasn't fast enough. He backhanded her hard enough to knock her to the ground, then tossed a plate of food on top of her. The ceramic plate hit the floor and shattered. She covered her face too late, feeling the sting of a cut on her cheek.

"Clean this mess up." The chair scraped as he got up. His boots were a heavy tread on the floor as he walked away.

It took a minute for her head to clear and the throbbing pain in her jaw to subside enough before she got off the floor and cleaned up the mess with shaky hands. There was a warm trickle of blood on her cheek to match her tears, but she ignored it. Once everything was picked up and the broken shards thrown away, she grabbed her jacket and went out the back door.

Getting away. It was always the goal when her da got like this. Too much drinking, too much heartbreak over her mum. Elizabeth had never been enough for him. His heart and soul had died with his wife. Tomorrow, she knew, he'd stand in the doorway of the kitchen while she prepared breakfast. He'd mutter an apology in a rough voice, to which she'd nod and reply, "It's fine," though really it wasn't. But it was all she'd ever known.

The night outside was chilly and dark as pitch. The sky was clear and the stars sparkled like diamonds tossed onto black velvet.

Elizabeth walked down the hill to where the trees met the small creek that ran through the back of the small village. It was her favorite spot—a quiet spot—and she came here often when she needed to escape.

The cold air felt good against her skin and eased the ache in her head. She settled down on the cool grass, pulling her knees to her chest and staring at the dark water.

"I wondered if I'd ever see you again."

Elizabeth started at the voice, nearly jumping to her feet, but he spoke again.

"Take it easy, it's all right. It's just me, your new neighbor." He moved into the dim light cast from the moon, which filtered through the trees. "Mark."

Stunned, Elizabeth thought he looked even more perfect in the moonlight. To her amazement, he sat down beside her with a sigh, staring at the water as she had been.

"So are you gonna tell me your name?" he asked. "Or shall I attempt to guess?"

Her tongue didn't seem to remember how to work, but she managed to croak out, "Lizzie."

"Lizzie?" he asked. She nodded. "Is that short for Elizabeth?" She nodded again. "Which do you prefer?"

She'd always hated being called Lizzie, so she didn't hesitate now that someone had actually asked. "Elizabeth."

"It's a pleasure to meet you, Elizabeth," he said, extending a hand.

She looked at it, then tentatively gave him her own. His hand closed around hers, warm and strong, yet gentle.

"What are you doing out here this time of night?" he asked. "It's a bit late for a stroll."

"I just needed some air," she said.

He nodded, as though that was a perfectly good reason for her to be wandering in the dark.

They sat there for a few minutes. She was no longer looking at the water, though. Her every focus was on the boy next to her. She fancied she could smell the slightly musky scent of his skin. It was invigorating and addicting.

Too nervous to speak, she clutched her knees to her chest as he turned and looked at her. He was smiling slightly and she tentatively smiled back. But then his smile faded and his brows drew together in a frown.

"What's this?" he asked, reaching out to touch her cheek. "You're bleeding. Did you hurt yourself?"

She'd completely forgotten. So taken aback by his appearance, Elizabeth hadn't given a thought as to how she must look. Reflexively, she jerked away.

"A cut, that's all," she said, starting to panic. Most of the townspeople suspected her da's temper, though she'd been careful to hide any evidence the best she could. Why she protected him, she didn't know. Maybe it wasn't so much protecting him as preserving her own self-respect.

"Odd place to get cut," he mused, leaning closer. "How'd it happen?"

Elizabeth jumped to her feet. "I have to go," she said, but Mark was on his feet as well.

"Please stay," he said. "I'm sorry. I won't mention it again."

"No, no. I need to go." In a blink, she was off, hurrying away from him. She looked back once, only to see his body silhouetted in the moonlight, gazing after her.

As she'd predicted, her da apologized the next morning, glancing at her bruised face once before quickly looking away. He left for the pub shortly after that, and Elizabeth knew he'd be there all day, which left her blissfully alone.

It was tempting to go back to the creek from last night to see if Mark would show up again, but she resisted. If he found out about her father, *she might just die of mortification. So instead, she was curled up reading a book when there came a knock on the door, and was taken aback to find Mark standing on the stoop.*

"What are you doing here?" she blurted.

"Now that's a fine way to greet a friend," he said with an easy smile, though his gaze was shrewd as he took in her face. Belatedly, she stepped back into the shadows of the hallway.

"We're not friends," she said.

"We can be." To her dismay, he followed her, stepping inside. "I'd like to be."

"Whatever for?"

"Maybe because it'd be nice to have someone who knew what it was like to have to hide marks that are hard to explain."

She'd been edging backward, but now she stopped, fixing him with a look. He didn't flinch from her probing gaze. A beat passed.

"I don't know what you're talking about," she said.

"Oh, don't you?" He reached forward and brushed her cheek with his fingers. She sucked in a breath at the gentle touch. "I think you're lying."

"What's it to you?" she asked. She was suddenly angry. She hadn't wanted to be this—someone to be pitied—and he was making her feel like a victim.

He didn't answer. Instead, he turned his back to her. Confused, she watched him, then realized he was pulling his shirt up, exposing his back . . .

Which was covered in red welts and bruises.

"He likes the belt mainly," Mark said after a charged moment of silence.

Elizabeth swallowed, saying nothing as Mark dropped his shirt and turned back to face her.

"So you wanna talk about it?"

"Not particularly."

"Me, neither."

They stared at each other for a moment and for the first time ever, Elizabeth felt a kinship with another living soul.

"Let's go back out to the creek," he said. "Bring your book along. You can read to me."

She didn't think to disobey, just got her book and slipped on her shoes before following him out the door. His hand found hers, slotting their fingers together like it was nothing out of the ordinary. Since he didn't seem to think it was, she struggled for the same nonchalance.

And so the days of summer break passed, meeting Mark at their spot by the creek whenever she could get away. Some nights she waited for hours and he wouldn't appear. Those were the nights when she knew the next day he'd be moving stiffly and he wouldn't lie down in the grass.

They talked about everything and nothing. Sometimes they sat in silence. Sometimes she read to him. Occasionally she'd bring a few biscuits she'd made, or a piece of cake. He had a sweet tooth and liked that a lot.

It wasn't until the next time Elizabeth had incurred the ire of her sole-remaining parent and showed up late with a split lip and bruises on her arms that Mark kissed her.

Tentative at first, as though he wasn't sure what she'd do, then more confident when she didn't pull away. His hands gently cupped her jaw and the world faded away around them as they kissed. It was as though they'd found solace together, a bit of healing and comfort, and it was the best thing she'd ever had in her young life.

Two months later, she realized she was pregnant.

She wasn't completely ignorant of how these things happened, and as she stood there, counting again the days of the calendar, she knew she should be terrified. And she was. But she was also the tiniest bit elated.

Elizabeth told Mark that night as the summer moon shone down on them, lying on the soft grass. His hand was drifting across her stomach and it froze.

"Pregnant?" he asked. "Are you sure?"

"I'm two weeks late," she said.

"You're underage," he said. "We can't get married."

Her heart sank a little. She hadn't known what she'd expected him to do, but the idea of having a baby by herself, of telling her da . . . A shudder went through her at the thought.

"But we can run away," Mark continued. "Just you and me. Bide our time until you're sixteen. When will that be?"

"Three months."

"Then we only have to hide until then. We can do that. Then we'll marry and there's nothing anyone can do about it."

Marriage and a baby to a man she'd fallen in love with . . . it seemed too good to be true. And she should've known it would be because just then her da stepped out from behind a tree.

"So this is where you been coming every night," he said, advancing on them.

Elizabeth gasped in dismay, grabbing up her clothes as Mark jumped to his feet. He had no time to say anything before her father's fist shot out, knocking him in the jaw with a powerful crack of knuckles against bone. Mark dropped to the ground like a rock and didn't move.

"Mark!" In moments, she was crouched next to him, trying to shake him awake. He was still breathing, thank goodness, just out cold.

"Pregnant, eh? Spreading your legs for the first boy who pays you a bit of attention?" Her da grabbed her arm and dragged her to her feet and up the hill.

"Let me go!" She fought him, but a fist upside her head that made her see stars put an end to that.

She was forced to dress while her da packed her things, then he drove her out of town. For the next nine months, she was mostly a prisoner at a convent, growing and birthing her baby boy far away from the prying eyes of neighbors and friends. She railed and screamed when they took the boy from her, not even letting her hold him. Tears poured down her cheeks as she cursed them every vile way she knew how, until the Head Mother of the convent gave her cheek a stinging slap.

The hope that had kept her going—hope that she'd see Mark again—was dashed the moment she was returned to her home. He'd been sent away, into the military, never to return.

"Sucha sad tale, but ye ken, that's how things were in those days," Elva said, adding more tea to her cup. "Girls her age did'nae hae babies oot o' wedlock. The baby was ge'en up fur adoption."

"Do you know what happened to her?" Alexa asked.

I was stunned, still in emotional turmoil over the story I'd just heard.

"I'm afraid I dinna." Elva said. "One day, they were just gone. Both her and her faether. They did'na leave a note nor tell anybidy whaur they wir ga'an. They've nivver returned. If she's still alive, she'd be, oh I dinna, most likely in her sixties by now? I do wish I ken whit happened ta her."

"Do you know what happened to Mark?" I asked. I didn't dare turn to look at Devon to see how he was handling all this.

"Mark? Och, aye. The Clay family moved awa' soon after the Percys left. No one's seen them since."

"Then who buried Dillon McGewan there?" It was the first time Devon had spoken.

"Naebiddy really kens," Elva said. "It jist appeared one day, the grave freshly dug. Seemed best no' tae disturb the deed, so nae-biddy did."

What had happened? It couldn't have been coincidence that Devon had the same last name as the boy Vega had fallen in love with, could it?

Abruptly, Devon stood and I hastened to follow suit.

"Thank you for your time," he said to Elva. His words were cordial but I could feel the tension in his body. "We'll just be off now."

Beau and Alexa said their goodbyes as well and followed us out, but I was mostly concentrating on Devon. I wasn't sure what to make of everything Elva had said to us and couldn't imagine what must be going through Devon's head at the moment either.

"Let's take a walk," he said to me, his hand taking mine.

I glanced back at Alexa as we started walking and she gave a nod of understanding, grabbing Beau's arm and tugging him back when he began to follow us.

We walked without speaking, and I thought maybe Devon was following the sound and scent of the ocean, as our path was a gradual descent. Finally, we crested the last hill and looked down onto water, gently lapping at the sandy pebbles that made up the beach.

"I've always loved the water," he said. "Especially here. Deserted and cold . . . the water is more indifferent here than elsewhere, I think. It continues on its way, no matter what tries to impede its path. It demands respect for its beauty and power. Can you feel it?"

I was too worried about him to answer. I tightened my hand around his, and he glanced down at me.

"Can you?" he repeated. "You can almost feel it in your blood, getting stronger and colder with each wave that comes in."

"What's wrong, Devon?" I asked. "Please talk to me."

He sighed, turning again to look out at the water. I waited, watching him and just being there.

"You haven't sorted it yet?" he asked.

"Sorted what?"

"Dillon Clay. My father. He was her son. She named him after his father, Mark Clay. Which makes me Vega's grandson."

CHAPTER
THIRTEEN

Once upon a time, my stepbrother had been a monster. A monster who had hidden behind family ties and assumptions of trust and loyalty. He'd done horrible things to me and the one small comfort I'd had was that we didn't share the same blood. That which made him into what he was didn't run in my veins, too.

Devon had no such comfort.

I didn't know what to say, what words of advice or understanding to offer. Once the shock had worn off, so much became clear. Vega's constant protection of Devon. Her obsession with him. The murder of Kira, the one other woman who'd gotten too close. Her threats to me, and finally, her inability to shoot Devon point-blank in the hotel room when we'd been cornered.

So I just held on to him, and I wasn't sure really who was holding on to whom at that point. I felt for him, tears stinging my eyes, and rested my head against his arm as we stared out into the ocean, which didn't know or care what turmoil was wreaking havoc on our lives at the moment.

"Are you all right?" I asked after a while. My voice was nearly lost in the sound of the surf against the shore.

He nodded immediately. "Oh yes. I'm fine."

I cringed inside at that. Yes, I'd been "fine" for years upon years . . . then Devon had walked into my life and shown me just how *not* fine I was.

"Is that how you're going to play this?" I asked.

I could feel him look down at me, but I kept watching the waves. "What do you mean?"

"You're shutting me out. Keeping it all inside. And if that's what you want to do, that's your decision." I looked up at him. "But you don't have to. I don't want you to."

"My . . . grandmother . . . tortured and murdered my wife," he said with obvious difficulty. "Has tried to kill you. Has lied to me for years about who I really am. I don't think I've even been able to process how that is affecting me. I'm stunned. I feel betrayed . . . used. And I have no idea why she did it."

Okay, he was talking. This was good. "Alexa said your parents were murdered," I said. "We need to figure out what she meant by that. Then maybe you'll know more about why Vega . . . Elizabeth . . . did what she did." *Other than her being a complete sociopath*, I wanted to add, but knew that wouldn't be exactly helpful.

"They were random victims. Not murdered. I can't imagine Vega would kill her own son. Surely to God . . ." He didn't continue, and I understood.

"Let's go ask her. We'll hear what she has to say . . . together. You and me."

I tugged his arm and he looked down at me. His face was hard to read but his eyes . . . his eyes held naked pain. I wrapped my arms around his neck, and was surprised to feel his arms go tight around my waist. His weight pressed on me and his face was buried in my neck. I held on to him as his shoulders shook and my skin grew damp. He held me so tightly, it was hard to breathe, but it felt good to be able to be strong for someone else. And I was grateful beyond words that Devon allowed himself to be vulnerable with me.

After a few minutes, his grip on me eased and he stepped back. Other than his eyes being slightly red and a tiny bit swollen, you couldn't tell at all that he'd been upset.

Without a word, he took my hand and began retracing our steps up the hills to where we'd left Beau and Alexa. Though they weren't at the car, there was a pub nearby and Devon guided us toward it. Once we'd entered, I saw Beau and Alexa seated opposite each other at a corner table. Their heads were close together and they were talking. When Devon and I approached, they immediately clammed up, looking like two teenagers who'd been caught by their parents.

Devon held the chair for me and I sat down. He sat across from me, next to Beau. They already had drinks, and the waitress was on us in seconds, asking what we wanted. Devon ordered a bottle of wine . . . and two shots of vodka, straight up. I didn't complain and those shots went down pretty darn smooth.

"What happened to my grandfather?"

Devon's first shot across the bow took me by surprise, but Alexa seemed prepared.

"Mark Clay served his time in the Royal Marine Commandos and did very well. Unfortunately, he was reported Killed In Action a few years into his service. He never married."

I felt a wave of disappointment. It would've been really great for Devon to try and track him down and meet him.

"So you're saying that Mark and Elizabeth—Vega—had a son together, Dillon Clay McGewan, my father."

Alexa nodded. "I figured you'd work it out on your own."

"Then why did you say my parents were murdered?"

Alexa glanced at Beau, who gave her a nod.

"That bombing . . . Devon, it wasn't a coincidence that your family was there."

"What are you talking about?"

I could tell he was agitated and I rested my hand on his knee underneath the table. His palm settled over mine and his body relaxed slightly.

"We think it was a targeted assassination . . . on your father," Beau said. "Disguised as a mass bombing."

Devon's hand was like ice.

I was horrified. "How many people lost their lives . . . just to kill one man?"

"Twenty-three," Devon said, his voice flat. "So someone knew who my father was. It was a revenge killing."

"Most likely."

There was a moment of heavy silence. "Did my father know who his parents were?" Devon asked. "Did he even have a clue as to the who and why?"

"I don't know, man," Beau said with a sigh and helpless shrug. "There's just no way we can know. The only ones who do are Mark and Vega, and Mark's dead."

The fact that Vega would know loomed large, though no one spoke the words.

"I want to go further north," Devon said. "There's a place I'd like to visit."

No one argued with that pronouncement, and though I wondered where he was talking about, I decided to hold my tongue until we were alone.

Suddenly, I felt Devon's eyes on me. Glancing up, I was taken aback by the look of horror on his face. I was about to ask him what was wrong when I felt it.

The warm trickle of blood from my nose.

My hand flew up to my face just as a dull ache started inside my head. Both Beau and Alexa were staring at me—Alexa in confusion and Beau with a look of sad resignation.

"I thought you said she was better," he said to Devon.

"I am. I was," I cut in, grabbing a napkin to staunch the flow. "I don't know what this is—"

"She lied."

We all looked at Devon. His face was a mask of cold fury.

"She lied to the agent, who then lied to us. It wasn't a cure, merely another delaying tactic. Something to allay the symptoms for a short while."

I felt sick to my stomach, and it had absolutely nothing to do with the pain in my head.

"We leave in the morning, at first light."

No one questioned Devon, and I said nothing as he took my hand and led me from the pub.

Beau had checked us in to a little hotel next door that looked like it had been around since the days of William the Conqueror. But the inside was nice and clean, and I knew that I was concentrating on anything else other than what had happened.

Devon was going to be a widower again, nearly as quickly as he'd been the last time.

I'd never forget the look on his face at the table, and my heart ached.

I showered, wrapping one towel around me and drying my hair with another. I caught sight of Devon in the mirror. He was leaning, one arm against the doorjamb, watching me.

"Don't," I warned.

"Don't what?"

"Weren't you the one who said not to give up?"

He didn't reply, but he didn't have to. I could see I wasn't getting through to him. His eyes had always been the most expressive part of him and now the blue depths held an anguish I could feel. I set aside the towel in my hands and turned toward him.

"It'll be okay," I said. "No matter what happens. You'll be okay." My smile was a little too sad, but it was the best I could do. I had to be strong . . . for both of us. Devon had been through so much today.

Reaching up, I cupped his cheek in my hand. His hand circled my wrist and he turned his lips into my palm.

"I don't want to live without you."

My eyes went wide at that. "What do you mean?" I asked carefully, almost afraid of his response.

"You're my world," he said, his blue gaze meeting mine. "And I'm tired. Tired of fighting the good fight, which may not have been the good fight after all. I thought perhaps I'd done enough, seen enough horror and blood to redeem myself and gain a quiet life. It seems fate won't be kind, or forgiving."

I stared at him, aghast. "Please don't say that," I begged. "You're a good man. I can't bear to think of you feeling so fatalistic."

He was quiet, studying me. I prayed he'd see that what he was thinking just wasn't going to happen. I couldn't think that if I died—as it seemed certain now—he wouldn't go on.

"Let's just go to bed," I said. "We're tired and everything looks worse when you're tired."

Devon brushed his lips to my forehead. "You go ahead, darling. I think I'm going out for a bit."

I watched in dismay as he grabbed his jacket and walked out the door, letting it swing shut behind him.

Well, shit. Now what?

I shrugged into one of Devon's shirts and my underwear, doing up the buttons to between my breasts. Though the sleeves were too long and the garment overly large, it made me feel closer to him.

I lay down in the bed, but I couldn't sleep. Didn't want to sleep. I wanted Devon, but didn't know what *he* needed. Did he need space? Did he need me, but didn't want to put pressure on me? I had no idea.

Time passed as I watched the hands of the clock moving inexorably onward. My worry started as a kernel of concern, growing larger with each passing moment until I could no longer lie there waiting for him.

Just then, the hotel room phone rang. I snatched it up without a second thought. It was Beau.

"Can you come down to the hotel bar?" he asked without any preliminaries. "Devon . . . well, just come down, okay?"

I said I was on my way and hung up. Grabbing the bathrobe provided by the hotel—an unexpected touch considering the place—I shrugged it on as I hurried out the door. I hadn't even bothered with shoes. My worry for Devon was too great.

The elevator seemed to move with agonizing slowness, the ancient relic groaning and sighing as though I'd woken it from its slumber. Finally, it deposited me on the first floor. I peeked out, but the lobby was deserted.

I'd caught sight of where the bar was earlier when Devon and I had arrived, and I hurried there. Beau was waiting at the door for me, arms crossed. The only people in the place were the bartender and Devon, seated on one of the leather stools. His back was to me and he was hunched slightly, his head resting in one palm.

"I think you can take it from here," Beau said, pushing himself off the wall where he'd been leaning. "Though if he passes out before you can get him back to the room, give me a shout. Room 212."

"Okay, thanks," I murmured. I took note of the room number, then headed for Devon.

The bartender gave me a solemn nod when I approached. He was dressed very nicely in a long-sleeved button-down shirt, black pants, and black vest. He even had a black tie.

"I'll have another," Devon said, his voice raw.

I slipped onto the stool next to him. "And what are we drinking?" I asked.

The bartender was the one who answered. "Gin, straight up, twist of lemon. Splash of vermouth with three olives." He paused. "Five of them."

Holy bejesus.

Devon had noted my arrival and didn't seem surprised. "Figured Beau would ring you," he said. "Bloody sod."

"Looks like he was right," I replied. "What are you trying to do? Get completely drunk?"

"It seemed like a good idea at the time."

If I'd drunk five gin martinis, I'd be passed out cold on the floor. But with Devon, the only thing that gave him away was his eyes—which were bloodshot—and the slight slurring of his words along with his more pronounced accent.

The bartender fixed another drink, which he set in front of Devon. I quickly slid it in front of me and took a sip, then coughed.

"It's a little strong," I managed to get out past my burning throat.

Devon took the drink from me and downed it, setting the empty glass carefully back on the granite bar. His hand was resting on the counter, and I laid my palm atop his, slotting our fingers together. I turned his hand over so I could see the plain wedding band around his finger.

"You don't have to do this alone," I said. "We're together. For however long we have. Don't push me away."

The bartender discreetly walked away and I heard the door to the bar close behind him, leaving us alone.

Devon was quiet for a moment. His elbow was bent, braced on the bar, and his fingers touched his temple, rubbing slightly as he stared at our joined hands.

"But that's how it's always been," he said.

"That's how what's always been?"

"Alone. Always. I've always been alone. And now . . . just this once . . . I thought I'd gotten to a place where I wouldn't be alone. Yet, you're being taken from me."

Okay, alcohol was bad, true, especially in copious amounts. But nothing beat it as a tool that got men like Devon to open up. Men who kept things to themselves, who didn't discuss feelings and instead carried everything around, locked deep inside. So at the moment, I couldn't be too upset that he'd been drinking. Not if I'd hear what he was really thinking and feeling . . . things he'd keep from me in an effort to protect me.

"I don't deserve you," he said.

"Wait, hold on," I interrupted. "That's total crap, Devon. You know that, right? Why in the world would you say such a thing?"

"The things I've seen . . . the things I've done. Too much . . ." His voice trailed away, and he glanced around, as though just then realizing the bartender had left.

With a shrug, he pushed himself up and over the bar, grabbing one of the bottles of bourbon and setting it down. With a quick twist of his wrist, the bottle opened and he grabbed a tumbler. I watched him pour in two fingers worth of the amber liquid.

"What do you mean, Devon?" I asked. "What kinds of things?" I couldn't help it. I was curious. Devon never *ever* discussed missions he'd been on or what he'd done. The temptation now to learn was too strong to pass up.

"I've killed so many," he said grimly. He turned and his blue gaze was fierce on mine. "And I will never . . . *never* . . . tell you how many."

I swallowed at his vehemence even as sympathy rose in me. He lifted the glass and took a large swallow.

"This is undoubtedly the gods' way of meting out justice," he mused. "Not that I can blame them. Much more satisfying than killing me outright, is it not? Torturing me instead with the pain of something almost within my grasp."

"Don't say such things," I said. "You're a good man. You've just had to do some bad things in the name of protecting the innocent."

"No one is innocent. Not really. All have sinned . . ."

He was staring into the mirror behind the bar, the look on his face so tortured and filled with regret, I couldn't stand it.

I leaned against Devon's shoulder and slid an arm around his waist. "I'm tired," I said, hoping to distract him. "We should go to bed."

"You go on ahead, darling," he said, finally looking away from his reflection in the mirror. "I'll be up shortly." He refilled his glass.

I snatched it from him and tossed the shot back. If I thought the gin was bad, the whiskey burned a blazing trail of fire down into my belly. I noticed Devon's eyes following the movement of my throat as I swallowed.

"I'm not going without you," I said, reaching down to untie the robe. I slipped it down my arms and let it fall around me. "I'd really like you to take me to bed, Devon." I gave him as seductive a look as I was capable.

The Look came into his eyes. The kind of look I'd become quite familiar with over the time we'd been together. It was lust and affection tinged with urgency and passion. I loved when he looked at me like that. It made me feel wanted, desirable—a woman clear to my bones.

"I don't think I can make it to the bedroom, my love."

My heart sank. He couldn't walk. What room had Beau said he was in? I'd have to call him to come help me get Devon back upstairs.

"I just can't wait that long," he continued, breaking into my frantic thoughts as he picked me up, his hands circling my waist, and set me on the bar in front of him.

The granite was cold on the backs of my bare thighs. He settled his hands on my knees, spreading them.

"Take off the shirt."

I didn't think to disobey, my eyes transfixed on him and the way he was looking at me. My fingers moved to the buttons, undoing them clumsily. He watched me, his gaze burning my flesh as each inch of skin was revealed.

I wore panties, but no bra. The chill of air brushed my breasts, tightening my nipples into hard points. Devon parted the shirt but didn't remove it. I sucked in my breath as his hands settled on my waist.

"Lift," he murmured, tugging on my panties. I squirmed as he tugged the garment down and off my legs, spreading my thighs again.

It wasn't as bright as daylight in the bar, but there was plenty of light, and I felt a blush stain my cheeks as he gazed between my legs. I saw his Adam's apple move up and down as he swallowed hard. I was wet already, getting wetter and needier by the moment as he stared at my body.

He placed a hand on my abdomen, pushing me back. I leaned back, resting on my elbows. His palm trailed down my stomach, flat against my skin. He was darker than I was, my skin a pale shade of ivory compared to his sun-kissed tan.

Devon leaned down, putting his mouth between my legs with no preliminaries whatsoever. I gasped at the sensation. The sight of him doing this to me was almost more erotic and intimate than the act itself. He pushed my thighs farther apart, then slid a thick finger inside me as his tongue flicked hard against my clit.

I couldn't keep my eyes open any longer, and they slammed shut, my head falling back as Devon kissed me with unreserved passion, marking my body as his possession. My fingers were in his hair, holding him to me. Moans and cries fell from my lips as my orgasm crashed over me. He knew just the right way to touch me, prolonging my pleasure until I couldn't take any more.

Tugging on his hair, I pulled him up so I could kiss him. My legs circled his chest and he pulled me closer to him, scooting me to the edge. I heard the sound of metal clanking as he undid his belt, but I was too consumed with his tongue in my mouth to pay much attention. I wanted him, and didn't particularly care that we were in a public place. No one was around. That was all that mattered.

Devon picked me up, carrying me to one of the tables, which was a much more suitable height for what we both had in mind. He lay me down and I grasped his cock, hard and thick between us, guiding it into me.

It was sweet relief and intoxication, being with him like this. His urgency and passion fueled the fire between us. His lips on mine, his hands gripping my hips, holding me. He possessed me utterly, as he had from the first time we'd been together. I was his. Would be only his.

Sweat covered his skin like a thin blanket and I pushed my fingers through his hair, reveling in the damp strands as he made love to me with a desperation I knew had been fueled by the alcohol and bad memories. I didn't mind being his solace and comfort. I wanted it. Wanted to be able to provide that to him. I didn't know and couldn't possibly understand everything he'd seen and done. But this . . . this I could give and maybe it would be enough to comfort him.

He kissed my throat, licking the skin there. I lifted my hips to meet his thrusts. He made a noise, deep in his throat, moving faster and harder, which was just fine with me. I could feel myself hovering on the edge and I tried to hold back, waiting for him.

When his fingers tightened on me, I knew he was close and I couldn't hold back any longer. Waves of pleasure spiraled out from where we were joined, like ripples from a stone thrown into a pool of water. I could feel my body clutching at his. He gasped, groaning as his orgasm was ripped from him. I knew I might have bruises tomorrow from his fingers, but I didn't mind.

He rested on top of me, his chest heaving from exertion. I could feel his heart hammering against my chest and I didn't know if it was my pulse or his. I held him to me, my arms and legs circling him, until he pulled back slightly and looked in my eyes.

Brushing the hair back from my face, he said, "Don't think I don't know what you're doing."

I was silent, gazing back into the blue of his eyes.

"And I thank you."

I smiled a little as he brushed a kiss to my forehead. He seemed more sober now, not that he'd behaved all that drunkenly before. It amazed me. How his body processed alcohol the way it did, I had no idea.

He pulled me up and we spent a few seconds righting our clothing, then he held the robe so I could slip my arms into the sleeves.

No one was around when we came out of the bar, the lobby area completely deserted. Taking my hand, Devon pulled me close as we rode the elevator to our floor and meandered down the hallway to our room. I loved when he did this, touching me as we walked, his arm around me and his lips by my ear, alternatively whispering to me and kissing my neck.

We undressed each other and climbed under the covers. He wrapped his arms around me and I smiled. Yes, I was still sick and the future looked bleak. But the here and now? Well, the here and now was pretty darn good. I fell asleep listening to the sound of Devon's slow, steady breathing.

And when I woke in the morning, he was gone.

CHAPTER FOURTEEN

At first, it didn't occur to me that he was actually gone. I assumed he'd gone downstairs for coffee or breakfast or goodness knows what. So I showered and dressed, ignoring the ache in my head that boded ill. It wasn't until I stepped into the little restaurant attached to the hotel and saw Beau and Alexa sitting alone together that a frisson of alarm went through me.

"Good morning," I said, sliding into the empty chair next to Beau. I was trying to ignore what my gut was telling me. "Have you seen Devon?"

I could sense immediately from the looks on their faces that it was bad.

"What?" I asked. "What is it? Where is he? Is he all right?" My hands gripped the edge of the table, my body wanting to jump and do something, go find him—but I didn't know where to start looking.

"I'm sure he's fine," Alexa said. Oddly phrased, considering.

"Why do you say it like that?" I asked. "Where is he?"

"He left," Beau said. I swung my gaze to his. "Earlier this morning."

I swallowed hard, trying to get a grip on my emotions so I wouldn't either burst into tears or throw one of the heavy mugs of coffee on the table. I couldn't decide if I was furious or heartbroken. Probably both.

"And where did he go exactly?" I was proud of how controlled my voice was.

"He went to find Vega."

My hands clenched into fists. "Why? Why would he do that? What if she decides to kill him?"

"I don't think she'll kill her own flesh and blood," Alexa said, though she didn't sound one hundred percent sure. "I mean, she hasn't yet."

That wasn't very comforting.

"He went to try and get her to give me more medicine, didn't he," I said, and it wasn't a question. That was the only thing that would've made Devon leave my side. Nothing else.

Alexa glanced at Beau, then back at me. "I think so, yes."

I covered my face with my hands and just breathed. I was so angry I wanted to spit nails. And I clung to that feeling. I didn't want to feel hurt or hopeless.

After a moment, I had control and I put my hands down. Took a deep breath.

"I want to talk to her."

"To who? Vega?" Beau looked appalled. "No fucking way. She wants you dead, Ivy. Is at this moment making sure you die slowly and in pain. The only thing you'll achieve by talking to her is a quicker death."

"I don't think so," I said. "I have an idea. Now how do we find her?"

"No, I'm not—" Beau started, but Alexa interrupted.

"Why can't she?" she asked. "It's her life, her decision."

I was surprised at the support . . . and the source.

"You have no say in this," Beau retorted. "I'm in charge here."

"Oh, really?" Alexa's eyes narrowed. "You're *in charge*?"

"Yeah," he said, doubling down.

More irritated than amused at their bickering, I demanded, "One of you tell me how to find her."

That shut them both up. Beau gave Alexa a belligerent look, then waved his hand like *Go on then, tell her.*

"Vega has her own headquarters for the Shadow, north of here, at Cape Wrath."

"Cape Wrath?" Yeah, that didn't sound intimidating or anything. I'd bet dollars to donuts it was exactly where Devon was headed.

"The military sometimes uses the area for training," Alexa explained. "But the Shadow built underground there. It's pretty remote."

"Then that's where I'm going." I signaled the waiter for a cup of coffee because hot on Devon's trail or not, I needed the caffeine.

"You can't go alone," Alexa said. "Not in your condition. I'll come with you."

"The hell you are!"

Beau's outburst had Alexa's gaze spitting fire at him again.

"Pardon me, Mister I'm-In-Charge," she said. "Was I supposed to ask your permission first?"

"You're in the custody of the CIA," he said. "You can't just get up and leave."

"I'm only in your custody because I'm allowing it," she sneered. "I want to take Vega down as much as you do, and I'm not going to stand idly by and let the child go by herself."

Whoa there, hold on. Did she just call me a child? But even as I opened my mouth, Beau was arguing with her.

"So even though she's put numerous hits out on you, you're just going to waltz right in there," he said.

"Americans waltz. I prefer the silent approach."

"You—"

"Enough!" I said, holding up my hands, palms out. "Enough of your arguing!" I looked at Alexa. "You know the way, so you're taking me." I looked at Beau. "And we're doing this partly for the CIA. So shouldn't you get some backup and come riding to the rescue in the nick of time?"

He didn't look pleased, but he nodded. "I can see what I can do."

"Okay then. Now I'm going to finish my coffee"—I dumped some cream in the mug the waitress had just set down in front of me—"then we'll get our things and head out."

"You have no idea what you're getting in to," Beau said, glancing from her to me.

"Probably not, but I have no choice."

Devon was out there, and we weren't going down without a fight.

I had one call to make before I left and I made it quickly, from my room. Once that was done, I met Alexa in the lobby.

"You'd better wear this," she said, handing me a heavy jacket. "It's cold up there."

Beau had already gone so it was just her and me.

"We need to rent a car or something," I said, glancing around the lobby for the desk clerk. He'd probably be able to tell us how to do that.

"No need," Alexa said, hoisting her duffel bag on her shoulder. "Follow me."

Curious, I followed her outside. It was a gray day, no sunshine, and the air smelled damp. There was a definite chill in the air and I was glad for the jacket.

"You have a car already?" I asked, glancing around. I didn't see one idling at the curb, just several parked along the narrow road.

"Something like that." She headed for a nicer sedan, slightly larger than most of the cars. "This one will do." Reaching into her pocket, she took something out that I couldn't see. Standing in front of the driver's side door, she fiddled until the lock clicked. Pulling open the door, she hit the locks. "Get in."

I knew what she was doing and wanted to say something, but Devon was waiting. So I clamped my lips shut and got in. In seconds, she had started the engine.

"How are you doing that?" I asked. It was one of those keyless entry cars. You had to have a key in the passenger compartment for it to start.

She showed me what she was holding. It was smaller than her palm and there were several lights blinking.

"It's a transmitter," she said. "It sends thousands of signals per second to the car until it finds the right one that'll do the trick. A little pricey, but worth it when I'm in a bind."

"How much head start does Devon have on us?" I asked.

"A couple of hours."

"How long will it take to get there?"

"All fucking day."

Nice.

It took more patience than I thought I had to endure the hours we drove. Eventually, the silence and uncertainty of what awaited Devon—and us—got to me. So I tried to make conversation.

"You never did say why you didn't send Devon back in a body bag, too," I said, recalling Devon's story about finding Alexa.

"I'd had enough," she said with a shrug. "Killing people gets easier, but it wears on you. And Devon was such an ignorant sap, in the dark about so many things. I took pity on him."

I didn't think Devon would like it very much if he knew Alexa had taken pity on him.

"I hope you don't mind me saying this," I began, "but . . . you don't look like much of an assassin. You're just so . . . little."

Alexa glanced at me and grinned. "I know. Makes it so much easier sometimes. People don't expect it. And there are more ways of killing than brute force. I'm pretty adept at them all. Besides, people don't want to believe I'm an assassin sent to kill them, even when it's obvious. They'd rather believe a lie than the truth, though it's staring them in the face."

"That's kind of a universal truth, though, isn't it?" I said. I was trying everything I could to keep my mind off Devon, but it was hopeless.

"What will we be able to do when we get there?" I asked. "If she's going to kill him, it won't be right away, will it?" *Please tell me no*, though logically I understood she couldn't possibly know.

"I thought you had a plan," she said, frowning as she glanced at me yet again. I wished she'd keep her eyes on the road. It twisted and turned, the heavy clouds obscuring the sun as a light mist began to fall.

"I do, but not on how to get inside. I was hoping you'd know how to do that. Once we're in, I can talk to her."

"You're planning on talking to her?" Alexa asked in disbelief. "That's your big plan?"

"What did you think I was going to do?" I snapped back, stung. "It's not as though I'm some kind of tiny, freak assassin."

"Watch it, Beauty Queen. I'll dump your skinny ass on the side of the road and not look back."

I bit my tongue, not just because I thought she'd do it—she totally would—but it wasn't her causing me to be snappy and on edge.

"I'm sorry," I said. "I'm so worried about Devon . . . and so pissed off, I want to kill him myself."

"Yeah, I'd be pretty fucking pissed, too," she said. "I told him not to go, that he was making the wrong decision. But like a typical man, he wouldn't listen."

"So how do you get by?" I asked. "Do you just . . . freelance now?" I didn't know what other euphemism to use for: *So hey, do you hire yourself out to kill people?*

"I don't kill people anymore, if that's what you're asking," she said. "I work in intelligence."

"Intelligence?"

She looked at me like I was a total idiot.

"I'm a spy. I specialize in honey traps."

My eyes widened. I'd seen enough movies to know what they were. A woman finds a target, gets him to sleep with her, and uses pillow talk to find out classified information. I was shocked, but tried not to show it.

Alexa laughed, the sound slightly bitter. "Yeah, that's the usual reaction. Believe it or not, it's harder than it looks. It's the oldest trick in the book, so the high-profile targets—the ones who really have the information you want and aren't just spouting bullshit to make themselves look more important than they really are—they're trained on how to spot it. So it's quite difficult to get them to trust me enough to talk."

"I can't imagine . . ." I said, looking at her in a whole different way. Not a bad way, because I thought she was probably right. "Sex," I said. "A woman's greatest weapon, or so I'd been told. Difficult to wield, though, without being hurt yourself." I watched her closely and could tell I'd hit a sore spot because she winced, ever so slightly.

She shrugged. "Some things are worth being hurt for."

I sensed she wasn't going to say anything more about it, so I changed the subject.

"Beau seems to really like you."

She looked at me, her expression one of disbelief. "You've got to be kidding me!" she said with a small laugh. "He hates me. He knows exactly what I do and it disgusts him."

I'd seen the way Beau had looked at Alexa, at how he'd touched her when she was hurt, and disgust was the furthest thing from his mind.

"I don't think so," I said slowly, wondering at how she could possibly not see it when her livelihood depended on her ability to read men.

"Trust me. I know."

I didn't want to argue with her—after all, it's not like it was my business.

"How much further?" I asked. Night was falling. It had been hours since we'd eaten, but instead of hunger my stomach was churning with anxiety and nausea.

"Well, we could park and walk the last couple of miles . . ."

I looked outside at the mist, which had transformed into rain, at the dark and forbidding landscape, and the utter lack of civilization. Then back at Alexa.

"Yeah, it was just a thought," she said. "We'll drive right on up to the front door. We won't have to wait long for them to take us in, though I do hope they ask questions before they start shooting . . ."

Yeah, me, too.

It took another thirty excruciating minutes for us to reach the end of the road. And by "end of the road," it was literally the end of anything you could drive on. There was a one-story building on our right, and straight ahead was a lighthouse, its strobe light turning slowly and sending its ray through the darkness. At its base was a small structure, not big enough to be a home but large enough to hold one person comfortably.

"You ready for this, Beauty Queen?"

I didn't know why she persisted in calling me that, but it irritated me, and perhaps that was her intent: to get my mind off worrying and fear, and to focus. Because nothing quite made someone focus like being angry.

"I'm ready to save Devon, then kick his ass," I said.

She grinned. "I am totally on board with that."

Alexa drove the last couple of hundred yards and pulled to a stop. I reached for the door handle as she turned off the engine, but the door flew open. Dark figures cloaked in black stood outside and I had no idea where they'd come from. I hadn't seen them when the headlights had bounced over the landscape. But I could see them now . . . as well as the long assault rifles they held, several of which were pointed at me.

I could hear Alexa's door open, too, and assumed the same thing was happening on her side of the car.

The muzzle of the closest rifle was about six inches from the center of my forehead and I broke out in a cold sweat. I swallowed, slowly lifting my hands in surrender even as my gaze was riveted to that relatively small, though deadly, black hole.

They didn't speak, but they didn't have to, now, did they.

I got out of the car, wincing as the cold rain hit my face in sharp, stinging blows. The wind had picked up, too, whipping my hair around. I was suddenly glad for the shorter haircut. It would've really gotten in the way had it been as long as when it was blonde.

The men—I counted five—prodded Alexa toward me. Her hands were similarly raised. The figures moved behind us and I felt the cold metal push against my back.

Their silence was unnerving, as was the howl of the wind and rain. It felt as though we were on the edge of the planet. I could hear the pounding of the surf against the rocks below the cliff just past the lighthouse. A bit of spray was visible from below, and I knew the ocean had to be churning something fierce for water to hit so hard that I could see it. What meager light there was glinted off some large cylindrical objects half-buried in the ground.

"What's that?" I asked Alexa.

"UXO," she said. "Unexploded ordnance. The military mainly use this area as an artillery and mortar range, large caliber ammunition since the Second World War. Stay away from them. They're old and volatile, easily set off."

I digested this as the men took us into the small structure at the base of the lighthouse and I shuddered once we were inside. My clothes were soaked through and I was freezing.

Rain beat against the windows, and I wondered where in the world we were all going—it was quite crowded in the small space— then I remembered what Alexa had said about it being underground. The guy beside me moved forward to a panel in the wall and pressed his hand to it. There was a blue light under what had seemed to be an opaque surface, which scanned down his palm, before the panel slid open.

He entered an elevator, then Alexa and I were herded in. The panel slid shut and we began descending.

"Mercenaries, eh?" Alexa mused. "I guess the Shadow isn't what it used to be."

None of the men replied or even acknowledged that they'd heard her speak.

The ride seemed long, making me wonder how far underground we were going. I was tense and scared, but also angry. Vega had controlled so many lives—including Devon's and my own. It had to stop. She had to be stopped. And if the British government was too afraid to take care of its dirty laundry itself, then Devon and I would do it for them.

When the doors slid open, I thought I was prepared to see her again, thought I knew how I would feel. I was wrong.

I barely glanced at the room as the mercenary soldiers moved us out of the elevator. Two of them stayed and three went back upstairs. But all my attention was focused on the woman standing in front of a wall covered entirely in LCD screens. She wasn't looking at us, but was watching the screens as intently as I was watching her.

Her blonde hair was swept up neatly in a French roll, and she wore a pale-pink skirt with a matching jacket. A white blouse and pearls peeked from underneath. It was incongruous. She looked like a straight-laced British grandmother about to take tea somewhere posh, not the coldly calculating woman I knew her to be.

"We picked up these women outside," one of the men said. "Neither was armed."

Vega took her time responding, and her obvious disdain for any threat we might pose rankled me. My entire life had been upended because of what she'd done. I was a wanted fugitive in my own country due to her.

My hands curled into fists, the nails biting into the flesh of my palms.

"Are we interrupting you?" I sneered. "I wouldn't think you'd be very busy, forced into retirement as you are. The Shadow's days— *your* days—are over."

That got a reaction. She finally turned, her steely-blue gaze narrowing as she focused on me. It was chilling because now I could see the resemblance between her and Devon.

She smiled, her lips thin and her eyes cold. "Ivy. How are you feeling, my dear?"

I gritted my teeth, my whole body tense with the need to attack her.

"Easy," Alexa murmured. "They'll shoot you if you go after her."

"Alexa," Vega said. "I must say, I didn't expect to see you again. Not with a price on your head."

Alexa shrugged. "Maybe I just missed your warm hospitality."

"Where's Devon?" I asked. "He's here. I know he is. What have you done with him?" My skin itched with the need to find him, to make sure he was all right.

Something flickered in her eyes, but I couldn't tell what.

"Devon isn't your concern," Vega said. She walked slowly toward us, her hands clasped behind her back. Her face was flawless, age and the years marking her, but you could still see the beauty she must've been when she was young. "He's returned to me and will be dealt with. I do, however, question why I am expected to endure *your* presence."

"I've been learning a lot about you . . . Elizabeth. So much that it almost made me feel sorry for you."

Only the slight widening of her eyes betrayed her reaction to my saying her real name.

"Is that why you've come?" she asked. "Because you think you have something on me? Trust me, if the British government can't pin any crimes on me, you certainly won't be able to."

"You've been careful over the years, making other people do your dirty work," Alexa said. "You're quite clever."

"Tell me something I don't know." Vega's retort was said with utter disdain.

I noticed she glanced back at the screens on the wall again. The deliberate casualness of her actions made me suspicious. I scrutinized the wall but couldn't see the images properly. We were too far away and the angle was wrong.

"Devon knows he's your grandson," I said. "We found your hometown, heard all about Mark Clay. And the son you had to give up." I couldn't help feeling a pang of sympathy despite everything.

Vega's eyes narrowed and she got right up in my face. "Don't you dare feel sorry for me," she hissed.

"That's why you took Devon in, isn't it?" I asked, ignoring her anger. "Somehow you found out what had happened to your son, and when he and his family were killed, you took in Devon."

"It doesn't take a bloody genius to work that out," she said. Turning on her heel, she walked away, back to stand in front of the screens. Her arms were crossed protectively over her thin chest and for just a moment, I saw a flash of how she must've been years ago. Young and vulnerable.

"Devon came to see you," I said. "He wants you to give me the cure." I really hoped that had been what he'd said. His continued absence was worrying me.

"I'd imagine he would," she said somewhat absently, still watching the screens.

"I'd think you'd want to as well," I said. "Since I'm carrying your great-grandchild."

And that was the bomb I wanted to drop, my one and only play. No, I wasn't really pregnant, but Vega didn't know that.

Her head whipped around, the screens forgotten.

"What did you say?"

"I said I'm pregnant. And if you don't cure me, your flesh and blood will die right along with me." I held my breath, hoping my instincts about why Vega had kept Devon around were right.

"You're lying."

"Maybe I am," I said. "But maybe I'm not."

The room was silent as Vega and I stared at each other. At last, a bitter smile crossed her face.

"I would cure you," she said, "not for your sake, you know of course. But I can't. My scientist has left me. I have no way of forging the vaccine."

Her words settled deep in my gut. So this was it then. Which really meant I had nothing left to lose.

I leapt at the guard on my right and Alexa followed suit with the guard on her left. We'd talked in the car about what to do, and she'd given me some tips on how to at least bide some time for her to take one of them out before moving on to the next.

I struck with the heel of my hand, getting him at the base of the nose and pushing upward. He stumbled back in surprise and pain, and I followed.

"If you're up close, he won't be able to swing his rifle around," Alexa had told me. *"Hand-to-hand is best for a short-term fight, though a woman can't take the prolonged beating a man can. So best get it over with quickly."*

I hoped she'd take care of the "get it over with" part because I'd got him in the groin with my knee, but was rapidly running out of ideas.

There was a heavy thud behind me and Alexa's guard hit the floor out cold, then she was a blinding speed of movement, shoving me out of the way and striking two blows to my guy that had him slumped on the ground in three seconds flat.

I froze, speechless at seeing her in action. Devon hadn't been exaggerating when he'd said she was lethal. Never judge someone by their size, obviously.

Spinning around to confront Vega, I was momentarily nonplussed. She was completely ignoring us, still watching the screens. Breathing hard, I glanced at Alexa in question. She, I noticed, *wasn't* breathing hard. In fact, she looked like she'd just finished tying her shoe.

"Your guards seem to be having a bit of a lie-down," Alexa said. "It's so hard to find good help these days."

"What's on the screens?" I asked. "Because you're looking at them very hard. Is there a program I'm missing tonight?"

"You want to see what I'm watching?" Vega asked without turning. "Then come here, child."

Being called *child* again rankled me, but I bit my tongue against the snide retort that sprang to my lips. Antagonizing her would get me nowhere.

I walked forward until I stood next to her. Alexa followed, but at a slight distance, as though she didn't trust Vega. She'd also taken the rifles from the fallen men. One was in her hands, the other slung over her back.

Glancing up at the screens, I searched them all. They were different security camera views of the exterior. One of them showed waves crashing against the cliff, which I thought a strange thing to capture . . . until I saw a man was strapped to the rocks, being pummeled with each wave.

"Devon! Oh my God!"

It was him. She'd manacled his wrists to the cliff on either side. He looked soaked through, but conscious.

"What the hell are you doing?" I cried, grabbing Vega's shoulder and spinning her around. "Are you trying to kill him?"

"He's proving his loyalty to me," she said. She looked at my hand on her shoulder. "Don't touch me."

Her snarl didn't faze me. "Oh I'll do a lot more than touch you if you don't get him off that cliff."

"Threaten me all you like," she dismissed. "You're not going to kill me. You don't have it in you."

"But I do." Alexa's rifle was pointed at Vega. "And there's not a soul who'd arrest me for it."

"I always thought you had more panache, more style, than that," Vega said. "Though you've turned into a whore since your Shadow days, so I could be wrong."

I turned to Alexa. "Keep her here. I need to go get Devon."

Alexa swung the rifle from over her shoulder and gave it to me. "There are three guards out there," she said. "You'll need this."

Since I had no other option, I took it. I didn't want to shoot anyone, but if it came down to their lives or saving Devon's, there was no choice at all.

"Do you know how to use it?" she asked, then went on as if I'd said no. "The safety is here," she pointed. "It's off at the moment. The trigger is here and brace yourself when you shoot. It'll knock you back some."

"Okay." Hopefully, it wouldn't knock me on my ass.

Hurrying to the elevator, I punched the button and waited impatiently for it to rise. When I stepped out, I had my first encounter with one of the guards. His back was to me, which gave me a split-second advantage before he turned to see who was getting out.

I didn't shoot him. Instead, I turned the butt of the rifle toward him and jabbed at his face. It made contact with his nose and blood spurted. He stumbled back, his hands flying upward to his face, which was a mistake.

I used the butt again, shoving it as hard as I could into his solar plexus. He bent over and I used it again on the back of his neck like I'd seen Alexa do. He went down and didn't get up.

My hands were shaking with adrenaline and fear, but terror for Devon outweighed them all. I'd do whatever I needed to do in order to get him off that cliff.

The rain hadn't let up and I started shivering as the icy drops hit me. The other two guards were nowhere around, and I wondered if they had deserted Vega, too.

In the dark and rain, it was nearly impossible to see. But what did capture my attention were the headlights bouncing down the road toward me.

Shit! Now what?

I hurried to the side of the building so the headlights wouldn't illuminate me, and waited. I wanted to gnash my teeth in frustration at the delay. But my getting caught or captured might leave Devon to die.

The car doors slammed and I heard voices as men got out. I couldn't discern their words over the rain, but one voice was familiar.

Beau. He could help me.

Peeking out from my hiding place, I saw it was him and another man, an older man, who looked vaguely familiar, but I couldn't recognize him at this distance or in the dark.

"Beau!" I called, stepping out. His head whipped toward me, as did his gun arm. I swallowed, holding up my arms. "It's me. Ivy."

The other man had stopped to look, too, as I approached. Beau lowered his weapon.

"How'd you get here so fast?" I asked. "I thought you went to bring help."

"I did," he said, then pointed at the man with him. "I brought Mark Clay, Devon's grandfather."

CHAPTER FIFTEEN

Devon's grandfather?" I echoed in stunned disbelief. "But how . . . ?"

"Mark worked as an informant for the CIA for a while under another name," Beau said. "Once Elva told us the story, I remembered something about a high-value informant from the Shadow. So I got a hold of my station chief and went and picked up Mark here. Thought maybe he could help us."

"We need to help Devon first," I said, then explained what I'd seen on the screen. "So he's somewhere off the side of the cliff, but I don't know where, and I know I'm not strong enough to pull him up."

"I know where he is," Mark said, his jaw tight. "Follow me."

For a man in his sixties, he was spry and attractive, tall with salt-and-pepper hair and the lean, muscular frame of a younger man.

The rain had finally let up to a heavy mist, so it was easier to follow Mark down the hill toward the cliffs. To my surprise, he found his way unerringly in the dark to a nearly obscured path that wound downward. Wide enough for only one person at a time, we went single file. To my right was a sheer drop onto the waves pounding against the rocks. On my left was the sheer face of the cliff.

I swallowed hard as I brought up the rear. I was terrified of heights and on the verge of panic. I had to focus on Devon and getting to him—that was the only way I'd get through this.

It seemed to take forever, each step perhaps being my last, when finally Mark halted.

"He's there," he said, pointing.

Beyond the end of the path was an empty space, then a platform where Devon was bound. His head hung low on his chest and I caught my breath in dismay.

"Okay, I'll go over and unlock him," Beau said to Mark. "You be ready to grab him from me."

Mark nodded and Beau took a running leap across the chasm, landing at Devon's feet. I held my breath as he skidded on the wet rocks, but he caught himself. Devon stirred then, his head lifting. I realized he wasn't shivering, which was a bad sign. Hypothermia could've set in by now.

"'Bout time you showed up," Devon said weakly. "It's been a bit dull without you."

"Yeah, I can see that," Beau replied, getting to his feet. He pulled something out of his pocket and went to work on the manacles. He had them undone in moments and Devon collapsed against him, his knees buckling.

"Easy there, buddy," Beau said. "Let's get you out of here. C'mon, wake up. Your girl is right there, waiting for you. You don't want to look like a pussy, right? Man up."

I knew Beau was trying to get a reaction from Devon so he'd have the strength to jump the empty space to where Mark and I stood. Devon lifted his head and peered our way. He looked past Mark, his gaze finding mine.

"You were supposed to look after her," he rasped to Beau. "Not drag her here."

"Talk to Alexa. I didn't have a choice."

"I'm going to need to collect your man card, my friend."

"Since you're well enough to insult me, then you're well enough to haul your ass back over there," Beau said, nodding toward the chasm. "I'd advise a running start at it."

Devon nodded and I was terrified as he took a couple of steps back. He swiped a hand over his face to remove some of the water and rain, then I saw his shoulders rise and fall with a deep breath. He took off and I stopped breathing altogether.

He didn't go far enough. His hands caught at the edge of where we stood and I screamed. Mark was there, though, flat on his stomach and his hands around Devon's wrists. I hurried to help, dropping down and holding on to Mark's legs. I felt him pulling on Devon and I held on with everything I had. I couldn't lose Devon. Not like this.

Inch by agonizing inch, Mark pulled Devon up until Devon was able to grab a better hold and pull himself onto the path. He rolled over onto his back, just breathing. His clothes were soaked and torn, mud streaking the cloth as well as his skin.

Beau landed next to him a moment later, having made the jump back easily, and helped Devon to his feet. Devon looked at Mark.

"I should thank you, but I don't know who you are."

"Mark Clay." Mark held his hand, but Devon just stared at him.

"Mark . . . Clay," Devon repeated. "My . . . grandfather."

Mark's nod was solemn. "Indeed."

"Where the fuck have you been?"

"I'm sorry," Mark said. "Elizabeth never told me you survived the attack on Dillon . . . on our son."

"So my parents *were* killed because of you both," Devon argued. "Why?"

"I was the first commander of the Shadow," Mark answered me. "Begun during the Cold War, it was meant to be more secret and black than even MI6. Politicians talk and too many people knew too much. The Shadow had only one commander, with agents at my disposal, and no one knew more than was necessary.

"In the eighties, the Shadow had infiltrated the IRA and our source was very highly placed. It wasn't until Elizabeth came to work for me that I realized that our agent was also our son."

Devon's father had been a Shadow agent. Suddenly, it all began to make sense.

Mark continued his story. "Elizabeth wanted him pulled out— the situation was dangerous—but he refused and I backed him. It was the wrong decision. His cover was blown, and before we could warn him, they killed him."

"My father was an agent?"

"Yes, he was. After he was killed, Elizabeth and I had a terrible falling out. She blamed me for Dillon's death. In the end she orchestrated a coup and took over the Shadow and put a hit out on me.

"I faked my death, let her think she got me, and went to work for the CIA, spending the rest of the eighties and early nineties fighting the Cold War. Frankly, I never expected to see Elizabeth again, and she never told me that you'd survived. If she had, I swear, Devon, I would have come for you. Raised you properly."

The two men stared at each other and Devon finally gave a curt nod, then held out his hand. Mark clasped it, then pulled Devon toward him for an ever-so-brief British man-hug.

"Can we finish this touching family reunion up above?" Beau asked. "I'd rather not meet my maker tonight."

"Don't worry," Devon said. "You'd be heading somewhere further south."

I smiled tightly at his joke, glad he could still give Beau a hard time even though he was as white as a sheet and had to be freezing.

Mark led the way back up again and I breathed a sigh of relief when we reached the top.

"Let me have that, darling," Devon said quietly, taking the rifle from me. I let him. It wasn't like I didn't know how to use it, but I was positive if a situation came up where we needed it, he'd be a better shot than me.

I was following the men, lagging a little because, hello, I wasn't in as good shape as they were. When we got to the top, I paused to catch my breath.

Suddenly, an arm went around my neck and I was hauled back. I started to struggle, but felt the cold muzzle of a gun pressing against my temple.

"I'd love to shoot you, child, so I'd suggest you start cooperating and don't give me an excuse."

Vega. I froze. Where was Alexa? What had happened to her?

"I see you didn't learn your lesson, Devon," Vega called out. All three men turned around. I heard Vega's sharp intake of breath. Then she pressed the gun deeper into my skin and I winced at the pain. "No . . ." she whispered. "It can't be . . ."

"Elizabeth," Mark said, walking back toward us, stopping while still a few yards away. "It's good to see you again."

Vega didn't immediately reply.

"But . . . you're dead," she said.

"As you can see, I'm in perfect health."

"Maybe I should shoot you instead," she said bitterly.

"After all these years, you still blame me for Dillon's death?"

"I told you to get him out!"

"And it was his choice to stay," Mark countered. "He knew the dangers of the job."

"He was our son—"

"And this is our *grandson*," Mark interrupted. "Your fear of losing him has consumed you. You've got to let Devon go."

Beau and Devon inched farther apart to flank Mark, Devon's rifle at the ready.

"Don't move!" Vega cried out, obviously spotting their intentions. "Move one step further and I'll blow her head off." Her arm tightened around my neck so it was hard to breathe.

The men stopped in their tracks. Devon's hard gaze was on Vega, his jaw locked tight. He held the rifle steady despite what he'd just endured.

"But I found him, Mark," she said. "I found Devon—"

"And now what are you doing? Torturing him? Holding the girl with a gun to her head?"

"I've lost everyone," Vega said, and her voice sounded strangled. "My mother, Dillon, you. Devon's all I have left."

Vega might have been having an epiphany or existential crisis or whatever, but I'd had just about enough of her using me as a hostage. God only knew what she would do next. And my life was already forfeit, so it wasn't as though I was really losing anything that wouldn't be lost anyway. Only this way, I'd be choosing the manner and time of my death.

I wanted to take a deep breath, but didn't dare. That might alert her that I was about to move. Instead, I sent up a quick prayer, then acted.

Jerking my head back toward Vega, I grabbed her wrist just as she reflexively pulled the trigger. The shot went wide, thank God, because my head was now out of the direct line of fire. I twisted her wrist and arm around and down behind her back and she cried out in pain, dropping the weapon. In a flash, I'd snatched it up and was pointing it at her.

She stepped backward, away from me, and I saw the cliff behind her.

"No, stop!" I called, but it was too late. Her heel hit the edge and the ground crumbled beneath her feet. In the blink of an eye, she was lost to view.

I ran forward and fell to my knees at the cliff's edge. Peering over, I saw Vega had managed to grab on to an outcropping of rock. She hung, suspended in midair. Quickly, I set aside the pistol and reached for her.

"Take my hand," I said. "I'll pull you up."

But she didn't. Instead, she looked past me to Mark and Devon.

"Move," Devon said to me, but he didn't wait for me to respond. He picked me up and set me aside.

Mark was already down on the ground, reaching for Vega. Devon held on to his legs as Mark hauled her up until they were both lying on the sodden grass, panting from exertion and adrenaline.

Devon rose and took me in his arms. We held each other so tight, I would've crawled inside his skin, if I could've. He was soaked and so was I, but I could feel warmth from his skin. For a moment, I just closed my eyes and savored it. I hadn't told him what Vega had said about the vaccine. It could wait. Nothing could change what was going to happen anyway.

"All these years," I heard Vega saying to Mark, "you let me believe I was alone, that you were dead. How could you do that to me?"

"You couldn't forgive me," Mark said.

"I couldn't forgive you, but I never stopped loving you." I was shocked to hear tears in Vega's voice. "I just couldn't be weak anymore. Being weak cost me our baby. It cost me you, for a long time. And then we lost our son all over again."

I felt an unwilling pang of empathy. I knew what it felt like to be weak and at the mercy of others.

Sirens, in the distance, approached us. I knew who it was, because I had called them. Extradition to America was easy if you were a wanted fugitive.

"They'll arrest you, darling," Mark said. "For your father's murder and a thousand other things. You'll be vilified in the press and the trial will drag on for years."

"Not exactly the ending I'd had in mind," she said, a bit of her wry sarcasm back as she glanced at the headlights, still a ways off.

"I'd hoped one day we'd find our way back to each other," Mark said, taking her hands in his. "Every second without you over the years has been excruciating."

Vega looked at him. "I don't want to go to prison."

"Then you know what we have to do," Mark said. Vega nodded.

"Wait, what are you going to do?" Devon asked, letting go of me and taking a few steps toward the couple. Mark had an arm around her shoulders and Vega had both hers around his waist. That's when I noticed he'd picked up the revolver I'd left on the ground.

"Stop right there, Devon," Mark said. "Don't come any closer."

"What are you doing?" Devon asked again. He had to speak louder because the sirens were almost upon us.

"What we should've done a long time ago," Mark said, gazing down fondly into Vega's eyes. The look on her face was one of peace. "Ready, my love?"

"No! Wait—"

But Mark had already raised the revolver, and instead of shooting Vega, then himself, as I'd expected, he aimed for something on the ground. I had a split second to see it was one of those artillery shells Alexa had told me about. Then Devon was knocking me to the ground, his body covering mine.

The report of the revolver was immediately followed by an explosion that shook the ground. Bits of mud and rock rained down on us, Devon taking the brunt of it. When it finally stopped, my ears were ringing.

I sat up, afraid to look to the spot where Vega and Mark had stood. I expected . . . I don't know. Blood? Body parts? Something. Instead, there was nothing there but burnt grass.

Devon got to his feet and helped me up, too. The sirens were muted now, the cars parked and men in uniform filing toward us. Devon and I walked to the edge of the cliff.

"The impact must have blown them off the cliff," he said, peering down at the crashing waves.

I didn't reply, too busy scrutinizing the rocks and waves. Had Mark and Vega really pulled a Thelma and Louise?

"Or maybe it didn't," I said, pointing. There was a clear footprint, the size of a man's shoe, in the soft mud and sand.

Devon and I looked at each other. For his sake, I wanted them to still be alive. They were his only living blood relatives, after all. We didn't say what we were both thinking.

"What's going on? What was that explosion? Put your hands up where we can see them!"

The commanding voices and scurry of boots on gravel had both Devon and me turning and lifting our empty hands. Uniformed men with rifles were directly in front of us, but made way for a man in a suit to walk forward.

"You must be Ivy Mason," he said, flashing his ID. He worked for the US Department of Homeland Security. "I've been sent to extradite you back to the States."

Devon stiffened immediately. "You have no authority for that," he said. "She's on British soil."

The man looked at Devon. "Ms. Mason called us to turn herself in," he said. "Do you really think we would've come looking for her here in this godforsaken place?"

"You turned yourself in?" Devon asked me in disbelief. "Why would you do that?"

Now for the news he didn't want to know. "Because Vega didn't have the cure, Devon," I said sadly. "She never did. My only chance is to get back to the lab at the FBI and see if they can help me."

He looked stricken and didn't speak.

A helicopter was landing, and when it did, a team of four people wearing hazmat suits jumped out.

"We need to get Ms. Mason into the chopper," one of them said, his voice tinny through the suit.

"I'm coming with you," Devon said.

I didn't know if I wanted that, if I wanted him to see me die. "Devon, I don't think—"

"Do *not* attempt to argue with me." His tone was resolute, and I thought I'd pushed him about as far as I could, so I nodded.

"I want to make sure Alexa is okay," I said. "She was guarding Vega."

"Beau went to check on her," Devon said.

Just as he said that, I saw Beau emerge, supporting Alexa with an arm around her back. She seemed okay, though a bit dazed and weak. I wondered what had happened, but had no time to ask her. I was just glad she was still alive and appeared unhurt.

"The chopper's waiting," the man said. The other two flanked me, herding me toward the helicopter.

Maybe it was because the threat was over, that Devon was safe and Vega gone, possibly dead, that made my body decide it now had permission to collapse. For whatever reason, I'd only taken two steps when my knees gave out and pain erupted inside my head.

The suits tried to catch me, but were hampered by their gear. Instead, it was into Devon's arms that I landed. For some reason, I felt more like this was really it . . . that I wouldn't be waking up this time.

Devon hoisted me up into his arms and started for the helicopter again. I kept my gaze on him.

"I want you to know that I love you," I said. "The time we've been together . . . . I wouldn't have traded it for anything."

"Except perhaps your life," Devon replied, despair lurking in his voice.

"It was better to have a short life *with* you, than a long one *without*," I said.

Devon bundled me into the helicopter onto a stretcher while the hazmat guys climbed up and buckled in, too. He crouched next to me, eschewing a seat or buckle, and took my hand in his. One of the hazmat guys started taking my vitals while the other two recorded the readings.

It was too loud to talk over the noise of the blades, so I just looked into his eyes and he into mine, saying silently all the things we hadn't yet had a chance to voice. I held on as long as I could, but the pain was increasing until finally, I had to shut my eyes.

"Can you give her anything for the pain?" Devon asked, his voice loud enough to be heard.

One of the guys nodded, producing an IV needle. I hated needles and IVs were the worst, but the prick of the IV was nothing compared to the pain in my head. He hooked up a saline drip, then shot something from a syringe into the IV cord.

After a few minutes, the pain began to subside, but with it came a wave of exhaustion. I fought to stay awake. I wanted to look at Devon for as long as we had. And I was also terrified that if I closed my eyes . . . I'd never reopen them.

"Shh, my darling," Devon said. "Go to sleep." His hand brushed my hair.

I was too tired to speak, so I gave a small shake of my head. Sleeping could wait until I was dead. But despite the will I had to stay awake and the fear permeating me at the idea of never waking, I found my eyelids drooping. At last, sleep overtook me.

CHAPTER
SIXTEEN

They say that being in a coma is like sleeping, that you're not really aware of what's going on around you. I have to disagree. It's much, much worse.

I felt like a prisoner inside my own body, sensing things going on around me, but unable to respond. I could hear conversations and machines whirring. Sometimes I could make sense of it, sometimes I couldn't.

Devon's voice stood out from everyone else's, though, and was rarely not there. Even when I sensed it was late at night, he was there. He talked to me—told me story after story about his past, things he'd done, places and people he'd seen. He spoke long into the nights, until his voice was nearly gone.

He held my hand, I could feel it, but I couldn't make my hand curl around his. It was incredibly frustrating, and if I could've cried, I would have.

"Beau is well," he was saying now. "And Alexa fully recovered. I believe he's quite smitten, though he won't admit it. Alexa's decided to help out the CIA for a time, so I imagine he'll be inflicting his rather dubious company on her for the immediate future.

"I spoke to your grandparents," he continued. "I didn't want to inform them of your . . . health . . . until absolutely necessary. However, the doctors . . ." He stopped and had to clear his throat before going on. "The doctors seem to think I should ring them up straightaway, which means . . ."

His voice trailed off, but I knew what that meant. It meant that I was dying and it wouldn't be long now. My heart ached for the pain in Devon's voice and the pain inside me at leaving him alone.

"Beau found the journal pages amongst Vega's things," Devon was saying now. "The scientists are working to re-create the vaccine encrypted on those pages." A pause. "You lied to me, you know. Well, of course you know you did, it's just that I didn't realize. You told me you'd destroyed the diary, when in fact you kept those encrypted pages." Another long pause. "I can't fault you for that. It may very well save your life, if they can work fast enough. I just wish you'd told me."

I could feel myself drifting off again into that weird place between slumber and awake, and I struggled not to. I wanted to stay with Devon—I didn't want to leave him to face his nightmares alone. But it was pointless to resist and the darkness dragged me under.

A harsh light invaded my eyes and I winced, turning aside and making a noise of protest.

"She's responsive. That's a very good sign."

A man was talking and it wasn't muffled like before, but sounded very near. I felt a hand slide into my palm. I squeezed, instinctively knowing it was Devon, then I realized: I could move.

My eyes shot open and I immediately squinted at the brightness around me. I was in a hospital—if the white walls and fluorescent lighting didn't give it away, the man in the white coat with a stetho-scope around his neck certainly did. My mouth and tongue felt swollen and dry, plus my entire body ached as though I'd gone ten rounds in a boxing ring and lost.

I tried to think of the last thing I remembered . . . Devon talk-ing, saying he needed to call Grams because I was going to die.

"I thought I'd be dead," I said, my voice a rasp of sound.

"You almost were," the doctor said, motioning to a nurse stand-ing at the foot of the bed. In a flash, she was holding a cup with a straw to my mouth as he fiddled with the bed controls to sit me more upright.

"Have a drink of water," the nurse said, "but just little sips, not big gulps."

I wanted to tip the whole thing down my throat, but did as I was told, taking a few small sips that eased the sawdust in my mouth. When I was finished, she stepped away and I could see Devon behind her.

An overwhelming relief swept over me, sweet and heady, at the mere sight of him. I couldn't help it—my face creased in a smile as tears stung my eyes.

"You're here," I said. Duh, stating the obvious. And he must've read my mind because his lips twisted slightly, too.

"So I am."

I drank him in, from the clear ocean-blue of his eyes, to the breadth of his shoulders, to his hand wrapped around mine. His jaw was heavily shadowed with stubble, so I could tell he hadn't shaved in a few days, and there were dark circles under his eyes.

"You're a very lucky woman," the doctor said. "It was a close call."

"What happened?" I asked, still staring at Devon. "How did you fix me?"

"The vaccine on those sheets they brought to us wasn't quite right," the doctor said. "The closest it could do was send the virus

271

into remission, and only that for a short time. So I'm afraid you were our guinea pig as we tested different variations on you.

"It's taken nearly three weeks, but we finally hit on the right one," he finished.

Now I did look at him, twisting around in astonishment. "Three weeks? I've been out for three weeks?"

"We induced a coma-like state to help your body fight the virus," he explained. "We also did a blood transfusion. Today you were showing no further signs of the virus in your blood so we believe that we found the correct formula, and went ahead with plans to wake you."

Time passing with me unaware. It was a bizarre feeling. And Devon, by my side the entire time. My hand gripped his tighter.

"We'll keep you for another couple of days, make sure everything checks out," the doctor said. "But I think you're out of the woods." He smiled.

"That's . . . I'm overwhelmed . . . thank you," I said. I'd survived. Somehow, through the tenacity of strangers determined to save me, I wasn't dead. Emotion overwhelmed me, and I looked up at the ceiling, blinking rapidly to dispel the tears in my eyes.

The doctor patted me on the arm, then he and the nurse left the room. I cleared my throat a few times, then glanced at Devon.

His eyes were bright with unshed tears and he was smiling.

"I wasn't about to let them give up on you," he said, his voice rough. "I need you." Lifting my hand, he pressed his lips to the back of my knuckles. "It would've been just too tragic to lose the love of my life once I'd found her. Fortunately, they agreed."

I'd had close calls before, sudden brushes with death that had come out of nowhere and left no time to reflect on the precious gift of life. But not this time. I drank in Devon and the way he looked at me, acutely aware of how lucky I was.

"Tell me what I missed," I said, after an embarrassingly long time of staring into each other's eyes and holding hands. "Is Alexa okay?" Vaguely I recalled listening to Devon talk while I'd been unconscious, but now I couldn't recall the details.

"She's fine," he said. "Vega had a bomb on remote that went off. It wasn't a massive explosion, but enough to knock Alexa out so Vega could get away. Beau found her and pulled her out."

Rescued by Beau. Knowing Alexa, I'm sure that had to have rankled her. I couldn't help a smile, though. Perhaps it would do her a bit of good to be rescued.

"So did Vega get away?" I asked. "Or did the explosion kill her and Mark?"

Devon's expression turned slightly grim. "They didn't find any bodies," he said. "But the sea there is very rough. It's possible they could've been lost in the water and washed away and we'd never find them."

I couldn't tell how he felt about that—the possibility that Vega might still be alive. She'd killed Kira, or had her killed, and I knew Devon wanted vengeance. Yet . . . she was his flesh and blood.

"Do you want her to be dead?" I asked.

Devon frowned, glancing down at our joined hands. His thumb brushed my skin as he thought.

"What she did to Kira, and to you, is unforgivable," he said. "I think what happened to her when she was young warped her in a way that's difficult for me to understand. Frankly, she's a high-functioning sociopath. She needs help. Perhaps Mark can get her what she needs. If they survived."

There was a knock on the door before it swung open. I looked up to see my Grams and Grandpa rushing toward me.

"Ivy! Oh my goodness! I can't believe you've been so sick and no one told us!"

Then she was hugging me, and I was engulfed in the scent of home—bread baking and the fresh air of the farm. Like a trigger that the child inside me had been waiting for, I started sobbing. I didn't know what it was in particular that moms and grandmas had that allowed an adult to take a breath and revert to the nine-year-old who just wanted to hear it was all going to be okay, I just knew that's exactly how I felt.

We were both crying and holding each other, and I was grateful I'd been given the opportunity to have this again. I hadn't gotten to say goodbye to my grandparents when Devon and I had left the farm several months ago.

When we could breathe again, she stepped back a little, but took my hand tight in hers. Grandpa hugged me hard, his eyes bright with unshed tears.

"Glad you're okay, Ivy-girl," he said. A master of understatement, but that was the Kansas farmer in him, and I didn't mind.

"What's this?" Grams said, looking at my wedding rings. "You're married?"

"I'm afraid that's my fault," Devon said. "But I believe I was just following some very sage advice I'd been given." He nodded toward Grandpa. "Ivy did me the extreme honor of becoming my bride. It was rather sudden, so you have my utmost apologies for not being at the wedding."

"So long as you're married, we'll get over not being there," Grandpa said.

"Married! My little Ivy! I can't believe it." Grams started tearing up all over again and Grandpa gave her a handful of hospital tissues.

They stayed for a while, until Grams could tell I was tiring, then hugged me and promised to be back the next day. Devon had flown them in and was putting them up in a hotel nearby.

"You should go, too," I said to him. "You must be exhausted."

"I'm fine," he said. "I'll sleep when you do."

"Have you been sleeping in that chair?"

"Darling, I can sleep anywhere. It doesn't matter."

But it mattered to me. "Come up here with me," I said, scooting to one side of the bed.

He did as I asked, carefully untangling my IV cords until he could take me in his arms. I let out a deep sigh. With my head against his chest, I could hear his heart beating. I closed my eyes and let the sound soothe me.

"I am sorry," he said after a while.

"For what?"

"You've been through so much . . . most of it dreadful . . . because of me."

I twisted so I could look up at him. He was looking at my face, his brow creased, and I could see regret in his eyes.

"Don't be sorry," I said. "I'm not. No one said the path to true love was paved with rainbows and unicorns. I'd much rather focus on now and the future, than dwell on the past. Wouldn't you?"

He studied me, his fingers brushing my cheek as he looked in my eyes.

"I'd like that very much," he said at last. "I've never considered my future as being anything but an ephemeral thing, bound to be quite short and likely painful. Now, I find myself dreaming of you and our life together. But it makes me terrified, too."

"Why?" I asked. "Why would that terrify you?"

"Because I love you so much, it hurts," he said. "And I can't imagine what I'd do if I lost you. I've never felt this way before. For someone used to putting my feelings in a box, it's rather . . . disconcerting."

"Well, you're not going to lose me," I said with a smile. "We've paid enough to the karma gods. We're going to be together, and be safe and healthy, and have our happily-ever-after."

"How do you know?"

I smiled, snuggling back into him. His arms pulled me closer.

"Because that's how these things go," I said. "Love stories don't really end, they just go on, don't they. And whatever happens, we'll handle it, as we've handled everything else. Together."

His lips brushed my forehead.

"My sweet Ivy, I do believe you're right."

Of course I was.

 EPILOGUE

"Warm enough, darling?"

I glanced up to see Devon hovering, yet another blanket in his hands.

"You've already put two blankets on me," I said with a smile. "I'm fine."

"It's quite chilly out here," he said. "I don't want you to catch cold."

Out here was outside our home off Lake Tahoe. We'd moved here nearly two years ago, falling in love immediately with the two-story log "cabin" (I'd told Devon it was way too big of a home for the word *cabin*, but he still called it that) right off the lake. I loved sitting near the water's edge, the huge pine trees watching over me as I gazed at the deep blue water. But it was cold today so I'd bundled up.

"I'm not going to catch cold," I said. "Now stop hovering and sit with me."

He sat in the twin Adirondack chair next to me. "How are you feeling?"

"I'm fine," I said with a patient smile. "And yes, the baby's fine, too."

I was six months pregnant, a circumstance that both Devon and I were thrilled about, but that also managed to send him into paroxysms of worry. Like now.

"Have you thought about the name I suggested?" I asked, wanting to get his mind off worrying about me and onto something more pleasant.

"I'm not sure about it," he said. "I don't think it's going to be a girl."

We'd elected to not find out the gender, which was a little frustrating, but also fun to speculate.

"Have you gotten someone to take over for you at the home for a few months?" he asked.

Shortly after we'd moved to Lake Tahoe, I'd opened up a charity home for abused women and children. Devon had helped and it had been cathartic to be able to help those in need. We provided a safe place to stay as well as life necessities until those women were able to put their lives back together. But with the baby on the way, I couldn't be there for the day-to-day operations. I had volunteers, but Devon and I had decided to hire a full-time person as well.

"I have two interviews scheduled for tomorrow," I said. "What about you? Are you still going to DC this week?"

Devon had taken up consulting for private and government security agencies. Sometimes it required that he travel, but with technology being what it was, he could do a lot from our home.

"They ended up moving the meeting," he said. "Rescheduling it for another couple of weeks."

I nodded, taking a sip of the coffee in my travel mug. It kept it warmer a lot longer than in just a ceramic cup.

"Logan called earlier," I said. "He and Marcia are planning to come visit at the end of June. The baby should be here by then."

Marcia and Logan had begun dating shortly after I'd left my job at the bank. Though they'd casually known each other for a while with me as the common friend, they'd never dated. When they finally did, they'd hit it off and had recently gotten engaged. I was happy for Logan, and glad that we'd been able to maintain our friendship despite the rough patch we'd gone through.

"Good. You should be glad of that."

I smiled at Devon's careful nonchalance. He and Logan were never going to be best friends, but they'd reached a truce, and that was good enough for me.

We sat together, watching the water. Devon reached for my hand. I smiled at him. Sometimes I thought both of us were overwhelmed at how things had turned out. Life had been so dark for so long, for both of us. At last, I had a life I'd only fantasized about—married to an amazing, fascinating man who loved me; living in a beautiful, peaceful place; doing something near and dear to my heart; and now bringing our child into the world.

It just goes to show you, I thought. Sometimes when life seems not worth living—when darkness is all around and it's hard to face another day, you have to hang on. Because sunshine does break through the clouds, and better days do come, and dreams really can come true.

THE END

Acknowledgments

I owe a huge thank-you to my amazing editor, Maria Gomez, for holding my hand not only during the writing of this book, but this entire series. I can't thank you enough for your patience and encouragement when I was sure everything I wrote was a huge pile of excrement.

Thank you to Melody Guy for her incredible work on pointing out my many plot failings. I love your attention to detail and you made the series a thousand times better than it would've been without you.

I couldn't have written this book or this series without the wonderful support of my family. Thank you all for loving encouragement and patience as mommy orders take-out pizza for dinner . . . again.

Thank you to my agent, Kevan Lyon, for keeping me going when it was hard for me to see the light at the end of the tunnel.

Thank you to Montlake Romance and the incredible team of people there. I'm blessed to be with Montlake and to get to work with the very best in the business.

Lastly, thank you to Maj. M.G. "Mac" McLellan of the British Army for fact-checking (and correcting) my Briticisms and attending to numerous other details. Your time was greatly appreciated.

About the Author

Photo © 2014 Karen Lynn

Tiffany Snow has been reading romance novels since she was too young to read romance novels. After a career in the Information Technology field, Tiffany now has her dream job of writing full time.

Tiffany makes her home in the Midwest with her husband and two daughters. She can be reached at Tiffany@TiffanyASnow.com. Visit her website, www.Tiffany-Snow.com, to keep up with her latest projects.

Made in the USA
Middletown, DE
25 January 2021